Retribution
TransCanada Killer Series
Book 2

J E Friend

ISBN 978-1-9991192-5-6

Publisher: Dark Cellar Publications, darkcellarpublications@yahoo.com

Author: J. E. Friend

www.jefriend.com

Cover Designer: A. E. Hellstorm at Flying Elk Photography

http://www.flying-elk-photography.com/about-book-covers

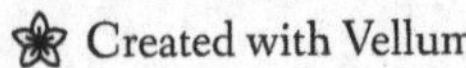 Created with Vellum

For my mother, Judy, who has read and re-read each of my books before they were ready for publishing and encouraged me to keep going.

1

Maggie awoke with a scream on her lips, her body slick with sweat. She trembled, pulling the covers up to her neck and curled into the fetal position. Blinking in the darkness to chase away the images that flashed before her. Her father's body didn't lie on the floor of her cab. That was a lifetime ago, when she was a child, too young to defend herself. She took long, deep, calming breaths, trying to put the nightmares at bay and flicked on the lights.

She swung her feet over the edge of the bed, rose and stepped over to use the bucket in the corner to relieve herself, and checked the time. 3 am. It was too early to start her day, so she crawled back under the covers. She hoped that watching Frank Carter die would end her nightmares, but less than 48 hours later, another nightmare brought back memories of the night she witnessed her father's murder. Her hand slipped under her pillow, searching for the evidence she'd rescued from Carter's truck. As her fingers wrapped around it, she wondered if the ribbon of children's hair clips she found were the reason behind tonight's nightmare. The horror of what that man was capable of brought her own wounds to the surface.

Maggie held the ribbon up and counted the hair clips. Twenty-one. Her own, which she removed and stored with the one he'd left behind, made twenty-two. There were so many children who suffered at Carter's hands! She felt the rage fill her as her free hand curled into a fist.

She thought of Audrey and how Carter's actions had taken everything away from her, too. Audrey's daughter Sara's faded yellow hair clip was near the top of the ribbon. At least now, she'd know who killed Sara, and that justice was served. He may not be rotting away in a prison, but he'd never harm another child again. She'd watched as the first flames licked at his cab. Listened to his screams as he begged for his life when it became engulfed in flames and she left the scene.

'*These families need closure.*' Maggie thought, wondering how many more victims there were who wouldn't get closure, the ones without hair clips. She felt she had to help the families find peace. She couldn't go to the police with the evidence. That wasn't an option. '*How could I explain where the ribbon came from without incriminating myself?*' She wondered. '*I left enough evidence at the accident scene to link Carter to the crime the press dubbed the 'Trans-Canada Serial Killer.' But if I went to the police, they'd know I was at the accident site and didn't report it.*'

Maggie lay on the bed with the ribbon clasped in her hand, allowing the pent-up tension to leave her body as she thought of ways to bring closure to the families. Her eyes scanned the rainbow of colours in front of her, the symbol of innocence lost, and tears pooled in her eyes before breaking free and seeping from the corners in tiny streams, cleansing her shattered soul as she made a plan.

2

After her call to Dr. Coleman, Maggie leaned back and sighed. She felt her body sag into her seat as the reality of her situation sank in. The hunt was over and she'd found the man that killed her father. She reached up to retrieve a cigarette from the package in her visor. Her fingers trembled, causing the package to drop to the floor of the rig. Feeling her chest tighten, she gasped for breath. Sweat beaded her forehead and her mouth went dry. She leaned forward, placing her head on the steering wheel, and waited for the sensation to pass. She knew what was happening. It had happened before and would happen again. She was having a full-blown panic attack. The last time she had one was after she killed her first victim. She hadn't planned on killing him. She seized the opportunity at hand, but this death was different. This time she'd killed the monster who destroyed her life, ending the hunt that had dominated her existence.

With the carnage of the burnt Mack truck and the corpse she left inside well behind her, her body relaxed for the first time in years, maybe even decades. The panic attack eased as a sense of finality spread through her. Her mind slipped back to the anguished sounds from his screams as the flames closed in on him and she shuddered. All the visits to her father's grave, the promises she made to him over the years, had come to fruition. For as long as she lived, she'd remember the look of shock on Frank Carter's face when he realized who she was and that he was going to die. A tear formed in the corner of her eye, which she brushed away with the back of her hand. He had destroyed so many lives and she'd stopped him. She ended the monster's reign.

Maggie knew it was a stroke of genius planting all the evidence that tied her to being the serial killer in the tangled mess from the accident, making sure everything was far enough from the wreckage and flames, but not too far. She hadn't framed an innocent man. He was still a killer. Instead, she framed a different serial killer, one whose perversions destroyed lives. Her victims deserved their fate. They were the dregs of society who slipped through unnoticed. There was a definite sense of satisfaction in knowing that. Over the years, she'd lost count of how many lives she ended, but with each kill she knew she spared dozens of children from suffering her own fate.

Maggie didn't think when the police found the evidence, the turn of events would surprise the Detective investigating the case. She watched his face when he interviewed Carter in Chilliwack. She knew the detective sensed there was something wrong with the man and had she bumped into Carter sooner, the Detective would have Carter's murder to investigate too. Now they'll discover the 'accident' scene and the scattered debris, and they'd assume they'd found their man.

Maggie looked out at the open road ahead of her and decided she needed a break from this lifestyle. A break from the road she loved so much but only followed to seek redemption. Her next call was to Adam in dispatch. She needed to tell him that when she returned; she was taking some time off.

On the phone, he argued with her, informing her she needed to give notice when taking vacation, but the tone of her voice told him not to pursue it. She knew he wasn't happy, but he couldn't say anything other than to grumble. She was an owner/operator and that gave her the right to decide when and where she drove. After she hung up with Adam, she called her Aunt Julie and told her she was coming home for a while. This time she told Julie about the body at the Husky in Chilliwack, and used the excuse that it was too close for comfort and she needed some time off to regroup. It thrilled her aunt that she was coming home, no matter what the reason. Her aunt would let her uncle know, so that when he got home, he could arrange time off so they could have some family time.

A few days later, Maggie pulled into the yard at her aunt's truck repair shop. She chose to bobtail home instead of taking the trailer with a paying load. She was rethinking trucking and didn't know what her next move was, or even if she was going to continue driving, so she left the trailer in the yard back in Toronto. The company she signed on with wouldn't send it out with another driver, so it would wait there until she decided.

Maggie took a deep breath and unclipped the two hair clips that were with the childhood photo of her and her father, and slipped them into the pocket of her jacket. Maggie had Frank's collection of hair clips secured in a baggie in her duffle bag. She vowed to find the families of the children who belonged to the clips and return them with a single note stating "He's Dead," or something similar. She also knew the perfect person to help with the task.

Maggie climbed out of her truck, reached up to pull down her duffle bag and prepared to head inside the shop to say hello before continuing on to the house. She turned, her step faltered as she found her aunt right behind her.

"Aunt Julie! I didn't see you come up."

Julie's eyes narrowed, and she eyed Maggie up and down. "Tell me what's going on, Maggie." Julie had a sixth sense about things that Maggie found uncanny.

Maggie's eyes flew open. "What do you mean, what's going on?"

"Maggie. I've known you since you were a baby, and I took you in after that monster killed your father. I know you better than most people. Something's up."

Maggie sighed. "I'm thinking about getting out of trucking. I'm good at it, but I only went into it because of dad. It was a way for me to feel close to him. Things are getting bad out there, and I thought I'd take some time off to think about what I'd like to do next. I'm only 28. I have lots of time to decide. Maybe I'll use this brain you keep reminding me I have and go back to school." She finished with a chuckle.

Julie wrapped Maggie in her arms, pulled her tight, and kissed her brow. "Whatever you decide to do, we're here for you. We want the best for you."

3

The next morning, Maggie pulled her car out of the garage where she'd stored it while on the road and took the back roads to Dr. Coleman's house. She didn't want the nosey neighbours to see which direction she went. There were already enough rumours about her past and her time spent in Dr. Coleman's office.

When they spoke last, they agreed it was best to meet at the house and away from prying eyes. Dr. Coleman told Maggie she had cleared her schedule, so she'd be free to devote herself to Maggie without interruptions. There was a lot Dr. Coleman didn't know, and Maggie felt it was time to fill her in if she was going to gain Audrey's assistance.

Maggie pulled up in front of Audrey's quaint cottage-style house on the lake and parked her car. A neat stone path led from the gravel laneway to the front door. Perfectly trimmed shrubs and colourful flowers lined the walkway. Everyone in town knew where the doctor lived, but this was Maggie's first visit to her home. Maggie checked her purse one last time to verify that the ribbon of hair clips was still inside. She'd place her own hair clip back on the ribbon in the position she'd found it. It would help Audrey see how horrific things were, especially if Maggie was going to tell her everything and ask for her to take part in gaining closure for so many families.

After her meeting with Audrey, Maggie planned to go to the cemetery and visit with her dad. She wanted to bury her hair clips with him, putting an end to the rage that had overshadowed her life since childhood. She needed him to know she'd put an end to the decades of violence that families had suffered at the hands of Frank Carter. Just thinking about his name caused her stomach to clench. She hoped by doing so she'd find the peace for which she'd been searching.

Maggie stepped out of the car and pulled her shoulders back, steeling herself for the difficult conversation that lay ahead. She knew old wounds would open up for them both, and they'd have to relive the trauma that had changed each of their lives.

She had her hand raised to knock, but before she could, the door swung open. Dr. Coleman stood before her wearing a t-shirt and jeans. Maggie had never seen her out of her work clothes, and her eyes widened. It was then that she realized the humanity of the doctor. She wasn't just a doctor; she was a mother who lost a child and who had become a friend over the years since Maggie stopped going for counselling.

"You're looking well, Maggie. Quick, come in before my cats try to escape." Audrey said, motioning Maggie inside.

Maggie nodded, stepped inside, and closed the door behind her. She looked around at the furnishings and felt the room reflected Audrey's personality. Something rubbed against her leg and she peered down to see a seal-point Siamese cat weaving between her legs. The audible sound of purring drifted up.

Audrey bent down, scooped up the cat, and placed her on the back of the sofa. "That's Blue. Ash is around here somewhere. I hope you're not allergic to cats! I didn't think to ask."

Maggie shook her head. Still unable to find the words she needed to begin the conversation.

"Come and have a seat. I've made some tea. But I can make you something stronger if you'd prefer."

Maggie smiled. "Tea is fine, but we may want something stronger by the time I finish my story."

Maggie waited while Audrey poured them each a cup before she reached into her purse and pulled out the ribbon of children's hair clips she'd found in Frank Carter's truck. Bile rose in her throat as she thought of all those lost children at the hands of that man.

As Maggie smoothed it out across her lap, the reality of what Maggie had registered on Audrey's face, her jaw dropped and her eyes widened. "Oh my God!" was all Audrey could say. Her hand trembled as she reached out to touch it, before snatching her hand back and balling it up into a fist on her lap.

Maggie took a deep breath and began.

"Audrey, the man who collected these 'souvenirs', is dead. I watched him die. When I was in Chilliwack last, I bumped into him and although I didn't see his face, the sound of his voice brought the memories of the night my father died flooding back. He didn't recognize me. Why would he? I was no longer a terrified, vulnerable child anymore. Someone he'd left for dead. I was now a grown woman."

Audrey's eyes concentrated on the ribbon, looking at each clip until she came to the one she recognized. She unfurled her fist, reached out and touched the worn plastic yellow clip near the top of the ribbon. Sara's name although, faded, was still visible. Tears welled up in Audrey's eyes. Maggie reached out and clasped her hand around Audrey's. Unable to find the words, Audrey motioned for Maggie to continue.

"I watched him pull out of the parking lot and as he left, I recorded his license plate. I wasn't sure what I planned to do with it, but it made sense to me. It's not as if the police would believe me if I called in and reported that the man who killed my father and attacked me was heading towards the Coquihalla. It happened years ago. But I knew I had to do something. On my route back to Ontario, I saw he was ahead of me. It was early in the morning and the roads were empty. So I forced him off the road and pulled over to confront him. His truck landed on its side, and I had to climb up to come face-to-face with him. I didn't expect to find this." Maggie said, clutching the ribbon, her eyes brimmed with tears.

"Enraged, I yanked it down. The souvenirs of his monstrous deeds! Can you imagine Audrey? He had it clipped to the roof of his cab! There were so many! I had to stop him before there were more victims. Then saw Sara's and my hair clips, and I knew the same man destroyed both of our lives." Maggie paused and looked into Audrey's eyes before continuing.

"Before for he died, I told him who I was. You should have seen the look of shock on his face. Ignoring his cries for help, I left. It wasn't until I noticed the smell of diesel that I realized his fuel tank had ruptured. This was my opportunity to kill him! I lit a cigarette and dropped it into the spilt fuel and watched it ignite. His screams when the flames reached him still echo in my ears. I was far away when fire and rescue showed up."

Maggie's shoulders sagged. Her neck ached from the tension she'd felt. The weight she'd been carrying around on her shoulders slid off with her admission. She reached for her cup and took a sip to ease the parched feeling in her throat.

"Maggie," Audrey paused, searching for the right words. "I'm glad he's dead, but if you left the clips there, the police would know who and what he was."

"If he survived the fire, which was improbable, the clips wouldn't have. There'd be nothing left to indicate his true nature. So, I left evidence to frame him for another crime. I thought it was better to take the clips to ease your mind and let you know I'd caught him."

"Another crime? What other crime could you frame him for?"

Maggie tossed a loonie on the table. "I'm now paying for your service. Are we under patient/doctor confidentiality?"

Audrey's eyes flicked from the one-dollar coin and up to Maggie's earnest face. "Always."

"You remember asking me about the serial killer? The one who was killing truck drivers?" Maggie watched as Audrey nodded. "It was me. I'm the one who was killing the truck drivers. They were all deviants fascinated by little girls. The first time I killed someone, I didn't plan on it." She took a deep breath before revealing how it all began. "When I started trucking, I did it to search for my rapist, and in doing so I discovered other truckers whose perversions focused on young children. I centred my rage on them. My first victim was by circumstance. I was at a truck stop when I overheard two truckers talking. One had picked up a copy of penthouse and asked the other if he'd seen the centrefold. The other responded with 'my tastes in girls runs a little younger, if you know what I mean'. He even winked. My stomach lurched. I could see the expression on the man holding the penthouse magazine and the shock that registered on his face. I went back to my truck and pulled out the ceramic knife I used for preparing meals. In the meantime, the driver returned to his truck and got in. I slipped out of my cab, my knife in hand, and waited. I knew before he got into his bunk for the night, he'd get out and go to the back of his truck to pee, and when he did, I'd be there. It didn't take long before he stepped outside and went around to the back of his trailer. I stepped out of the shadows and surprised him, his cock in his hand. 'Looking for a little piece of old Mike, are ya?' he asked. When he said that, I couldn't control the rage I felt."

Maggie's face revealed how repulsed his words made her feel. Her mouth was dry but she continued.

"'You look a little sweeter than the usual girls working the lots.' Bile rose in my throat, but I swallowed hard and responded. 'I'm a little old for your tastes, aren't I?' He looked me up and down before replying, 'Sure, but you're so tiny you could pass for younger,' then he sneered. He actually sneered at me. He'd finished peeing and was now stroking himself. 'Here, little lady, I got it ready for you.' I couldn't help myself. The rage boiled from somewhere deep inside me. I swung my knife at him, the sharp blade severed his penis in one stroke. 'What the fuck?' He said as he stared at his blood-soaked hands and the now flaccid member laying on the pavement. Before he could say anything else, I took the blade and sliced it across his throat. His blood spattered all over me. The look of shock that registered on his face before he fell to the ground was satisfying. I should have felt horrified, but I didn't. Instead, I returned to my truck and wiped the blood from my face and hands on my t-shirt. Then I rolled the ruined shirt into a ball and tossed it into the garbage in my truck. I used a mirror to survey how much blood was still on me before taking baby wipes and cleaning off the rest. I used the same wipes to clean off the knife and wipe down the outside of my door. He wasn't the man I wanted to suffer, but he was sick and still deserved it."

Maggie's heart raced and her chest heaved as she fought against the anger that bubbled out, reliving the experience. Audrey remained silent, knowing Maggie hadn't finished her story. But her expression revealed what Maggie already knew in her heart: Audrey had suspected Maggie was the killer.

"I realized in that moment that if I found the man who murdered my father, I was going to kill him. That meant in the future, I'd need to be better prepared. So, I sourced out long veterinary gloves which are available at any livestock supply store. Most truck stops and dollar stores carried disposable rain ponchos. They were the perfect way to protect my clothing. I replaced my ceramic knife for inside the truck and kept that one for the hunt. I always carried a hunting knife for protection, but I liked how easily the ceramic cut through flesh. When I drove away, the adrenaline pumped through my body. I revelled in the sense of horror and accomplishment I felt. It gave me a new sense of purpose."

Maggie leaned back on the sofa. There was still more to discuss, but she needed a minute to compose herself before she continued. Audrey's face was void of emotion as she got up and went to the bar. She turned to Maggie and held up a bottle of gin. Maggie nodded. Audrey poured them both a shot, sat down, and braced herself to hear the rest of Maggie's confession.

4

Maggie and Audrey continued sitting in silence as they sipped their shots of gin, allowing the liquid to warm their blood. Now that the worst of the conversation was over, Maggie felt her body relax. She looked up and noticed that Audrey was staring at her and realized Audrey had something she wanted to say, but was struggling to find the words, so Maggie waited, allowing Audrey time to gather her thoughts.

After a few minutes, Audrey sighed, took a deep breath and began. "So, tell me what your plan is for the rest of the hair clips? You could have just taken yours and Sara's and left the rest to burn." Audrey swallowed the last of her gin and leaned back, studying Maggie.

"There are a few reasons I took them. First, if I left them, the fire would have destroyed them and none of the victims' families would have closure. You know all too well how devastating that is. Second, a person who killed pedophiles wouldn't keep a ribbon of children's hair clips. If they survived the fire, how could I frame him for my crimes? And third, I want to be the one to give the families closure. I want some good to come out of this madness."

"Closure? How do you propose to do that? You have the clips and the police have no clue what Frank Carter did."

"Does the exact nature of his crimes matter? The police will think he's the serial killer. There is nothing left to link those crimes to me. He is a serial killer, but for different crimes than the police know, that's what's important. As for closure for the families, I thought maybe you could help me with that." Maggie replied as she laid the ribbon on the coffee table so that Audrey had no choice but to look at it.

Audrey ran her hand through her silvered hair and looked down at the ribbon. In her other hand, she had Sara's clip tight in her grasp. Audrey felt the ends digging into her flesh. She opened her mouth to respond, but shut it. She stood up and walked back to the bar, grabbed the bottle of gin and poured them each another measure, this time leaving the bottle on the coffee table. Her hand wrapped around her glass and she took a long pull from the clear liquid before speaking.

"I want to help. The not knowing was unsettling. Losing a child is a parent's worst nightmare. These families all need closure. I've known what he did to my little girl for years, but not who he was. I thought they couldn't catch him," Audrey paused. "That was what haunted me. Knowing the monster was still out there to harm other children." Audrey wiped a tear from the corner of her eye. "Do you have a plan as to how we'll find out who the clips belong to?"

Maggie grabbed her glass, stood up, and paced. Her tiny frame shook as she tried to form the words.

"He haunted my life since that night. How many more victims did he leave alive without knowing? I should have died. I almost did. He killed my father before my eyes, then he beat me, raped me and strangled me. It was the thought of him doing what he did to me, to someone else that fuelled my rage. Do you see how many clips are on the ribbon? What about the children who weren't wearing hair clips? How many more families will never get the closure they need?"

Maggie sobbed. Tears brimmed her eyes before breaking free to slide down her cheeks.

Audrey stood and went to Maggie, wrapped her arms around her, and allowed Maggie to cry. Offering her a 'mother's' comfort. After years of therapy, this was the first time she'd witnessed Maggie's tears, and it tore at her heart.

"I can't say it will be ok, but it will get better. We will work together and help ease the sorrow of other families." Audrey reassured her.

Maggie stepped back from Audrey's embrace, wiped the tears from her eyes with the back of her hand, and chugged back the glass of gin. When Audrey motioned for her to pour herself another, Maggie shook her head and continued.

"We need to start with newspaper archives. We have to look for stories of missing, murdered, and/or abused girls. When we find possibilities, we will have to reach out to them. Let them know about Sara and myself, without giving our names. If the stories don't include information about missing hair clips, we'll mention that he took Sara's and mine. Lead in by describing our hair clips. They might open up. We will have to do this from afar. We can't risk being tied to the clips and families. When we find a clip that matches a victim, we will return it anonymously and include a simple note saying 'he's dead' or 'the monster responsible is dead'. Nothing more. That will give the families the peace of mind they deserve. It will take time, but the families need closure."

Audrey smiled at Maggie. "You've given this a lot of thought. Your plan might work. I'm in. I'll use my connections as a psychiatrist to see what I can find out. We have to assume because he was a trucker that the victims can be from both the USA and Canada."

They continued chatting and planning their next steps until Maggie looked at the clock and announced she needed to leave. She still wanted to visit her father's grave, and she'd promised her aunt she'd be back in time to prepare supper. Maggie stood to leave and on impulse hugged Audrey and whispered in her ear, "You're the reason I'm still here." Then she left.

5

Maggie felt a sense of peace spread through her after her meeting with Audrey and also a newfound purpose. They'd agreed to search together for the victims of Frank Carter and return the hair clips to the families with a card that read 'Justice. He's Dead.' She knew it would take time, even years, but it needed to be done. The families needed to know that the monster was dead and justice prevailed.

She pulled her car along the side of Highway 17 and parked before she climbed the hill to the Cobden Union Cemetery. Maggie could have pulled into the parking area, but old habits die hard, and she was used to pulling her rig to the side of the road during her visits and even though today she was in her car, it just felt right. She pulled out a beer and a Redbull before grabbing the plastic bag that contained both of the hair clips she wore that fateful day.

Maggie made her way through the gravestones until she stood in front of the one that read 'Bradley "Butch" Hopkins, loving husband and father.' Her mother's grave was beside his, 'Alison Hopkins, loving wife and mother', but her memories of her mother were sparse. She was 3 when her mother died of cancer. After that, it was just her father and her. Of course, Aunt Julie and Uncle Bobby were there too, but she struggled to remember the simple things about her mother. Her father was her whole life when Carter killed him. Sometimes she still woke up screaming when thoughts of that night crept into her subconscious. He'd taken everything from her. Now she'd ended his miserable life, and she felt elated, knowing he'd never be able to harm another child.

Maggie kissed her fingertips and touched them to her mother's headstone, then sat on the grass in front of her father's. After the gin at Audrey's, she didn't want more to drink, so she cracked open her Redbull after twisting off the top of the beer for her father. The beer she would pour on the ground of her father's grave, as was her regular habit. One she started doing as soon as she turned 19 and was old enough to drink. She brought her first legal beer up to the gravesite to have one with her dad and repeated it whenever she was in the area.

"Hi dad." Maggie whispered as she made herself comfortable, taking a long jolt from her can. "I can't believe you've been gone twenty years. That bastard took everything from us. It took me a while, but I made him pay." She picked at some weeds in the grass as she spoke. "He's dead and now I can help bring justice to the other families whose lives he ruined."

Maggie pulled out her pocketknife and cut a small square of grass away from the base of the headstone. She used the blade to loosen the soil and pushed the small bag with both of the hair clips inside it, into the earth. Then she poured some of the beer on the dirt to moisten it, put the piece of sod back on top, and added some more beer to the grass.

"These belong with you, dad. I may not have died that day, but part of me did. The child I was before that day died. I'm burying my innocence with you dad, now a part of me will always be with you. I miss you so much." She finished with a sob.

Maggie wiped the tears from her eyes and drank the last of her Redbull. She poured the last of the beer out on her father's grave, then she lay down on the grass between the two graves, one hand rested on each grave, as if she was holding her parents' hands. She lay there under the warm sun, searching for peace, instead she found a new resolve as her mind rambled with what was ahead. Maggie closed her eyes and sensed her father's pride, while she lay basking in the mid-afternoon sun, and decided what her next move was.

6

Maggie left the cemetery and returned to her aunt and uncle's house. Her body had relaxed as a sense of calm and purpose enveloped her during her visit to the cemetery. While she lay between her parents' graves, she'd considered her options and decided on her next move. The most important thing was to squash the dark urges that threatened her future. If she continued down her current path, she'd end up dead or in jail. Her primary goal was to find and stop the monster who ruined her life, and she'd done that when she watched Frank Carter die. With Audrey's help, she'd be able to put her demons to bed. Only one thing remained to do before moving on. She needed to thank the person who had saved her life all those years ago.

Later, Maggie would sit down with her aunt and uncle and tell them what she'd decided, but first, she needed to call Ryan. He was the reason she was alive today, and she wanted to thank him. She couldn't bring herself to say anything when she first learned who he was. Emotions had overwhelmed her, and she needed time. But now she'd come to terms with everything and she had a proposal for him.

She knew getting him to accept it would take some persuading, but she wasn't taking no for an answer.

Maggie pulled her car into the driveway and smiled when she noted she'd be alone in the house. She wanted the solitude. Aunt Julie was still working at the shop and Uncle Bobbie wasn't due home until sometime tomorrow.

She grabbed a bottle of water and made her way to the back deck. She needed privacy for the phone call she was about to make and from the deck, she could see when her aunt approached the house. Maggie pulled a cushioned Adirondack chair under the shade of the umbrella and settled in to make her call.

She took a sip of the cool water to relieve her parched throat before calling Ryan. Her stomach knotted when she heard the first ring. Thankfully, he answered on the second. Even though he saved her life as a child, they hadn't known each other long. They'd met on the road but had become friends through their common interests. She knew he checked the caller ID before answering when he greeted her by name.

"Hey Maggie, how's it going?"

Maggie chuckled to herself at the friendly sound of his voice, realizing how much she missed hearing it. "Everything's great! I'm at home, taking some time off for myself. What about you? Are you on the road or at home?"

"I just loaded my gear into my truck. I'm getting ready to hit the road in a few minutes."

Maggie breathed a sigh of relief. "That's perfect. I have a couple of things I'd like to discuss with you, and it'll be best if you're stationary. Maybe even sitting down, but not driving."

"That sounds rather ominous, Maggie. Is everything alright?"

"Everything's fine Ryan. Let me jump right in and tell you what's on my mind."

"Ok."

"Do you remember when we were in Chilliwack and you told

that story about finding the dead trucker and his daughter?" She asked, pausing for him to respond.

"Yes," she could hear the hesitation in his voice as he replied. "I also remember that you had a strange reaction to that story. Was it someone you knew?"

"Yes," Maggie's voice caught, her eyes welled up, but she continued, her voice just more than a whisper. "There is no easy way to say it. I was the little girl."

Ryan went silent on the other end. Maggie heard him gasp and swallow before he responded. "Oh, my god Maggie! I always wondered what happened to her. Anytime I see a girl with strawberry hair, my thoughts flood with what ifs."

Maggie cut him off. "You saved my life, Ryan. I've always wondered who the driver was that first found my dad's body and me in the back. The man who took the time to call 911 instead of thinking it was someone else's problem. I spent weeks in the hospital and from what my aunt told me, it was touch and go for a while, but what I know is if you didn't find me when you did, I'd be dead."

"If I'm being honest, when I first found you, I thought you were dead. I couldn't go past your father's body and check on you because the sight of you tore at my heart. You looked so battered and bruised I figured you had to be dead, too. You weren't moving. I didn't know you were alive until the paramedics rushed you to the hospital." Ryan choked back a sob.

"I've always hoped to find you and thank you, but when I heard you tell the story when we were in Chilliwack, I couldn't say anything. I was in shock. None of the guys I work with know what happened to me. I told no one. It was my cross to bear, the dark shadow that has surrounded me my whole life. Thank you. You don't know how much it means to me to say that."

"You don't have to thank me, Maggie. I wish I could have done more for you. I'm so happy you survived and continue to thrive."

Maggie felt the heat of shame creep across her cheeks as she wondered how happy he'd be if he knew what she'd done in her search for redemption. She took a deep breath and continued. "Well, that brings me to the second reason for my call."

"Oh?"

"I'm going back to school and getting out of trucking. To find the person who saved my life was the only reason I went into it," she lied with ease, "and to be close to my dad's memory, of course, which I've done. I'm trading trucking for journalism and I'm getting rid of my rig. I remember you mentioned you were thinking of becoming an owner operator. So, I'd like to give you my truck as a thank you."

"You, you, you can't just give me your truck, Maggie." Ryan sputtered. "I did what anyone would have done. Sell your truck to pay for school."

Maggie chuckled, "My aunt and uncle invested everything my parents left me to provide for my future. I don't need the money and it would make me happy. Do me a favour! Talk it over with Krissy and get back to me. There's no hurry. I've parked my truck at my aunt's shop in Cobden, Ontario. Talk to your boss. If you can sign it on to the company you're with, all you'll need to do is pick it up."

"Maggie, I have to pay you something for it."

"No, I won't take anything for it. It's how my father would want it too." Maggie finished. "What you did was worth more than the truck. To me, it's still not enough. Think about it and get back to me."

Ryan called Krissy and told her who Maggie was and her offer to him. After he talked with Krissy and many back-and-forth conversations between himself and Maggie, he agreed. He continued the argument that he wanted to pay for the truck and Maggie told him if he did, she'd put the money into a trust for his kids, so they agreed he'd take what he'd wanted to pay her and put money into a RESP for his children.

When they came to terms, Ryan, Krissy, and the kids drove to

Cobden for a mini vacation. Cobden didn't have a hotel, so Ryan's family stayed with Maggie and her aunt, while her uncle was on the road. They took care of the paperwork and switched the ownership over, then Ryan drove 'Big Red' back to Fergus, Ontario, where he would take a few days to set the truck up his way. Krissy and the kids followed him in their car.

Before he left, Ryan tried again to get Maggie to accept payment for the truck. She refused, reminded him of their agreement, and asked him to stay in touch. Maggie also worked out a deal with her aunt that Ryan could get the friend and family rate whenever he used her shop for services. Her aunt couldn't do enough for the man who saved Maggie's life, and she agreed.

Before Maggie told her aunt and uncle about Ryan and his visit, she told them what her plans were. Maggie was worried about how they'd react, but when she saw the relief on their faces she knew they supported her. They told her it surprised them when she started trucking, especially after what she'd been through, but they respected her choice and remained silent. It was with their blessing and encouragement that Maggie fired off a late application to Dalhousie's School of Journalism and crossed her fingers while she waited to hear from the university.

When she received her acceptance package to the program, the house was a flurry of preparations for her to move to Halifax and to attend Dalhousie. Taking care of the arrangements occupied most of the summer, but Maggie managed regular visits with Audrey as they worked on finding the families of Carter's victims.

In late August, Maggie found herself a two-bedroom condo in the downtown core and purchased it. The condo was close to campus. Maggie didn't want to live in the dorms, and felt the condo was an excellent investment for the years of school she had ahead. When it was time for her to leave for Halifax, her aunt and uncle took some time off so they could drive out together to get her set up.

7

It didn't take long for Maggie to become well ensconced in her new life. Although it took some getting use to, Maggie moved past the events that haunted her for so many years and pushed down the rage that had filled her life. She'd reinvented herself and started over.

Maggie was a student at Dalhousie, living in Halifax's downtown core. She didn't fit in as the stereotypical student, but tried her best to acclimate. A part of her wanted to continue killing even now, but she wanted a 'normal' life and fought against the urges. Over the years, she'd learned there was an abundance of deserving victims, but she only killed to control the bloodlust she felt while she searched for the man responsible for her pain and suffering. It filled her with an inner sense of peace when she accomplished this. It was only then that she put down the knife and never looked back.

After everything she had been through, she felt she didn't deserve to have someone in her life and avoided close connections. She had trust issues and letting someone get near her threatened the walls she'd built up. Maggie believed she had too much blood on her hands to play the part of the naïve young coed, so she remained friendly but didn't make friends. With her dark past, she felt it was better that way. So, when she went to social events, she was civil, but not too friendly. When someone asked her out, and she declined, they went on to the next person of interest.

After she moved to Halifax, she made use of the motorcycle license she got after getting her Commercial license and bought herself an Indian Chieftain for the ease of getting around the city. It also came in handy when she needed to escape the confines of the concrete jungle and head out for a ride in the beautiful Annapolis Valley or along the South Shore. She owned a compact car, but only used it in the winter when the weather wasn't conducive to riding.

On the first day of her second year at school, she met Liam. She'd ridden past him on her bike and when he saw her, he followed her back to campus on his own bike. She had allowed her hair to go back to its natural copper colour and her curls whipping in the wind caught his eye. Also, she rode an Indian, and his own bike was an Indian Roadmaster. So, he pulled into the spot beside hers and struck up a conversation.

It took her aback when he did, and the contrast of his vibrant cobalt blue eyes set into his tanned face made her pause. The look was striking. He struck up the conversation by talking about her choice of ride. By the time she had to leave to get to class; he asked if she wanted to take a ride along the South Shore this coming week-end. The weather looked promising, and without thinking, she agreed. Riding even in a group was a solitary activity, so she knew she wouldn't have to talk to him. She told him she'd meet him back here at 8 am on Saturday morning. He asked for her number, but she just shook her head and promised to be there.

She arrived at the campus at 7:45 am on Saturday morning to find he was already waiting. He flashed a smile of even white teeth that were hidden behind his short-trimmed goatee and moustache.

"You made it!" He exclaimed as she put her bike up on the kickstand, swung her leg over and dismounted.

"I said I would." She replied with a hint of sharpness. She tsked to herself and regretted her tone when she saw the hurt look on his face. When Maggie said she'd be somewhere, she'd be there, but he didn't know that and she'd been unkind. This wasn't one of her road buddies from her trucking days; there was something different about him. There was something kind and genuine. It was only one ride and they wouldn't be chatting much, so she'd try to be nice. She felt he was interested in more than a riding buddy, but she wasn't the girl for him. Maggie considered herself damaged goods. There were too many skeletons hidden in her closet. But the allure of having someone to ride with under the warm September sunshine was too appealing to ditch him now.

"Sorry, it's been quite the week. I could use a long ride. Did you have anywhere particular in mind?"

"I was thinking of heading towards Peggy's Cove, through Mahone Bay and on to Lunenburg. Maybe find some place along the way to stop for lunch if that's ok."

"Sounds good."

Maggie twisted her hair into one long braid down her back to prevent it from ending up a tangled mess, put her helmet back on, fastened the chin strap and slid back on her bike. Liam, meanwhile, fired up his bike, his helmet still on his head, and backed out of his spot. He waited for her to pull up beside him before heading out.

They took a nice, leisurely ride along the coast. The roads were full of gentle twists and turns that were conducive to riding. Maggie loved the freedom she felt as the scenery whipped past her. The wind on her face, the scents of the road that assaulted her nostrils, the ones that you missed when you were in a car. She smiled when she discovered Liam was easy to ride with. He knew the rules of the road and was a considerate leader. Midway through their ride, they found a restaurant, stopped and had lunch.

Despite having nothing in common but riding, it surprised Maggie to find how easy he was to talk to. But even more surprising was how much she enjoyed herself.

When the ride was over and they'd returned to the city, she found herself a little sad. Liam suggested dinner as well, but Maggie didn't want to lead him on and claimed she had homework to finish. So, they headed back to the campus, where they said goodbye and headed off in their own separate directions.

Over the next week, Liam made a point of searching for her bike in the campus parking lot while she was in class. Every time she came out, she found he left something, brief notes, his phone number, and once a single rose. Maggie knew he was waiting for her to contact him, but she couldn't. His thoughtfulness touched her, and it took every ounce of restraint not to call him. A week later, she came out of the building to find him parked beside her bike, waiting.

Her step faltered, and she almost went back into the building, but she made her way towards him, her helmet swinging in one hand and her phone in the other. Her hair cascaded around her shoulders like shimmering flames in the late afternoon sun. She could tell that this time he wasn't taking no for an answer. She had to hand it to him. He was persistent.

Startled by his Cheshire grin and those amazing eyes, she couldn't help herself and smiled back at him. She'd been so wrapped up in reading an email from her professor that she hadn't prepared herself for the fluttering sensation she felt in her stomach when she saw him. His tenacity won her over, and she gave him a chance.

She figured if he knew the truth about her, he'd have run and not looked back, so she decided not to tell him anything about her past. She would move forward at a slow pace and see how things panned out, but no matter how close they became, she wouldn't let him know about her darkness.

One year to the day they met, Liam proposed. They married in a small ceremony the day after she graduated, with Uncle Bobby and Aunt Julie in attendance. Uncle Bobby walked her down the aisle and gave her away, beaming with pride as he did.

A year later, they discovered she was pregnant and went for a ride to celebrate. A ride that would change their lives forever.

8

Maggie struggled to open her eyes. The blinding glare from the overhead fluorescence lights forced her to snap them closed again. Pain radiated across her head from temple to temple, hazing her thoughts with confusion. The drone of machines whirred through the fog that surrounded her as she fought for consciousness. The unmistakable beeping of medical equipment drifted through into the misty recesses of her mind. Her nostrils flared as she recognized the aroma of disinfectant that permeated the surrounding air.

She fought through the pain that racked her body as she rubbed at her eyes, her movements impeded by the tangle of cords attached to her wrists and hands. Her head throbbed with the constant booming that pulsed with an unending violence. She shifted her weight and felt a searing sensation tear across her abdomen. She let out a wounded gasp and winced. Maggie slid her hand down along the crisp, cotton sheets beneath her touch, moving her hand lower to her swollen bandage covered stomach and the memory flashed. The blare of gunfire, then the blood, oh so much blood. Liam! Oh My God NO!

"Liam!" she screamed. Her eyes flew open as the memory that flooded in overwhelmed her.

She blinked at the sudden assault of bright lights as she looked around the room. In the corner she saw an officer who rose from his chair at the sound of her strangled scream and the nurse who jogged in with a needle. The nurse scowled at the officer and injected the sedative from the needle into her IV line.

Maggie felt the medicine as it entered her system. A sense of calm overcame her as she slumped back onto the pillow, allowing the fog to once again cloud her reasoning. She wanted to speak with the officer who walked towards her. She attempted to rise, struggling in vain to resist the medication that pumped through her veins, as she succumbed to the inevitable drug induced sleep.

The officer turned and frowned at the nurse before he spoke.

"Nurse, you knew I needed to speak with Mrs. Murphy. I have to ask her some questions about what happened. I'd appreciate if the next time she wakes up, you didn't give her a sedative right away." The officer complained as Maggie slipped back into unconsciousness.

"I'm not going against the doctor's orders, not even for the police! She was shot. You, of all people, should know that. It's my job to keep her comfortable and to prevent her from damaging her sutures. My responsibility is to my patient first." She quipped. "She has a concussion, with swelling on the brain from where her head contacted with the pavement. Even you can't be so dense not to understand why she has swelling and bruising on the left side of her face. Plus the surgery on her abdomen to remove the bullet, skull fragments, and brain matter from the other victim. It is amazing that she'd survived at all! The infection in her wound is another matter, but you know all of this. When we're sure she's recovered enough to speak with you, we'll let you know." The nurse turned in a huff and left the room.

The officer stared down at the petite woman in the hospital bed. He flipped his notebook, noted that she regained consciousness, closed the pad, and put it away. He'd leave word at the front desk for them to call him when she woke up again. She didn't need a guard, so he'd head back to the station to see what else they'd found at the crime scene. One thing was for sure; when she woke up, she'd be in a world of hurt.

As soon as they heard what happened, Julie left the shop in the hands of her trusted staff and Bobbie parked his truck. They'd stayed at Maggie's, taking turns sitting with Maggie. Bobbie and Julie planned to stay with Maggie after she was released, not wanting her to be alone in her grief. They tried to handle as much as they could after the shooting, so she could focus on the healing process.

9

Maggie lay prone in her hospital bed, staring up at the ceiling, unable to control the flood of tears that streamed down her face. She'd awakened to find the officer was gone, but the memory of the events that landed her in the hospital slammed forward in her consciousness with an agonizing force. She struggled to get up, but her brain felt loose as it sloshed inside her skull, which throbbed with an unbearable intensity and the stitches in her abdomen pulled, causing a searing pain. The sudden movement caused her to vomit and an alarm to sound. A nurse rushed in with a needle poised. She paused and wrinkled her nose at the sour scent of vomit.

"NO!" Maggie yelled. The sound caused the throbbing in her head to intensify.

The nurse paused and looked at Maggie as if realizing that she was awake for the first time. "I'll get someone in to clean that up." She said, motioning to the pile of vomit on the floor.

"I don't care about that. I need some answers. Tell me what happened." After not getting a response, Maggie continued, "If you won't tell me what's going on, then please get me someone who will."

The nurse hesitated before she nodded curtly and went off, Maggie presumed, to find the doctor.

The sombre look on the doctor's face as he entered the hospital room spoke volumes. Maggie's guts rolled. She knew the news wasn't good. The grave expression on his face told a story that words couldn't convey. Still, she hoped.

"Good morning Mrs. Murphy, I'm Dr. Polkowski. How are you feeling?"

"I'm in a hospital bed, hooked to machines. My head throbs and I have stitches in my abdomen. My whole body hurts. I think that sums it up. What I need to know is where is my husband? Where's Liam?"

The doctor hesitated and flipped through the file on his clipboard. Maggie watched him and a fresh wave of tears formed in the corners of her eyes. She knew the news wasn't good. She knotted her hands into the sheets on the bed and prepared for the worst.

"I wasn't the doctor on duty when they brought you and Mr. Murphy in. But I'm sorry to have to tell you, Mr. Murphy succumbed to his injuries at the scene."

A heart-wrenching wail escaped Maggie's lips. She struggled to get out of bed, but a wave of nausea and dizziness overcame her and she collapsed back onto the bed.

"You're wrong!" She screamed. "I need to see him!"

"I'm sorry you can't. He sustained a gunshot wound to the back of his head. The bullet exited through the front and lodged in your abdomen. He was dead on arrival. You don't want to see him the way he is. You'll want to remember him as he was."

Maggie's hands flew to the bandages on her stomach, cradling her womb. "My baby?" She whispered.

The doctor shook his head. "I'm sorry, the damage was extensive. When the bullet exited your husband, it lodged in your uterus.

There was nothing we could do. We had to remove it to save your life."

"My uterus? You took my uterus?"

"I'm sorry, Mrs. Murphy, it was necessary."

Maggie's breath hitched as her hand pressed against the bandages on her abdomen. She pressed harder to feel the searing pain from her injury, the hollowness of what would never be. "What else? I know there's more."

"You suffered a severe concussion, and a fractured cheekbone. These injuries resulted from your fall after the shooting. Unfortunately, for the last few days, your body has been battling an infection. We've kept you sedated to allow you to recover."

"Few days? How long have I been here?"

"They brought you in 10 days ago."

Maggie's jaw sagged. '10 *days! How had I lost 10 days?*' She thought, looking up at the ceiling, her eyes fixated on a smudge on the perforated tiles. Tears pooled in the corners of her eyes and broke free, cascading down her temples. She was so lost in her own grief, she was unaware as the nurse inserted the sedative into her IV, and she once again succumbed to the darkness.

10

Maggie recovered enough from her injuries to speak with the police, so they sent an officer over to question her. She told the officer what she remembered, and he filled her in on what they knew happened on the boardwalk in Halifax that day. Maggie's memory of the events was foggy and she could only give him bits and pieces. He hoped that by filling her in on some details, it would help jog her memory. Before he left, he gave her his card and told her to call him if she remembered anything else.

What Maggie remembered from that day was the weather. It was warm and sunny, so she and Liam had taken their bikes out for a ride and ended up by the boardwalk in Halifax. They'd stopped there to stretch their legs. The news they were going to be parents was exciting for them and they were in a celebratory mood. They parked their bikes and walked along the water's edge.

Not wanting to leave his helmet with his bike, Liam carried it with him. That day, she followed suit. They walked down to get a Beaver Tail, her first pregnancy craving, and Liam beamed as he walked beside his pregnant wife. With the sticky sweet pastry in hand, Maggie wanted to sit while she ate. She found a spot on a retaining wall looking out at the water while Liam stood in front of her, with that Cheshire grin of his spread across his face. As she licked the sticky remnants from her fingers, Liam squatted down in front of her and kissed her tummy, whispering to their unborn child. Maggie remembered radiating with happiness.

A commotion brought her attention to the boardwalk, where out of nowhere, a biker raced down the wooden path. It was the middle of the day on a weekend; the boardwalk was busy, and pedestrians screamed and jumped out of the way in fear of being run down. On the back of the motorcycle, was an armed passenger. Neither she nor Liam even saw it coming. The sound of bullets, the splatter of warm blood on her face as Liam crumpled before her, and then the searing pain of the bullet that pierced her uterus, killing their unborn child. She too slumped and fell to the ground, the side of her face connecting with the concrete with a sickening thud. Maggie's mind was stuck on an old newsreel of a scene that replayed over and over. Then nothing.

The police reviewed what she remembered and compared it to what they knew from ballistics and eyewitness accounts. The officer informed her they believed Liam's shooting was a case of mistaken identity. It seemed the shooter mistook Liam for the leader of a motorcycle gang, someone they called 'Patch'. He was the President of a local motorcycle club, The High Rollers. The police thought it was a rival club, The Dark Enders, that hired the hit and was the reason Liam died. The Dark Enders wanted Patch. Patch turned up dead three days later. Even though the police suspected what happened, there wasn't enough evidence to make an arrest.

Maggie looked at the grainy picture of Patch the officer showed her. Yes, from a distance they could be mistaken for one another, but Patch was a hardened criminal. She could see it in his eyes, where in Liam's kindness shone through.

When the officer left, Maggie felt the familiar rage slip in like an old friend, simmering beneath the surface. It wouldn't take much to fan the flames and let the feeling take over. For the last five years, she'd controlled it, keeping it dormant while she led a happy life. Now she'd allow the monster within her to come forward so she could seek her revenge.

11

Maggie's aunt and uncle arrived to pick her up from the hospital and bring her home on the day they released her. Julia and Bobby wanted to take her with them to Cobden, but she insisted on going home. Home to the house she'd shared with Liam.

Both of the motorcycles were back in the garage at her house. Her uncle had claimed them and ridden them back for her, cleaning and covering them, knowing it would be too much for Maggie to handle.

Maggie slid into the backseat of the car, sidestepping the hand her uncle extended to assist her. She slumped back and stared out the window as the car pulled into her driveway and the garage door opened. Maggie was slow to get out of the car. Her focus was on what was inside of the garage.

She couldn't tear her gaze away from the two bikes nestled side by side at the back of the garage. Her eyes filled with tears and her hands pressed into the wound on her abdomen, allowing the pain from the incision to cascade around her. Looking at the bikes, she wasn't sure she'd ever ride again. They now represented one of the

40

worst days of her life, but she couldn't deal with them yet, so for now, the bikes would stay where they were.

Bobby and Julie continued past Maggie into the house, allowing Maggie to take as much time in the garage as she needed. They knew she was struggling to deal with her loss. Bobby made his way to the kitchen to cook supper. Julie, meanwhile, hovered in the living room, trying to figure out how she could help. She knew to stay out of Bobbie's way when he was cooking and Maggie was so broken; she needed more than Julie could offer her. The haunted look in Maggie's eyes reminded Julie of those of the fragile, broken child from so many years ago.

There was an overwhelming sense of loneliness when Maggie entered the house, even though her aunt and uncle were there. This house was no longer a home, just a shell of what was and what could have been. Liam's shadow filled every room. Maggie fiddled with their wedding picture on the hall table before flipping it over so she wouldn't have to look at it. Instead of planning a future, she now had to make the funeral arrangements and bury the man she loved. The morgue kept Liam's body until she was well enough to make the arrangements, since he had no other family. The thought of his body laying in the cold room all alone tore at her. Exhausted, she plopped down on the sofa as the emotions she'd been withholding broke loose and she sobbed.

Julie took the seat beside her and pulled her close, comforting Maggie and allowing her to cry on her shoulder. Bobbie peered around the corner to see if they needed him before stepping back into the kitchen to give the women some time.

"Oh, Aunt Julie, what am I going to do? Liam was my every-thing." Maggie sobbed.

"I won't say everything's going to be all right. You and I both know it's not. But you're stronger than you know, Maggie. I won't sugar-coat it. It's going to be tough, but we're here for you."

"I have to plan for Liam's funeral. I don't know where to begin."

A fresh wave of tears followed.

"Don't worry, I'll help you." Julie soothed, rubbing Maggie's shoulder.

Julie now had a sense of purpose in all the loss and devastation. Her gruff, no-nonsense attitude served them well under the circumstances. She found a funeral home, helped Maggie decide on a simple service and cremation and before they knew it, it was over. The vase with Liam's ashes would sit on the mantel in Maggie's living room until she could decide what to do with them.

It wasn't long before Julie and Bobbie had to head back to Ontario, and Maggie was once again alone with her thoughts in the empty house she had shared with Liam.

Maggie wandering around the house, looking for purpose. She wasn't ready to go back to work and with nothing but time on her hands, Maggie turned to the skill set she'd gained with her job as an investigative reporter after graduating from Dalhousie. She needed to learn more about the motorcycle gang that had devastated her life. Maggie got a copy of the police report, and she pored over it in fine detail. Every time she did, her throat went dry and her hands shook. She could feel the rage slip back into her life like a familiar friend.

She knew Liam's physical appearance was like that of the High Roller's President. The same gang leader who turned up dead less than a week after Liam's murder. She read divers had fished him out of the harbour with a single bullet wound to the head. This time, the rival gang made sure they got the right man. The man they wanted was Parker "Patch" Cummings. Maggie looked at the grainy photograph in the Herald and realized how close in resemblance he was to

Liam. It was a tragic mistake, an easy one to make from the distance of the shooter and the speed of the bike, but it was one that changed her whole life.

Patch was the president of The High Roller's; his death resulted from a turf war with The Dark Enders. The president of The Dark Enders was a burly man with a grey beard and a thick stock of curly grey hair. Maggie couldn't find any reference to his real name, but discovered everyone knew him as Butch. This information curdled in her stomach like a rotten piece of meat. Butch had also been her father's nickname. The thought that two men so different could share the same nickname enraged her.

Maggie felt the shroud of the killer slip back over her shoulders. It was never far away, always just below the surface, simmering inside, just on the verge of coming to a boil. Her fist clenched as she considered her options. Maybe she couldn't outrun her past. Maybe she was and always would be a killer, not just a woman who hunted and killed the man the police couldn't catch. This time, if she was going to get justice, a knife wouldn't work. It was unlikely she'd be able to get close enough to this Butch to make him pay with her knife. She'd need a gun, one that wasn't registered and one that she could conceal.

Maggie flipped through her files and thought about where she could get an unregistered gun. Then she remembered she had written a piece on a man who ran guns not too long ago. She'd have to call him and see what he could offer. Maggie knew he trusted her. She'd kept his identity secret, and he'd be able to recommend the right gun for her. Maggie would tell him it was for self-defence. She'd also need to practice shooting as soon as she could. It was the only way to gain competency and accuracy. Maggie did a little research and discovered she could practice without a firearms license at a local shooting range. There was one in Dartmouth that offered hand gun rentals with ammunition for target practice.

After she spoke with her contact and told him what she was looking for, he recommended a 9 mm Glock. It would take some time for him to get her one, but he would contact her when he did. Knowing the type of gun, she headed to the gun range to practice with the 9mm's there. They had a special running where she could rent one for $74.99 with 30 rounds of ammunition.

Maggie found the staff friendly as they went over the safety information before giving her a gun to use. The first time she held it in her hand, it felt foreign. A staff member set up the target and handed her some protective eye and ear gear before she could begin practicing. She took her time, felt the weight of the weapon in her hand, and aimed at the target. The bullet went wide and missed. Maggie cursed under her breath. She steadied her hand and tried again, squeezing off a few quick shots. One of these hit the target in the bottom right corner.

Frustrated, Maggie rubbed the back of her neck and shook her head. Her chest tightened and her stomach clenched as sensations of frustration boiled within. Shooting and hitting a target was more difficult than she assumed. She'd already gone through the 30 rounds of ammunition and only tore the corner off the target.

In her determination to become proficient, she went to the shooting range daily until she could hit the target dead on every time. There were a couple of kill shots to the chest and, of course, the head. After a few weeks, she was hitting the target in the kill zones every time.

She explained her constant presence to the operators of the range by saying she was working on a piece for the paper and needed first-hand information on how long it would take to become proficient with a handgun. In the end, they only charged her for the ammunition she used as long as they got a favourable mention in the article. They even took the time to show her how to dismantle and clean the weapon.

Maggie felt a little guilty over her lie, so she wrote a small article and sold her editor on the idea, as a follow-up to the illegal gun trade article and the legitimate side of target ranges, which they published as a filler piece.

It was a few weeks later when her contact got in touch, saying he had the gun. He explained he had recommended the 9mm handgun to her because of its size and that it is now one of the most popular self-defence calibers for concealed and open carry in the US. The 9mm provided a good balance between the ease of firing and stopping power. It was a lightweight with a moderate recoil and had less chance of over penetration. She could find the ammunition everywhere, although because she didn't have a license to own a gun, she'd have to get her ammunition from him.

Maggie met up with him and paid for the gun. After he left, she sat holding the gun in her hands. She liked the way it felt. Knowing the weapon he was getting her; she'd done her research and understood the gun. She asked him for 5 boxes of ammunition. He raised his eyebrows, but supplied them to her. On her way home, she bought a gun safe to store her gun in and kept it under her bed.

Now she had to formulate a plan of action. Each day, she scanned news articles for information on The Dark Enders and especially on Butch. She soon learned his Vice President was Quinton Mars, who went by the nickname Quinn. Tattoos covered his body; he even had two small tear drops under one eye, a sign within the gang community that he'd killed someone. There seemed to be something about The Dark Enders or The High Rollers in the news daily, even if it was only a small article tucked in the back of the paper. She compiled all the articles into a file for reference. Now she had to figure out a way to get close to them.

Maggie wondered if there was a way she could infiltrate the gang. They didn't patch women in as members; the women were 'old ladies' to a member or a 'girl' that was available to whoever wanted her. Neither of these options sat well with Maggie. There had to be another way. She just had to think of it. The thought of having to sleep with one of the gang members caused her to shudder. But she knew it might come down to that. In the meantime, she had to find a way in and that way might be through Quinton Mars.

<h1 style="text-align:center">12</h1>

Maggie lay in the bed she'd shared with Liam, her hand resting on his pillow, as she tried to figure out her next move. Her whole life was a mess. She had worked very little since the shooting. All she could focus on was her overwhelming need for revenge. Her hand traced the puckered scar where the bullet entered her body.

A few weeks ago, she went to a tattoo parlour and got a tattoo over it, not to cover it, but to mark it as a reminder. It took a while to find what she wanted, but in the end, she found a picture of shattered glass that appeared to have a bullet hole in the middle. It was perfect. So, she incorporated the scar as the centre and had the shattered lines tattooed around it. It was symbolic of her shattered life and dreams and was a silent nod to the career Liam had devoted his life to.

Liam made her feel like she could have it all, even the child she was terrified of bringing into the world. She'd prayed that she could protect the life that grew inside from the atrocities that she herself had experienced as a child. Liam knew nothing about her devastating past other than her mother dying of cancer and her father's murder,

47

but not about what happened to her. The scars that were invisible to the naked eye. She never wanted to see the look in his eyes if he knew. She'd sworn her aunt and uncle to secrecy. They didn't agree with her decision, reasoning that honesty was important in a marriage, but they honoured it. Sometimes she wondered what they would think if they knew the truth about her. Her motive for going into trucking was to find the bastard that had killed her father, raped her and left her for dead and then to kill him. She didn't know she'd find so many deviants along the way, and by the time she found Frank Carter, she would have killed more than a dozen men. There were some secrets that needed to be kept.

She lit up a cigarette for the first time in 4 years, as she planned her next move. Liam hated her smoking, and she quit when he asked her to, but the killer inside of her liked how the first drag tasted and how calming it was to inhale the nicotine into her lungs. Smoking again would work for the person she needed to become in order to kill those responsible for Liam's murder.

She'd continued going to target practice, but also joined a gym to work on building some muscle for her slight frame. Her body ached after every session, but she revelled in the sensation. She also took boxing classes and learned how to fight, absorbing everything she'd need in order to give herself an edge. The exercise was therapeutic, and it wasn't long before she felt like an improved version of herself. She still didn't have a plan, but now she felt she'd be ready.

Maggie realized that in order to seek retribution, she'd have to ride again. Riding was her way in with the Dark Enders. The problem was, every time she entered the garage, her stomach clenched, and she broke out into a cold sweat. The motorcycles sat side-by-side in the same spot Bobby parked them. She'd stop and run her hand along Liam's bike, vowing those responsible for his death would pay. She pulled out her gear and looked at the purple jacket and other girly items Liam bought for her and decided she needed something a little darker in order to gain the trust of the gang. The fun colours Liam preferred on her wouldn't work.

So, she got fitted for custom black leather pants and chaps. Maggie ordered a fitted black leather jacket made so that it nipped in at the waist and flared out at the hips. She ordered a skull face protector, something she would never have worn with Liam. But she wanted to appear darker, more sinister. Her doo rag had a long sheath attached to control her copper curls for when she rode down the street. The final touch was the black half helmet emblazoned with skulls. She had to fight the instinct to just go out and kill as she had before. This needed more finesse. Maggie would need to infiltrate the gang, and get the information she needed, if she was going to take out as many members as she could, otherwise she'd end up dead before she could avenge Liam's death. In the end, if she died, she didn't care. She'd already lost everything.

Maggie vowed that by the time spring came around, she'd be ready. She was an excellent rider and could manoeuvre her bike in the toughest situations. Maggie just had to take her maiden ride since the shooting. Something she'd avoided long enough. She'd gain strength and talent with a gun and used the rest of her time to learn everything she could about both gangs. The High Rollers would also pay, but first The Dark Enders, they were the ones responsible for the shooting.

She'd work to infiltrate them, which meant being places they'd be, showing up at dive bars and any place that would put her in the position to meet members so she could find a way in. Deep down, she knew it meant she may have to be intimate with whoever she got close to. She shuddered as she thought about it, but knew there was no other way for a woman to get in. They didn't patch women in, even in this day and age. Quinton may be a hardened killer, but so was she, and at least he was attractive, so he was her targeted way in. She felt she could make the leap and prayed she didn't have an adverse reaction if it came to that.

13

Maggie knew if she was going to proceed with her plan, she needed to push aside the fears and doubts she'd developed about riding since the shooting. She didn't mean to, but she blamed what happened with riding. Liam would still be alive if they hadn't been out on the bikes. She steeled herself, stepped out into the garage, and stared at the two covered motorcycles. Her stomach dropped and her chest heaved as she neared Liam's, running her hand across the now dusty cover, leaving snake like finger trails on its surface. Her forehead beaded with sweat and her heart raced as she reached over to uncover both bikes. The sense of foreboding twisted at her intestines. It wasn't long ago that she'd felt at peace when she rode, but now everything had changed. If she was going to move forward, she needed to put her fears to rest, and this was an important first step.

With both bikes uncovered, she moved to stand beside Liam's flat black Indian Challenger and stared at the empty seat Liam would never sit on again. She ran her fingers across the leather, wishing he was there now, sitting on it. Her breath hitched as she swung her leg over and settled onto the seat. She could almost feel his energy vibrate beneath her. She reached over and turned the key. The rumbling vibrations of the engine sent shockwaves through her body. Tears streamed down her cheeks as she leaned forward to rest her chest on the gas tank, allowing herself to embrace it as she said goodbye to the man it belonged to.

One day she'd have to get rid of his bike, but she wasn't ready to face that decision yet. Instead, she'd hold on to it. It may come in handy in her quest for revenge. When she regained control of her emotions, she popped it into gear and moved the bike to the front of the garage, parking it for the last time. She shut the engine off and as the machine's sensations ebbed away, so did her tension.

Maggie grabbed the cover and secured it back in place. When she came out to the garage, she'd intended to wash both bikes. But the thought of washing Liam's and removing his imprint was something she couldn't bring herself to do. So, his bike would remain in place until she was ready to deal with it at a later date.

She turned to her own Indian Chieftain with its crimson metallic finish, a nod to Big Red. It was time to polish it up and take it for a ride before she began down the road of seeking justice for Liam and their unborn child.

She pushed her bike out onto the driveway and began polishing it, something she would have done before, but she couldn't bring herself to look at the bikes until now. They had always polished their bikes before covering them up and again when they uncovered them. She polished and rubbed until her bike shone in the midday sun. While she was at her task, a few neighbours stopped by, each offering her their condolences on her loss. Every time someone spoke, it felt as if they'd ripped open her wounds and left her bleeding on the street. It had been almost a year, but this was the first time she'd been out in the yard for more than a few minutes. Still, she mumbled thank you and focused on her task at hand. She figured they felt they needed to say something to her, even after all of this time.

She'd put off riding long enough. Now she needed to get on her bike and go. Maggie stared at the key in her hand, uncertain if she could ride again. Doubt crept in and her stomach heaved before she inserted it into the ignition. She turned it and felt the bike vibrate to life between her thighs. After tightening the chin strap on her helmet, she slipped a pair of sunglasses on and put it in gear. She turned left out of her driveway and headed down the street, feeling the familiar sensation of freedom wrap around her like a soft hug. As the wind whipped against her face, all of her fears and doubts peeled away and scattered to the wind. With a wild abandon she continued on the winding back roads.

When she returned home, she felt like one with her ride. Her trauma hadn't affected her ability to ride nor her skills on two wheels. It was time to move forward.

14

It didn't take long for Maggie to feel comfortable on her bike again. This was an important step if she was going to put her plan in motion. She laid her new gear out onto the bed she'd shared with Liam, including the gun in the shoulder holster she purchased. With a minor adjustment, it fit beneath her jacket without showing. Her weapon of preference, a knife, was in a sheath sewn to the right leg of her chaps. In order to make the leather appear worn, she'd thrown it all in her dryer to beat it down and soften it up. She didn't want to smell of new leather when she came in contact with someone from the Dark Enders. She'd also worn it around the house to create creases in the knees and elbows. Heading out with a polished look wasn't the persona she wanted to portray.

She made use of her journalism contacts and learned that tonight a group of The Dark Enders would be in a little out of the way bar just outside the city. She planned to ride out there and stop in for a drink. It was not the sort of place she'd frequent, but she hoped she'd get noticed by the members, and if she was lucky, she'd meet Quinn. She wasn't counting on it, but she knew she was bound to stand out,

54

just by her being there and holding her own in a room full of bikers. Of course, with her tiny frame and red hair, she wasn't hard to miss.

Maggie took her time with her shower as she prepared to go out. She kept her makeup to a minimum and dried her hair to allow her natural curls to set. Just as she finished, the doorbell rang. *'I'm not expecting anyone.'* She thought as she tightened the tie of her house-coat and went to answer it. She peered through the sidelight to see a man standing at her door. With the chain still engaged, she opened it.

"Yes? Can I help you?"

"Mrs. Murphy?"

Maggie nodded.

"I'm Detective Tate." He said, holding up his badge. "I'm doing some follow-up on the shooting. Do you have a few minutes to chat?"

The timing wasn't great, and it seemed odd that a detective would come to her house for a follow up so long after the shooting, so Maggie hesitated before she nodded and opened the door. She stepped aside and allowed him to enter, clutching the robe tight to her chest, lead him to the living room, and motioned for him to sit down.

"Do you have more information for me? Did you catch the killer?" She asked as she sat in the chair across from him.

The detective hesitated before he spoke, shaking his head. "First, let me tell you how sorry I am for your loss. Unfortunately, we haven't apprehended anyone yet."

Maggie tucked a strand of hair behind her ear and looked up into the detective's clear blue eyes. There was something familiar about him. She paused as she tried to place where she knew him from. Could he have been in the hospital while she was there? She could tell by the way he was staring back at her he recognized her as well.

She looked down and responded, "Thank you."

"I'm sorry, Mrs. Murphy. Have we met before?" Detective Tate asked.

Maggie looked back up at the detective.

"I was just thinking the same thing."

"This may be out of line, but did you used to be blonde?"

Maggie's eyes narrowed as she looked him over. *'Oh, my god!'* she thought, *'now I know where I know him from. It's the detective from Chilliwack!'*

She regained her composure and responded, "Yes, I was. And I just remembered where we met. You interviewed me in Chilliwack after they found a man murdered in the parking lot." Maggie smiled to herself as she watched the look of shock flash across his face.

"Now I remember you're the spunky truck driver. It was your eyes, I remembered. They stood out. I thought the jade green of your eyes was better suited to a redhead." He chuckled. "I'm glad to see I was right. Your natural colour suits you."

Maggie blushed and hated herself for enjoying the compliment. The smile left her lips as she changed her tone. She needed him to leave so she could finish getting ready.

"Why don't you tell me why you're here?"

Colby Tate noticed the change in her demeanour and got to the point. He asked her what she remembered about the shooting. After she filled him in, not telling him anything new, he told her what they knew and who they felt the gunman was working for based on the evidence. He explained to her they didn't know who the actual shooter was, but they had a few leads. He described what witnesses reported, hoping it would jog her memory. She told him everything she knew and accepted his business card before he got up to leave, promising to get in touch with him if she remembered anything else. As he left, Maggie asked him a random question.

"Detective?"

"Yes?"

"Do you have any children?"

"Yes, a four-year-old daughter." He replied with a smile. "Why?"

"You and your wife hold on to her. Life is too short." Maggie finished.

"I know that all too well. My wife died of cancer when Evelyn was a baby." Tate responded with a sad look in his eyes.

"I'm sorry." Was all she could say as he walked away.

Maggie shut and locked the door behind the detective. She stood just out of sight and watched as he got into his car and drove away. Now that he was gone, Maggie needed to finish getting ready. She dressed in her leathers, opting not to bring the gun tonight, but slid her hunting knife into the sheath in her chaps. Maggie applied a coat of lipstick to go with the light makeup and tamed her hair into the leather cover, which would protect it from the wind. She inspected herself in the mirror, satisfied that she appeared the way she intended, then went out and started her bike.

15

Maggie learned that the Dark Enders were going to be at the Capital bar tonight and she didn't want to miss this opportunity to run into them. She chose her full-face helmet, put it on and fastened the straps before she fired up the bike. She pulled to the bottom of the driveway, clicked the close button on the garage door remote and took a deep calming breath before heading out into the darkness.

When she pulled into the dimly lit parking lot, she noted there were many Harleys parked in it. She chose a spot near the exit and backed her bike in for a quick get-a-way if need be. Maggie knew that the number of bikes here would attract regular bikers, those without a gang affiliation, so her walking in wouldn't be too problematic. Still, she steeled herself for the uncertainty of what lay ahead.

She turned off the ignition and swung her leg to dismount the bike, choosing to keep her helmet on until after she entered the bar.

The effect of her removing her helmet and shaking out her hair would attract attention. Good or bad, she knew doing so would leave an impression on the men in the room. The women present were another story. But she wasn't interested in them.

She unzipped her leather jacket just enough to expose a glimpse of her cleavage and strode to the front door. With a single movement, she stepped into the room and removed her helmet and the sheath controlling her hair. She bent forward and shook out her hair, and swung her head back to allow the copper curls to fall into place, framing her face. Maggie's expression remained deadpan as she scanned the room.

As she did, she noticed the voices had stopped and, other than the background music, silence filled the room. Her eyes flicked across the faces that were turned towards her, and she went straight to the bar, ignoring the glares from the women and the catcalls that began in her wake from the men.

She slipped onto a stool and waited for the bartender to acknowledge her. She watched as he looked around the room before he made his way down to where she was sitting.

"What can I get you?" He asked.

"Whiskey neat." She replied, choosing to forgo her usual wine under the circumstances.

He was quick to pour her drink and place it in front of her. With her whiskey in hand, she spun her stool around and stared at the sea of faces that stared back at her. She lifted her glass in a mock salute and turned back to the bar. In the mirrored wall behind the bottles of liquor, she watched as two women approached her from behind and prepared herself for the inevitable onslaught headed her way.

"I think you're in the wrong place, bitch." One called out as she approached.

"Ya." Chimed in the other.

Maggie took a long pull from her glass before she turned around. She looked both women over before she responded.

She tipped her glass to them and said, "I'm just here for a drink."

The taller of the two scowled at her and then, without warning, swung her fist. Maggie slid off her stool before it could connect. She had to look up as the woman was several inches taller.

"I wouldn't do that again." She hissed between her teeth.

"What the fuck you say?" The shorter one challenged as she lunged at Maggie.

Maggie's right hand shot up and caught the woman around her neck at the base of her jaw and squeezed. "I said I'm just here for a drink."

The taller woman swung at her again, defending her friend, and Maggie used her left arm to deflect her. The look of shock that crossed the woman's face was well worth the bruise she knew she'd have tomorrow. She heard a round of laughter from some bikers at a nearby table. This seemed to infuriate the woman further. The one whose neck she held onto clawed at the leather gloves Maggie still wore, trying to get Maggie to release her.

With a swift movement, the bartender intervened by slamming a baseball bat on the top of the bar. "Enough of this bullshit. Either break it up or take it outside."

Maggie kept her eyes on the taller one, but she still didn't release the smaller one, waiting to see what would happen. The woman lunged at Maggie and before Maggie could react, a biker grabbed the woman from behind and pulled her away. Maggie turned her attention to the one whose neck she still held. Making and maintaining eye contact, she released her and watched her slither back to her table.

Maggie turned her back on the crowd, thankful for the mirrored wall behind the bar that enabled her to monitor the rest of the room, and breathed a sigh of relief at the defensive training she took. She raised her glass to take another sip, at the same time keeping a watchful eye on the two women who were complaining to the guy who broke up the fight when she noticed the bartender staring at her.

He moved closer. "You're either tough as nails or the stupidest woman I've seen." He whispered.

Maggie winked at him. "Maybe a little of both." And took

another small sip. The bartender smiled and moved back to the other end of the bar.

Through the mirror, Maggie watched as a man approached her. She'd done her research, and saw the scar down his right cheek, which gave his identity away. Maggie knew it was Dobby Cruise, aka Crusher, who was approaching her. His t-shirt stretched across his well-muscled body. She caught his eye in the mirror as he reached her seat.

"Seems we have a firecracker in our midst." He said as he nodded to the bartender, who cracked a Keith's and slid it down the bar to Crusher. He caught it, picked it up and took a swig as Maggie turned towards him.

She looked him up and down before replying, "I'm just here for a drink. I saw the other bikes and figured it was a biker friendly bar. I guess I figured wrong."

Crusher threw his head back and laughed, a rich baritone sound.

"Oh, it's biker friendly, just not the bikers you mean. I think you're out of your element here, missy."

Maggie chuckled. "I think I held my own with Frick and Frack over there," she replied, motioning with her head to where the two women sat, scowling at her.

"I'll give you that." He said as he finished his beer. "You should drink up and move on. I think you're more trouble than you're worth."

Maggie smiled and placed a mock look of shock on her face as she slid off her stool, giving the full effect of her tiny frame against his massive one. "Little old me?" She questioned.

He couldn't help himself and laughed again. This caused another biker to make his way towards them. Maggie watched him and grinned to herself. She may have hit pay dirt and waited for Quinton Mars to join them.

"Hey Crusher," he called out, "what do we have here?"

"I'd say we have a firecracker in our ranks, Quinn. I just suggested she should drink up."

"Now, let's not be too hasty. I think female bikers are hot, especially when they have fiery red hair." Quinn winked at Maggie as he moved to stand beside her.

Maggie saw the quick flare of anger that flashed across Crusher's face before he lifted his arms in surrender. "I'll leave you to it." He said as he turned and walked back to his table.

Maggie pulled some of her hair forward and examined it as Quinn slipped onto the stool next to hers. "I don't think it's fiery," she retorted, "more of a burnished copper."

Quinn glared at her. "You're kinda brazen for someone who coulda been in for a lot of hurt."

"This is a public bar, isn't it?" Maggie asked, looking around the room. She couldn't help herself and allowed her tone to be snarky.

"Yes," he replied, "but it's a private party."

"Oh, I'm sorry." Maggie allowed herself to look shocked. "I didn't see the sign." As she swivelled on her stool to look at the door for the sign she knew wasn't there, she caught the look of anger that flickered across Quinn's face and said. "I'll just get going. I'm sorry to have bothered you."

Quinn grabbed a hold of her shoulder and held her in place. If it wasn't for the thickness of the leather of her jacket, she was sure she'd find he'd left fingerprint bruises there. She allowed her eyes to widen and look up at him. His gaze softened.

"No need to rush off. Let me buy you a drink."

Maggie knew she should decline, but she felt she didn't have a choice, so instead, she nodded and smiled. Getting to know him would work to her advantage. She'd have to nurse the second drink. She didn't like to drink and ride and one was her limit if she did.

He stuck out a hand. "Name's Quinton, but my friends call me Quinn."

Maggie shook his hand. "Everyone calls me Maggie."

16

Colby pulled into the RCMP headquarters after his meeting with Maggie Murphy. She'd left an impression on him, but now he had more questions. He went to speak to her regarding her husband's murder, but now he pulled out his case files from the Trans-Canada killer case and checked his notes, especially the ones he made during his interview with her.

Colby flipped through his notebook and saw that her maiden name was Hopkins. He wanted to know more, so he keyed her married name into the search bar to see what came up.

The most recent information he found was about the shooting, which wasn't a surprise, but he also found a list of articles she'd written. He read a few of the articles and found that she was an accomplished journalist. She'd even won a few awards. Then he took her married name off the search and just searched for Maggie Hopkins. The articles he found caused his jaw to slacken and his eyes to widen. There was a reference to a murder. He couldn't find the details in a regular google search, so he switched to the RCMP database to find out more. Bingo.

He read the file that was attached to her name. The murder of her father, the assault and life-threatening injuries she sustained during the attack, and a part of him felt a deep sense of loss for the young girl she'd once been. She'd been through hell. He looked through the crime scene photos and those detailing her injuries. He noticed, according to the report, they didn't catch her attacker, which meant he was still out there somewhere. The father in him felt sickened by the trauma she endured. His own daughter was only a few years younger than Maggie would have been at the time of the attack. He felt rage bubble up within him at the injustice.

Colby took some deep breaths to allow himself to calm down before he selected and printed a few pages from the report, added some articles she'd written, and started a new file. He copied his notes from his notebook and added the recent shooting information. He wasn't sure why he did this. She wasn't a suspect, but her life and what she'd endured fascinated him. Deep down, he knew there was a lot more to Maggie Murphy below the surface.

He considered how strong of a woman she must be in order to survive so much trauma in her life, and then to continue on and succeed. Many abused girls end up on drugs, prostitution, or struggling within the system. She must have had a strong family support at home and undergone some extensive therapy, he figured. He couldn't help but wonder what made her give up trucking. All the evidence he found indicated it was after he interviewed her in Chilliwack. He wondered if a killer on the loose nearby was too close for comfort, especially after everything she'd gone through. He made a note to ask her about it when he saw her again, and he was going to make a point of seeing her again. There was something very intriguing about her.

He flipped through the notes from Chilliwack and looked over the conversation he'd had with Frank Carter. There was something about him that never sat right. His whole demeanour was a red flag. Then, they found the burned-out wreckage of his truck and the scattered debris from his trailer, and they knew they'd found their killer. The packages of pink hair clips mixed in with the other items were the last link to the crimes.

It bothered him how easy it was to link the serial killer crimes to Carter. It was too neat. He was dead, his truck burned beyond repair, but somehow the 'tools' used in his murders survived the fire and littered the gully. The other thing, his impression of Carter didn't fit that of a vigilante killer like the profile suggested. Carter felt to him more like the intended victim of the vigilante than the perpetrator.

But the case was closed. Still, Colby couldn't help but make a few notes regarding his thoughts and opinions of the case. He found he was still questioning the validity of Carter as being the killer. Could the actual killer have framed him? Were they getting too close to catching the killer? Unfortunately, the evidence didn't support his theory. The other thing of note was that since Carter's death, the murders stopped. Still, Colby had the sense there was more to the story, but he couldn't investigate his theories, not with the file marked closed.

17

Maggie huddled under the blanket, her knees drawn to her chest and her eyes red rimmed and swollen from crying. Her wedding album lay opened on the coffee table in front of her. She'd spent the last hour poring over the pages of pictures, focusing on how happy she and Liam were on their wedding day. On the floor, beside her, lay a pile of crumpled used tissues. She sighed as she looked at the photo on the open page. The one taken just before they kissed after the JP announced them man and wife. Liam looked at her in a way that made her heart melt, even now. The look spoke volumes of the depth of his adoration for her. She'd never felt so loved and safe as she had at that moment.

Maggie heard the phone ring and rubbed her eyes to remove the water that was leaking from the corners. She wasn't in the mood to talk to anyone right now, and almost ignored it, but when she checked the call display, she saw it was Audrey. Audrey was the only person who knew all of Maggie's secrets and yet still loved her. Maybe Audrey loved her despite the secrets. She was also the only person Maggie could seek solace from. Maggie hesitated, then answered it.

"Hi Audrey."

"Hi Maggie, how are you managing?"

Maggie's throat caught, and before she could answer, Audrey continued.

"I've found another one."

Those four words snapped Maggie out of her self-pitying feelings of woe. She sat up straight and put the phone on speaker, wiping her face with a fresh tissue.

"Another one? Are you sure?"

"Yes. I've just had confirmation. The details are the same and I just matched the hair-clip from the ribbon you gave me to the mother's post online."

Maggie heard Audrey take a sip of something and waited for her to continue.

"I was searching through the case files and found one that fit Carter's victimology. Then I began looking at the mother's social media accounts until I found a picture of her daughter wearing the hair clip. This morning she posted a tribute to her daughter and included a picture of the remaining hair clip."

"Can you send me the file and mother's social media links so I can look them over?"

"Of course, but..."

"Audrey, I trust you. It's just... I need this right now. I need something to distract me from my life before it swallows me up."

"Of course, Maggie, I understand. Can I help? You know first-hand that I'm a good listener."

"I need to work through this on my own, Audrey. I hope you understand. If things don't improve, I'll call you, I promise. In the meantime, I'll go through the evidence. When I'm done, I'd like to be the one to send out the card."

There was a pleading sound in Maggie's voice. Audrey knew Maggie was struggling with everything since Liam's death, and she made a mental note to check in more often.

"Maggie, of course you can, but remember, this is all because of you. None of these families would have closure if you hadn't found

Carter. What you did has allowed so many families to be at peace. You should be proud of yourself."

Maggie sighed, "It's hard to feel pride when you were also a victim. And you're as much a part of this as I am. You've done most of the research to find the victims and their families. I just made sure the monster responsible paid."

Audrey chuckled. "Let's say we make a great team. Maggie, take care of yourself. I worry about you. If you need anything, I'm only a phone call away."

"Thanks Audrey. And thank you for this. It's just what I needed right now."

18

Maggie put her coffee cup down and leaned back, she finished reviewing what Audrey had sent her and knew they'd found another one. The evidence confirmed that the clip belonged to Missy Randall, and the package arrived this morning in the mail from Audrey containing the hair clip and card they'd designed to inform families that the monster, Frank Carter, was dead. Audrey handled most of the investigating to find the families, but when she found one, she passed the information along to Maggie for a second pair of eyes, just to be sure. Then Audrey would address the envelope, include the card and hair clip, which she handed over to Maggie's Uncle Bobbie to mail. As a truck driver, he could drop them in mail boxes anywhere along his route. He never asked questions about what was in the packages, or what they were for, because he was doing it for Maggie.

Audrey and Maggie decided years ago that having the packages sent from different post marks made it more difficult if someone looked for the person who killed the monster or sent the cards. They wanted to bring closure for the families but still had to protect themselves.

Now that she knew the identity of the victim, Maggie repackaged the card and hair clip. She figured she could take a ride out to the Enfield Big Stop and find a post box along the way. The ride would do her good and help her clear the thoughts that still rattled around in her brain. The act of getting back on her bike aided in her healing, and she knew Liam would want her to ride for pleasure again.

Maggie tucked the little bubble wrapped envelope into her saddlebag. Her journalism skills came in handy and helped her in her search to find the address of a victim's family. Missy's mother, Etta, hadn't been too hard to find. She had regular posts on social media in her search for justice. The only thing that concerned Maggie was that Etta would also post a picture of the returned hair clip and postcard. This was another reason she didn't want the postmark to be too close to home and why Bobbie was such an integral part of the process. Maggie made a mental note to check online when she returned home to see if any of the other families had started a Facebook group about the returned hair clips.

Maggie hopped on her bike, felt the engine rumble between her thighs and made her way to highway 102. Traffic was light this time of the day, making the ride pleasant. Her initial apprehension about getting back on her Indian was long gone. Riding the open road was both an exhilarating and freeing feeling that she enjoyed. The more she rode again the more she realized that riding wasn't the reason for her loss. She rode before she met Liam, and she loved the way it felt to be back on her bike. He'd want her to continue doing what she loved. Maggie reasoned riding would help her catch his killer.

The sign for exit 7 loomed ahead, and she signalled her intent. She would continue on the number 2 until she hit the post office, mail the package and then turn around to fuel up at the Big Stop. If she was lucky, she'd run into a driver or two she knew from her trucking days. It would be nice to catch-up.

She fuelled, parked her bike and went through the store to the driver's lounge so she could cut through to the back on her way to the truck parking lot. She left her helmet on her bike, and she ran her fingers through her hair to free up some knots as she went. Today, Maggie wore her new leather pants to help break them in. She also wore her leather jacket with the hidden sheath built in for her knife. She didn't carry a ceramic one. Instead, she chose her large hunting knife, one whose hilt felt comfortable in her grasp. She'd taken the time to sharpen the edge to a fine razor finish so that it would accomplish whatever task she chose for it. Maggie didn't expect to need it, but wanted to get used to its presence inside the jacket.

She patted the knife through her jacket and stepped out into the parking lot. A smile swept across her face as she did. On the other side of the lot, she recognized Big Red and knew that Ryan was here. She hadn't seen him since she'd gone back to her natural hair colour and wondered if he would recognize her. As she made her way towards his truck, she saw him step out of the cab with his garbage in tow. She waved at him and saw the questioning look flash across his face. Maggie knew he didn't know who she was. She would remedy that in a hurry.

19

Maggie noticed Ryan hesitate. His eyes were downcast when he saw her wave. She didn't want him to turn back to his truck to avoid her. She knew he was shy, and if he didn't recognize her, he may not want a confrontation. Maggie called out, "Hi Ryan," As she came within earshot. He looked up at her and his eyes narrowed.

"Do I know you?" He asked.

She chuckled, "If you don't, I'm sure Big Red does."

She watched in amusement as his jaw sagged and recognition flashed across his eyes. His long legs were quick to close the gap between them as he wrapped his arms around her and pulled her into a big embrace.

"Oh my God Maggie, you look fantastic." He said as he stepped back and held her at arm's length.

"It's good to see you Ryan, do you have time for a coffee?"

"For you? Of course."

They made their way into the restaurant at the far end of the building and sat at a table facing the door. They stayed there for over an hour, chatting about everything and nothing. Ryan filled her in on how Big Red was running. He told her he was very thankful she'd hooked him up with her aunt Julie as his mechanic. She did most of his oil changes and annual inspections. She'd even taught him how to take care of some of the minor work himself. Maggie noticed the way his mannerism changed when he began talking about his newfound skills and felt pleased for him.

Ryan's face lit up with pride as he described some repairs he'd done on his own, things he wouldn't have known how to do a few years ago. Maggie smiled as she listened to him and made a mental note to thank her aunt for taking him under her wing. What she was most thankful for was that he didn't offer his condolences regarding Liam's death. It would have opened the wound again. He and Krissy sent flowers to the hospital with a kind note, but he had the good sense not to bring it up. Maggie couldn't help but notice as she talked to Ryan how much she missed the camaraderie of her fellow drivers, but that part of her life was in her past. There was a reason she was no longer trucking.

Her chest ached at how much she missed her road family. Maybe she needed to give a few of them a call and catch up, Josh and JD, for instance. It had been too long. She'd tried to distance herself from everything to do with trucking when she switched gears and went back to school. Now she realized it was a part of her, in her blood, so to speak. It was the world she grew up in. She wouldn't drive again, but it was time to reconnect with old friends.

When they finished their coffees, Maggie walked back with Ryan to his truck so he could show her what he'd done to it. She admired the new heated swivel seats he put in and the bits of chrome he'd added. She also noticed how clean he kept it. It confirmed that giving the truck to Ryan had been the best decision.

"She looks great, Ryan. I knew you were the right person to have her." Maggie teased with a slight bump of her shoulder.

Ryan beamed. "I wished you'd let me pay for her, but I appreciate you didn't. I started making money right away and Krissy and I have been able to put money away for the kids' education. Daniel is graduating from high school this year, and he's planning on McMaster for medicine! Can you imagine? I'm going to have a doctor in the family!"

"That's wonderful. Tell him congratulations from me. And say hello to Krissy."

They said their goodbyes and Maggie made her way back to the building when she saw a familiar figure heading towards her across the parking lot. An idea flashed through her mind, and Maggie went to speak to her.

20

Noelle stepped out of the building into the bright sunshine, as she prepared to search for a 'companion' for the night, when she noticed a petite woman with a mass of red curls heading her way. Noelle watched the woman's purposeful strides and wondered if she should step back inside, in case she'd serviced this woman's husband and she was out for blood. She heard the woman call out and use her name, and her stomach churned, but she braced herself for whatever lay ahead as the woman neared.

Maggie noticed the look on Noelle's face as she approached and wondered why she appeared to fear her. She smiled, hoping it would put Noelle at ease and let her know she meant no harm.

"Noelle, can we talk?" She asked as she got closer.

Noelle's eyes narrowed. "Do I know you?"

Once again, Maggie had to remind herself she looked very different from the trucker with the blonde bob. So, she explained who she was and noticed the look of surprise that flickered across Noelle's face before she agreed to chat.

Maggie led Noelle back inside the restaurant and offered to buy her supper for her time. Maggie was hungry and thought she might as well eat before heading home. She didn't have all the details of her plan worked out, but she knew everything would come together once she started talking. All she had to do was get Noelle to agree.

Maggie waited until they finished eating to tell Noelle why she wanted to speak to her. She allowed the idea to form while they ate and she listened to Noelle's plan to spend another month here before heading home. Noelle told Maggie she had sublet her apartment in Chilliwack and the woman staying there would like to stay as long as Noelle allowed her to. This piece of news would work out in Maggie's favour. She just hoped Noelle would agree to what she had in mind.

Noelle leaned back in her seat when she finished eating and waited for Maggie to explain why she wanted to talk to her. It was obvious this little impromptu dinner wasn't so they could get to know one another. Maggie hesitated, trying to find the right words, then dove in.

"Noelle, I have something I want to propose to you," Maggie said as she watched Noelle's eyes widen. She couldn't be honest with her about everything, so she embellished the truth.

"I'm doing an article for my newspaper, and I need someone with your special skill set to help me out."

Noelle burst out laughing, "Skill set? Do you mean my skills as a working girl? Are you writing an article about hookers?"

"No," Maggie paused, "I'm writing about biker gangs." Maggie finished watching the look of confusion flash across Noelle's face.

"As you can see," Maggie continued, waving her hand over her attire, "I ride. That doesn't guarantee me access to the biker's club-houses or meeting places. I know where they congregate, but women who enter these places are 'old ladies' of a member or girls who are 'available' to members. Do you see where I'm going with this?"

"You want me to 'give it away' to the bikers to help you write your story?"

"Well. Yes and no. I want to cover your living expenses while you stay here to help me, and I will cover your flight back to Chilliwack, or drive you there myself."

"And what will your position in all this be?"

"I'm hoping to get close enough so I can get to know a member of the gang. But I'll be honest, I haven't worked out all the details. The idea only came when I saw you here. I have things to figure out, and of course you need time to think about it, because if you agree, we will have to find a way for you to gain access to the club I'm looking into."

She watched Noelle as she digested the information. Maggie knew very well that what she was asking Noelle to do was huge, and possibly dangerous, but she had just the place to set her up. Maggie still had the condo she bought in downtown Halifax when she attended university. She rented it during the school year to a couple of students, but the school year had ended and it was vacant at the moment. By the looks of things, Noelle had little with her, and Maggie had no problem taking her shopping for an appropriate wardrobe for the job ahead.

"How long do I have to think about it?"

"Today's Wednesday. How about you let me know by the week-end? If you're in, I'll come pick you up and take you to a condo I own in downtown Halifax. You can stay there. You'll also need some more clothing, so I'll take you shopping and get you set up."

"This must be a big story if you're going to all of this trouble."

"It is." Replied Maggie without elaborating.

Maggie handed Noelle a card with her number on it before she headed back home. Based on Noelle's reaction, Maggie was certain she would help. There was something in her eyes that gave it away. Maybe it was the possibility of a little adventure.

As Maggie rode home, she thought about how her plan would work and mulled over the details. By the time she arrived at her house, she had figured much of it out. There was only one obstacle, and that was how to get Noelle into the clubhouse and then to gain access herself.

21

First thing Friday morning, Maggie's phone rang. She checked the call display, but didn't recognize the number. She considered letting it go to voice mail, but then realized it could be Noelle, so she answered it before it stopped ringing.

"Hello?"

"Hi...um...is this Maggie?"

Maggie heard the hesitant voice on the phone and knew it was Noelle's.

"Yes, it's Maggie, Noelle. Did you decide?"

"Yes. I'm going to do it. I could use a change of pace, so to speak, and this sounds interesting. I'm taking a break from my life back home, so why not switch things up?"

Maggie breathed a sigh of relief, realizing she'd been holding her breath, waiting for Noelle's answer. "That's wonderful Noelle! How about if I come now and pick you up? We can do some shopping, get some groceries for you and I'll get you set up at the condo."

"Ok," she paused, "when did you want me to get started with the biker gang?"

"Oh. Not right away. There are still some things I have to look at and plan for before we can move forward. We don't want to make a move unprepared and find ourselves in trouble."

"Did you want me to continue working the Big Stop while you get everything sorted out?" Noelle asked. Maggie could hear the apprehension in her voice.

"No. I think it's better to get you set up, for us to get to know each other and maybe together we can figure out the best way to move forward. Go inside and get yourself a coffee. I'll come in and find you when I get there."

When she arrived at the Big Stop, Maggie parked and went in search of Noelle. She found her right away. Noelle had positioned herself so that she was facing the door and waved at Maggie as she entered.

Maggie slipped into the chair across from Noelle after greeting her and made herself comfortable. The server came over to see if Maggie wanted anything, but she declined and asked for the check.

Maggie turned to Noelle. "We should get going. I want to stop at the Mic Mac Mall to get you some clothing, simple things like jeans, T-shirts, maybe a summer dress or two and whatever else you'll need for the next few months. Then we'll hit the Superstore for groceries and get you set up in the condo. It's furnished, so you'll have everything you need there."

Noelle just nodded as she listened to Maggie, then got up and followed her to her car. Maggie tossed some money on the table to pay for Noelle's coffee before they left the building, noting the small bag Noelle carried. She was right, Noelle had little with her, Noelle was going to need more clothes, etc., if her plan was going to work. Plus, Noelle couldn't look like a hooker. She had to look softer, but still keep her edge. The gang couldn't know what Noelle did for a living.

Shopping wasn't something Maggie typically enjoyed, so it surprised Maggie to find her time shopping pleasant. She didn't have many girlfriends growing up, and shopping with another woman was fun. They found some appropriate clothing to fit the persona Noelle would portray and some other nice, simple outfits to help her blend in with the downtown crowd when she went out to enjoy the city.

They packed the bags into the trunk and hit the Superstore for groceries. Maggie knew there was nothing, not even staples at the condo, so Noelle needed a lot. Maggie and Noelle finished packing everything into the trunk and headed to the condo. Laden with their purchases, it took Noelle and Maggie two trips to carry everything up to the apartment.

Maggie went into the kitchen and began putting away the groceries and directed Noelle to the guest bedroom to put away her clothes. Maggie wanted to keep the main bedroom available for herself in case there were times she couldn't make it home and needed to stay downtown. She'd already moved a few items into the bedroom. Things that would go along with her new biker chick personality and fit into the lifestyle she was trying to infiltrate. Luckily, both bedrooms had their own ensuite, which was the reason her condo was so popular with students.

Once Noelle stepped out of the bedroom, she pulled out a cigarette and motioned to Maggie to see where she could smoke.

"Oh. Please smoke on the balcony. I smoke occasionally too, but only outside. I don't like the way it gets into the furniture and renting it to students is harder if the place smells. Hold on," Maggie said, "On second thought, I'll come out with you."

22

Maggie ensured Noelle was set up and comfortable before she left for home. She got Noelle a pay-as-you-go cell phone so she could have a local number as they moved forward; she wanted the opportunity to contact Noelle whenever she needed to and a local number would benefit them when Noelle gained access to the Dark Enders. Maggie doubted she'd ever bring Noelle to the home she and Liam shared, and wondered if she should move into the condo with Noelle until this was over. It would simplify things and keep her home life separate from the lifestyle she was slipping into. She didn't want to bring any of the darkness to her home. It was something for her to think about.

Maggie rolled her shoulders before exiting her car, relieving some of the tension that built up, and walked up the path to the front door, noticing something on her front step. When she got closer, she saw it was a bouquet. She turned around and scanned the neighbourhood before she bent down to pick it up. The bouquet comprising 11 red roses surrounding a single black bud made her pause. Her stomach clenched, and she reached out for the wall to steady herself. She checked, but there wasn't a card enclosed. Whoever left them even removed the florist's information. A sense of ill ease spread through her as she held the wrapped blooms. She wouldn't take them inside. There was something off about the whole thing. Black represented death.

'*Who sent them? Could it be a death threat?*' She wondered. '*Maybe I should call the police.*'

She looked around, turned and walked to the side of the house, peeled the cello wrap away, and tossed them into the green bin. Then she tossed the cello wrap into her garbage can in the garage.

With her senses heightened, she went back to her car and removed the gun she'd locked into the glove box. She cocked it and made her way around the perimeter of her house. Maggie noticed that someone had removed the screen from one of the back windows. She tried sliding the window open, but the locks held. Nothing else seemed to be disturbed, so she went back around to the front of the house and entered the keyless code to unlock the door. With her gun still grasped in her hands, she made her way around the inside, turning on all the lights as she did.

Nothing seemed out of place, and she felt satisfied that no one had gained access to her house. She put the gun on the coffee table and plopped onto the sofa. Her heart raced. Someone had tried to break into her home and left what was an obvious threat on her doorstep.

Something or someone scared them off, or whoever was there was close by when she came home and they took off. She debated again calling the police, but it was only an attempt and she didn't want the police investigating anything else about her life. The roses concerned her the most. Who sent them? What did it mean? She knew it was a message, but she couldn't connect it to anything she had done.

But now she knew she needed to move into the condo. She'd

spend the day tomorrow putting blocker bars on her windows as an extra protection. Then she'd change the code to her locks and set up some cameras to record the perimeter.

She wanted her car at the condo, so she'd bring that first and then come back by Uber to get her bike. That way, she'd have her car when she needed it, for example, when she came to check on her house and it would help separate the biker life from her home life.

23

T he next morning, Maggie set to task placing one inch diameter dowels across each window and ensuring they were all locked. She added some more sensor lights around the house. Knowing it would annoy the neighbours if they went off, but it would also alert them to trouble. The last thing to do was install the cameras. Maggie set up one at the front door first, so she could identify anyone who dropped off a package and the second one in her backyard. It would go off with a motion detector.

She waited for the neighbours on either side of her and across the street to come home and then told them she was going on assignment and would be away for a while. Maggie gave them the number to a burner phone she'd picked up so they could call her if they noticed anything suspicious while she was gone. She knew they watched her as she pulled away. When they were at work, the next day, she would come back and collect her bike. She'd need access to both if she was going to maintain her double life.

With both her car and bike tucked away in the underground parking garage, she made her way up to her unit. It was time to have a chat with Noelle. When she went inside, she found Noelle on the balcony with a coffee and a cigarette. Maggie stepped out onto the balcony and her sudden appearance startled Noelle, who spilled her coffee down the front of her t-shirt.

"Shit!" Noelle exclaimed as she wiped at the spill. "I didn't hear you come in!"

"Sorry about that. I didn't mean to startle you! I've been thinking I should move in here while we work on my story together. That way, I can fill you in on the gang, what I know about them, and where they hang out when they're not at the clubhouse. Why don't you get changed," Maggie said, motioning to the now stained t-shirt, "and we can go for a walk while we talk, maybe find somewhere to have lunch?"

Noelle eyed Maggie before she nodded and went off to change.

They remained silent on the ride down the elevator, each lost in their own thoughts. Maggie and Noelle stepped out of the building into the bright sunshine, and their moods lightened. Maggie suggested they head towards the boardwalk as it offered a pretty view. The other reason she suggested it was she hadn't been back since the shooting and needed to push past her fears. As they neared the boardwalk, Maggie realized she'd been holding her breath and let out a deep sigh. Her stomach clenched as they passed the area where Liam died. Small bouquets of flowers still marked the spot, including a plush, although faded, teddy bear. Maggie averted her eyes as a tear formed in the corner. Seeing the teddy bear was more than she could bear right now, her loss was still too fresh. If Noelle noticed Maggie's reaction to the memorial, she said nothing.

They continued on, chatting as they went, until Maggie paused in front of The Bicycle Thief. She knew it served good food and was always busy. It would allow them to blend into the crowd and talk. If the plan was going to work, they had to be sure no one could recognize them as friends. But she doubted they'd run into any gang members here.

"Let's try this," Maggie said, motioning to the sign. Noelle nodded, and they spoke to the hostess before being shown to a seat on the patio. It was still early in the season, but the warm sunny weather was conducive to sitting outside. Maggie liked the idea of the patio. It served two purposes. One, she could watch her surroundings and ensure their safety and two, the noises from the boardwalk would drown out their voices in case anyone overheard them.

Maggie ordered a glass of Cabernet Sauvignon from Napa Valley and suggested to Noelle that if she liked red wine, it was a nice one. Noelle accepted Maggie's suggestion, ordered the same, and continued to look at the menu. Maggie could sense Noelle was ill-at-ease and realized that the prices were upscale to match the restaurant and location, so she reached over and touched Noelle's arm.

"This is my treat. I told you I would cover all of your expenses while you helped me. Don't worry about anything."

Noelle eyed Maggie before she leaned back and said what was on her mind. "Are you rich or something?"

A smile crept across Maggie's face before she broke into laugher and continued to laugh until she saw the hurt look in Noelle's eyes. She put her menu down and responded.

"No. I'm not rich. I'm comfortable. My parents died when I was young and my aunt and uncle invested the assets from their estate for my future. When I came of age, those investments were waiting for me and had grown. While I was trucking, I lived out of my truck, so most of my income went back into the bank after expenses."

"Wow, I'm sorry I asked." Noelle cut in before realizing Maggie had more to say.

"I also lost my husband last year, so there's insurance money added to my nest egg and I no longer have a mortgage. Tragedy seems to follow me, unfortunately. I'd give anything to have him back, but I have to move on."

Maggie took a sip of her wine. "Can I ask why you agreed to help me?"

It was Noelle's turn to chuckle.

"You know what I do, and the reason I travel in the warmer months is to get a change of pace. I was going to turn you down. Then I thought about it. It sounded exciting, and let me tell you, my life is anything but exciting. It seemed like an adventure where I could use my practical skills." Noelle wiggled her eyebrows and smiled at Maggie before continuing. "They'll come in handy."

Maggie lifted her glass to toast Noelle. "To adventure!"

"So, tell me what the plan is."

"Ok. Where to begin? I've already contacted some members of the gang. It went as well as I could have hoped for. I chatted with the VP and Sergeant-at-arms. I also got into a fight."

"A fight! You?" Noelle cut in.

Maggie chuckle, "I'm tougher than I look."

"I'm seeing that." Noelle responded, lifting her glass in a mock salute.

"So are you. That's why I knew we'd make the perfect team."

Maggie explained to Noelle what she had in mind. Omitting the details of her real reason for infiltrating the gang. She also explained that although she had a basic plan, some details wouldn't come to light until they made progress. Maggie told Noelle that she hoped to get close to the VP, but that it would take time. She wanted Noelle to show up at public places where the gang would be and to be friendly. If she was more than friendly, that was her choice. Maggie reiterated she didn't have to do more, but was honest that more would help. Maggie hated herself for saying that. She felt like she was pimping Noelle out, but Noelle's line of work would come in handy, except in this situation, she could sleep with someone because she chose to, not because they paid her to.

At one point, Noelle reached over and grabbed Maggie's hand.

"Don't worry, sex doesn't bother me. If it did, I'm in the wrong profession." She finished with a wink.

Maggie smiled back at her, taking another sip of her wine.

As their food arrived, a lobster roll for Noelle and the salmon for Maggie, their conversation had turned to more general topics, such as the night life in Halifax and some things Noelle would like to see and do while she was here. Maggie figured she could also be Noelle's tour guide, now that she'd be able to see more than just a truck stop.

24

After they returned to the condo, Maggie gave Noelle some spending money and told her to go out and enjoy herself. She wanted to go for a bike ride to clear her thoughts. Noelle told her to enjoy herself, but added that sometime, when Maggie was ready, she'd like to go for a ride with her if she didn't mind.

Maggie smiled. "I'll take you for a ride tomorrow. The weather looks good and we can do the South Shore and stop at some sights. Have you been to Peggy's Cove?"

Noelle looked down. "I'll be honest, I haven't been east of Enfield. Not enough reasons for truckers to go that far, and until now, all of my rides have been with truckers."

"Then we'll make a day of it. I'll stop somewhere today and pick you up a jacket and helmet. If you're home when I get back, we can open a bottle of wine and share a pizza."

Maggie grabbed her helmet and jacket and left the unit. She was looking forward to getting out on the road with the wind in her hair. As she adjusted the chin strap on her helmet, she thought of Noelle and found it surprising at how much she was enjoying Noelle's company. She also wondered what prompted Noelle to become a hooker. Maybe, on the ride tomorrow, she'd ask her.

Maggie rode for a couple of hours and found herself by the Acadia Park in Lower Sackville. She wanted to stretch her legs before heading back to the city, so she parked her bike, got off and stretched. Maggie hung her helmet on the handlebars and brushed out her hair before fastening it into a low ponytail. She took her ID and money out of the saddlebags and slipped it into the front pocket of her jeans before draping her jacket over the seat of the bike to keep it from getting too hot. Maggie slipped her sunglasses into place and walked towards the playground that was full of children at play.

She saw several benches that were near enough to the playground to watch the activities without appearing creepy. The thought of listening to the gleeful sounds of children at play would brighten her day. She loved children and was heartbroken to know she'd have none of her own. Without realizing it, her hand went to her abdomen and clutched at the emptiness within.

Maggie perched herself on a bench, leaned back, closed her eyes, and listened to the surrounding sounds. She felt a catch in her breath as she realized this would never be her life. She would never take her child to the park to play, never celebrate all the firsts she and Liam looked forward to. Suddenly, she felt she had to get out of here. She was suffocating from the sense of loss that overwhelmed her. Maggie sat bolt upright and prepared to leave when she heard a voice call out to her.

"Mrs. Murphy? Is that you?"

Maggie's head spun around in the voice's direction. She couldn't make out the features of the man and child heading her way. The sun was at his back. She shielded her eyes to get a better look.

"Colby Tate," He added. "Detective Tate."

Maggie sprung up and closed the distance between them, her hand outstretched to shake his.

"Call me Maggie." She said, squatting down so that she could look his daughter in the eyes. "And who's this?"

The child buried her face in her father's leg.

"This," Colby replied, "is my daughter, Evelyn. Say hi to the nice lady, Evelyn."

"Hi Evelyn, it's nice to meet you." Maggie said, watching as the child peeked out at her. Her big blue eyes blinked as she smiled shyly. Maggie smiled back at her, still squatting, then Evelyn left the shadows of her father's leg and dove into Maggie's arms. Stunned, Maggie hesitated for a second before hugging the child to her, inhaling the sweet scent of baby shampoo, feeling the child's kiss on her cheek. She scooped her up and stood with the child in her arms and looked at Colby.

Colby stood slack jawed at the sight before him. As he struggled for the right words, he shook his head.

"Evelyn's never done that before. She's wary of strangers."

"She's adorable. You're a very lucky man, detective." Maggie said, handing Evelyn back to him.

"Call me Colby." He replied as he took Evelyn from Maggie. "What are you doing here?"

"It's a beautiful day, so I went for a ride."

"A ride?"

"Yes, my motorcycle is over there." Maggie motioned to the parking lot.

"Oh, that's right, you ride a motorcycle. And drive trucks." He chuckled.

"Well, I used to drive trucks. Now I get called an annoying reporter who impedes detectives in their investigations. Or at least that's something I've been told." She teased.

"I can see that. You must be a stubborn go-getter, more than a pain in a detective's butt. I'm glad I haven't had to deal with the reporter in you." He responded as he put Evelyn back on the ground, clinging to her hand. Evelyn reached out her other hand to Maggie, who took hold of it, and smiled down at the child.

"How are you doing? I meant to come back to check on you, but there's been no new leads."

"That's ok. I've been as well as expected."

They chatted as they walked around the playground, swinging Evelyn between them.

"I should get Evelyn home for supper and bath time. Let us walk you back to your bike," Colby said as he bent down to pick up Evelyn, who yawned and carried her the rest of the way.

"Oh, you don't have to do that."

"It's no bother. I'm parked in the same lot. Can I have a look at your bike? I used to ride, but after Evelyn came and her mom died, I didn't want to risk not being there for her."

They continued on to the parking lot. Maggie, now eager to get moving, listened as Colby told her how much he liked her ride. Colby said his goodbyes and Evelyn asked for a kiss before they went to their own vehicle, melting Maggie's heart. She watched them head to his SUV while she donned her gear and thought he was a lucky man.

25

Bright and early the next morning, Maggie woke Noelle up to get dressed and ready to head out for a bike ride to the South Shore. Noelle donned the gear Maggie picked up for her and spun around to show her how the jacket fit. Maggie nodded her approval before they left the apartment, noticing how excited Noelle seemed.

"Have you ever ridden on the back of a motorcycle before?" Maggie asked as they headed down the elevator to the parking garage.

"No. But I've always wanted to."

"Well, it's a good thing we're going out today, then. You'll need to feel comfortable on the back of a bike if someone from the Dark Enders asks you to," Maggie said with a grin, and then gave Noelle some instructions so that they'd both feel safe on the ride.

Maggie backed her bike out of her spot and got it ready to leave. Then she held the bike in place while Noelle climbed on and got herself situated. The jacket Maggie purchased for Noelle fit well, and Noelle loved the purple skulls on the helmet. Maggie once again wore her black leather gear to break it in more.

When they were out of the city, Maggie headed to highway 333. The road had some nice bends and turns, for riding enthusiasts, straight is boring, making it a great riding road. Maggie's thought was to acquaint Noelle with some of the major attractions but give her some experience as a passenger. If her plan was going to work, Noelle needed to feel comfortable on the back of a bike in case one of the club members told her to ride with him.

When they pulled onto the road up to the lighthouse at Peggy's Cove, Maggie chose the first parking lot instead of the one by the lighthouse. She wanted to stretch her legs and give Noelle a break. Noelle had been hanging on for dear life and, although she'd become more relaxed as they went, Maggie felt the pressure from Noelle's grasp and knew she was uncomfortable.

"What are we doing here?" Noelle asked after she climbed off the back of the bike.

"We're going to walk up to the lighthouse, do the touristy things like look in shops, etc."

"Are we getting lunch here?"

Maggie laughed. "I guess I didn't give you time to eat breakfast before we left. We can get a snack and coffee at the top in the Sou'Wester. But I thought we'd have lunch further along in either Mahone Bay or Lunenburg."

"Mmm, coffee sounds great. Thank you."

They made their way up to the lighthouse, pausing at various shops along the way. Noelle liked the one called Hags on the Hill and even spent some time chatting with the woman at the till, asking questions before picking up a fairy door and buying it. When Maggie saw what she bought, she raised her eyebrows. To which Noelle replied, "It never hurts to have a little fairy dust to help when things get sticky," before giggling like a schoolgirl. Maggie liked this side of Noelle.

Noelle's exuberance shone through as she explored and experienced things for the first time. Once again, Maggie realized how little she knew about Noelle other than her profession. She had made assumptions based on what Noelle did for a living but didn't know who she was or what made her chose that line of work. She decided she would take the time to get to know her as a person. Since she'd invited Noelle to stay, she'd only considered what Noelle could do for her, not who she was. It was time to remedy that.

After finishing their coffees and some toast, they headed back to where they parked the bike and continue on their way.

"Do you think we can stop at the Flight 111 Memorial?" Noelle asked while tightening the strap on her helmet.

Maggie stopped to look at her. She'd been many times before, but it didn't occur to her that Noelle would want to see it. She cursed herself for her preconceived ideas and nodded as she responded, "Sure, we can. It's on our way."

They walked in silence as they wandered through the memorial site. Noelle stopped and took the time to read the plaques, while Maggie hung back, giving Noelle the freedom to read without her looking over her shoulder. Maggie glanced at Noelle and noticed the tears in her eyes as she read.

Maggie fumbled through her pockets, looking for a tissue, but came up empty. Noelle wiped the tears with the back of her hand and moved on. Noelle was a few inches taller than Maggie, so Maggie found she had to rush to keep up as Noelle headed back to the bike.

"Did you know someone on that flight?" Maggie asked.

"No, it's just a sad tragedy. Where to now?"

Maggie felt bewildered by Noelle's reaction to the memorial, but fired up the bike and replied, "Mahone Bay."

After a quick visit to Mahone Bay, they continued on to Lunenburg. While they were there, they'd had lunch at The Grand Banker Bar and Grill, and Noelle even convinced Maggie to take the horse and buggy tour through town with her. It continued to surprise Maggie at how much she enjoyed Noelle's company. She'd never had many friends growing up and for the first time realized what she'd missed out on.

They took their time while they ate lunch. During it, Maggie asked Noelle about her childhood and was brazen enough to ask why Noelle chose prostitution. Noelle told Maggie her story, that she'd bounced from foster home to foster home growing up. Her mother misused substances and died when she was young and she'd never met her dad. One of her mom's boyfriends had abused her, which was why she ended up in foster care. When she turned 18, the last home she lived in kicked her out because the money stopped. She found herself on the street with nowhere to go and prostitution seemed like the only answer. She tried working at a Tim Hortons, but she made more money from hooking. Now, she'd been at it for so long, it was a part of her. She tried to save money for her future, as she knew that one day, she'd be too old to hook, but that was a long way off.

Maggie revealed a little about her past, not her rape, but her father's murder and that the man beat her and left her for dead. She didn't elaborate about Liam's death, just skimmed over that it was an accident. Revealing too much might make Noelle suspicious about her real reason for trying to infiltrate the Dark Enders.

Maggie wondered if Noelle expected her to pass judgement on her life choices, and she sensed Noelle was relieved when she didn't. The conversation gave them a new understanding of each other and both realized they were forming a bonding relationship.

J E Friend

Exhausted from a full day of exploring, they headed back to the condo with cautious feelings about their budding friendship.

26

A week after their bike ride, Maggie sat in the living room with Noelle, telling her she learned the Dark Ender's were going to be at the Capital that night. She'd already informed Noelle that she'd met with some members when she showed up at the bar before. Her plan was for Noelle to arrive early by Uber, and have money available to Uber back. Maggie figured if Noelle was already at the bar eating a meal when the gang showed up, it wouldn't look suspicious. She suggested Noelle take a table at the back with her back to the wall so she could watch the entrance. Maggie reassured her she would show up later on her bike and always be a phone call away. She didn't want Noelle to acknowledge her presence because she didn't want the club members to know they knew each other, but if there was trouble, Maggie would come to Noelle's aid, no questions asked.

Maggie and Noelle worked on a back story. In the end, they decided Noelle would tell anyone that asked that she had recently moved from BC and was couch surfing with whomever she could while she looked for work and a place to live. This would serve them twofold. First, it would explain why she couldn't bring anyone home with her, and second, if a member trusted or took a liking to her, they may find her employment within the club.

Maggie cautioned Noelle not to reveal that she was a hooker. No one would care, but they'd treat her differently. They'd turn her to into a 'Lay' or 'Sweet Butt' meaning she'd be available for anyone anytime. Maggie hoped someone within the club would want Noelle for more than that. Noelle reassured Maggie that it didn't matter what she needed to do to get inside and get the information Maggie wanted. She'd do it. Sex was sex. Maggie rolled her eyes; this was something they didn't agree on.

Maggie sat in the bedroom and watched Noelle as she prepared to go out. She offered advice on what to wear based on what she saw the other girls wearing the last time she was there. She wanted Noelle to look a step above the other girls, but still like someone who would fit in. Maggie chose not to get ready until after Noelle left. Tonight, she was going to pair a leather halter with her leather pants and she'd leave her helmet with her bike. She didn't need to make a show when she entered the bar. She'd still stand out with her red hair and outfit. People assumed she was helpless because of her size, but that was far from the truth.

When Maggie arrived at the bar a few hours later, she scanned the room and found Noelle sitting at the back, as they discussed. She was already sitting with a club member engaged in conversation. Maggie searched her mind to see if she could recall which one, before deciding he was a minor player and not worth her attention. He was the perfect pick for Noelle, though. He'd be eager to show off and be chattier than some of the other more connected members.

Maggie noticed Noelle looked up as she entered, causing her companion to turn around, look her over and turned back to Noelle. She saw movement out of the corner of her eye and knew someone was approaching as she settled down at the bar, removed her jacket, exposing her bare back and ordered a whiskey neat.

"Let me guess," the voice beside her said, "troubles your middle name."

Maggie turned towards the voice and smiled. It was Quinn. *'This is perfect'* she thought.

"No, not that I can recall." She purred at him. "My mother gave me the middle name Maye."

Quinn laughed and nodded to the bartender, who placed an open bottle of Keith's on the bar in front of him.

"I suppose you saw the bikes and stopped in, thinking it looked like a friendly gathering." He said before taking a sip from his bottle.

"Something like that. Listen, as I told you the last time I was here. I just saw the bikes, knew it would be biker friendly and popped in for a drink. You seem friendly enough, but the girl coming up behind me doesn't." Maggie replied, keeping her eyes on the mirrored wall behind the bar.

Quinn spun his stool around. He'd been looking at Maggie and not at the reflection in the mirror. He scowled at the woman, who stopped dead in her tracks. Another member came up and led the woman back to her table. Maggie recognized her from the last time she was here. It was the woman she'd had trouble with.

"Why don't you tell me why you're here?" Quinn asked.

"I did. I'm just here for a drink. Although I don't mind some company, too." She said with a smile.

Quinn eyed her up and down before offering to buy her another drink. She accepted one more and continued to chat with him. When he suggested a third drink, she said she should get going. She'd didn't want to drink too much and then get on the bike.

Quinn offered to walk her out to her bike and told her she was welcome anytime they were here, running his hand up the flesh of her exposed arm, and, as an afterthought, invited her to a gathering they were having at the clubhouse in a week's time. Maggie couldn't believe her luck. Then he asked for her number and told her he'd call her with the details.

Smiling to herself, Maggie gave him the number to her disposable phone and stood to leave. She caught Noelle's eye, so she'd know Maggie was heading out. Noelle would find her own way home, but if she needed anything, Maggie would be there.

At home, Maggie poured herself a glass of wine and waited for Noelle to come back. She wanted to see how Noelle's night went and if she learned anything.

27

Maggie tried to stay awake and wait up for Noelle, but ended up falling asleep on the couch. When Noelle walked through the door, it was after 2 a.m.. The sound of the key in the lock and Noelle entering the apartment startled Maggie awake. She sat bolt upright, causing Noelle's steps to falter.

"Thank god!" Maggie exclaimed as she watched Noelle kick off her shoes.

Noelle's eyes narrowed as she quipped, "I'm not used to having a mother hen."

"I'm sorry, I was worried. They are a dangerous group. Things could have gone bad," Maggie replied, settling back on the couch and stretching.

"Ok, I guess I understand. But I couldn't just walk out like you did. Tiny, that's the guy I was talking to, well he seems to be interested in me, so I thought I'd spend some time getting to know him. You know, so I can help you."

"Good thinking. Did it help?"

"I think so. He invited me to a party they're having at the clubhouse."

103

Maggie laughed. "I got the same invitation. This is perfect. With both of us there, we can listen and try to get some information on what's going on inside."

"Tiny said something you should know." Noelle interrupted.

"What's that?"

"Tiny said that Quinton, the guy you were talking to, has laid claim to you. He's warned everyone else to stay away."

Maggie scowled. She didn't like being laid claim to, especially by a target, but then she realized how well this piece of information would benefit her.

"That's awesome!"

Noelle looked at Maggie with confusion. "Um, ok."

"No. Wait Noelle. Hear me out. Quinn approached me the last time I was in the bar. It's obvious I impressed him if after one brief meeting he's laying claim to me. It's my way in. Quinn is the VP. By getting close to him, I can get a lot of the information I need."

"But..." Noelle started

"But what?" Maggie cut in.

"He's a biker. Not only that, he's a man. He's going to want more than conversation."

Maggie frowned. "Yes, I supposed he will. I'll just have to make sure it doesn't come to that. Let him know that I'm not just a quick lay."

"I think you're underestimating the culture. I've done a little research while I've been here. And if you're the reporter you claim to be, you must know what he wants."

"Yes." Maggie snapped. "I know what he'll want. I'll cross that bridge when I get to it."

Noelle just shook her head. "I'm heading to bed. It's been a long day."

"Fine. We'll talk more in the morning." As an afterthought she added, "I'm sorry I snapped at you. I know you were trying to help."

From the doorway to her bedroom, Noelle paused and nodded before she closed the door, leaving Maggie alone with her thoughts.

28

Maggie stepped out of the shower the next morning and heard the distinctive sound of her personal phone ringing. She checked the caller ID and didn't recognize the number. She almost ignored it, thinking it was a telemarketer, but answered it.

"Hello?"

"Hi Mrs. Murphy, it's Detective Tate. Um, Colby."

"Hi Colby, what can I do for you?"

"I have someone here who wants to ask you a question."

Before Maggie could respond, she heard a tiny voice squeak, "wanna come to da park wiff us?"

Maggie's heart melted. She wasn't prepared to hear Evelyn's voice on the phone. Before she could answer, Colby cut in. "I'm sorry, she's been bugging me ever since we ran into you at the park to see the motorcycle lady. I couldn't put off calling you any longer. I hope I didn't put you on the spot."

Maggie held the phone in her hand and stared at it. Her heart raced. She broke out in a cold sweat and sank down onto the bed. She took a few deep calming breaths as she heard in the distance, "Maggie? Maggie, are you still there?"

She swallowed before responding, "Yes, sorry, I'm still here."

"Look, it's ok if you can't. I'll come up with an excuse for..."

"I'd love to."

"Really? That's great! Can you meet us in the same park in, let's say, an hour?"

"Make it an hour and a half and I'll pack us a picnic."

"Evelyn will love that, thank you. See you soon."

Maggie dried her hair and dressed in comfortable clothing, then stepped out into the living to find Noelle on the computer.

"Oh, good morning." Maggie muttered.

"Good morning. Are you going somewhere?" Noelle asked, noticing Maggie's attire.

"Um ya. A uh, friend called and I'm meeting him and his daughter at the park."

"Friend, eh? Well, don't let Quinn find out you have another 'friend'. I think he's the jealous type." Noelle teased.

Maggie couldn't help it, and felt the heat rise to her cheeks. She turned her back to Noelle so she couldn't see the pink hue on her face as she began going through the fridge searching for something to pack for lunch. Maggie pulled out some fruits and veggies and cut them up and placed them in segregated containers, thinking most children didn't like their food to touch. She had nothing to make sandwiches with, but she had some cheese, kielbasa, and scones, so she added those to her cooler bag. Maggie only had bottled water to pack, but she'd hit a store on the way and get some juice boxes for Evelyn.

"Call me if you need me. I'll be a few hours." Maggie smiled at her as she left the apartment.

"Have fun. I think I'll take a walk downtown and explore while you're gone." Noelle called out before the apartment door closed.

Maggie pulled her car into the parking lot and scanned the playground for Evelyn and Colby. As she pulled out the cooler bag, she saw him wave her over. He'd set up at a picnic table near the playground where he could keep a watchful eye on Evelyn while she played. Maggie couldn't help but admire how attractive he was. His hair was greying, and she figured he was in his forties, maybe late forties. The idea of getting too close to a cop with her background worried her, but it was just one playdate and the idea of seeing Evelyn again filled her heart with joy.

After she greeted him and deposited the bag on the table, she saw Evelyn running towards them. When she got close enough, she sprung up and wrapped her arms around Maggie before she tugged at her arm. "Come push me."

"Please!" Colby corrected as Maggie got up and followed her.

"Please," Evelyn added, dragging Maggie to the swings.

Evelyn kept Maggie busy, pushing her on the swings, spotting her at the bottom of the slide and holding her while she tried the overhead swinging bar. Maggie felt an incredible sense of joy as she interacted with Evelyn, but a deeper part of her felt the immense loss.

Colby left the cooler bag on the picnic table and joined them. The two adults chatted and got to know each other while they played with Evelyn until she announced she was hungry. Then they went back to the picnic table and pulled out the food Maggie had brought. When she stopped for the juice boxes, she also picked up some dip for the veggies, which Evelyn dug into with relish.

As she cracked a bottle of water, Maggie teased Colby. "I would have packed a bottle of wine for us, but I didn't feel like getting arrested."

Colby patted his chest and pants pockets then replied with a wink, "Seems I forgot my handcuffs."

It wasn't long before Evelyn had climbed up onto Maggie's lap and dozed off with her head on Maggie's shoulder. Colby put everything away and leaned over to take his sleeping daughter from her. As he did, Maggie smelled the woodsy scent of his cologne. His face was inches from hers, and she had to fight the urge to kiss his cheek, cursing to herself that she would even think that way. It was just a friendly play date, nothing more.

Before he left, Colby turned to her. "You're great with her. She misses not having a mom. Evelyn was so young when my wife died, she doesn't remember her. My mom tries, but she's getting older and can't keep up with an active child. Thank you for coming out and for the lunch. Maybe you'll want to do this again sometime, Evelyn would love it."

"Sure," Maggie replied, "just call me. You have my number."

29

Maggie could sense that Noelle was nervous as she watched her race around the apartment, trying to decide what to wear. In the end, she'd decided on a pair of skinny jeans, but couldn't decide on the right top. Maggie went to her closet and pulled out her denim halter and handed it to Noelle.

"Here, try this."

Noelle's eyes lit up as she grabbed the halter and put it on. She had a few inches on Maggie, so the top didn't meet the waistband of her jeans, but her figure was slender, and the pairing emphasized it. Maggie nodded in approval as Noelle spun around. With Noelle's back exposed, Maggie couldn't help but notice the tattoo of a hummingbird on her left shoulder, but chose not to comment. She had her own tattoo that she didn't want to talk about, either.

"It's perfect." Maggie said as she watched Noelle spike her hair. "No. Don't do that. Try something softer."

Noelle hesitated before adding some mousse and shaking her natural curls into place.

"Why should I look softer?" Noelle asked.

"I just think it will be a better contrast with the denim top. Plus, you don't want to be mistaken for someone they'll consider, every-one's girl."

Noelle used the diffuser on the hair blower to dry her hair without turning her curls into a frizzy mess.

Maggie nodded in approval. "There, you look great. Why are you so nervous?"

"Believe it or not, this is the first almost date I've had in years. The only guys interested in dating a working girl are looking for a percentage."

"Do you like him? This Tiny?"

"I'm only doing this to help you, but he is nice and interesting to talk to. And although I know he wants to fuck me, he also enjoys being with me. Did Quinn text you the time and location yet?"

"No." Maggie frowned, looking down at her phone. "I guess he's not as interested as I thought."

"There's still time. He told you the date, so maybe he's sending a last-minute message to see if you're interested. I'm not leaving for a few hours yet. I was just nervous and wanted to be ready. Why don't you put on what you plan to wear and get ready just in case? Maybe I'll have some pointers for you." She laughed.

Maggie hesitated before deciding Noelle had a point. She knew even if Quinn texted her halfway through the party, she'd show up. She wouldn't miss her chance to be inside the clubhouse and find out who ordered the hit that killed Liam. When she came out of the living room, she wore a pair of skin-tight pale denims with a dark denim bustier. She slung her leather jacket over her shoulder.

Noelle let out a low whistle. "You're gonna knock him dead. Are you planning on riding there?"

"To stay in 'character,' I will always ride to something hosted by the Dark Enders. If the weather's crappy, I'll take an Uber like you do, but separately, of course. We don't want anyone to know we're friends."

"Are we?" Questioned Noelle.

"Are we what?" Maggie asked.

"Friends."

Maggie looked up at Noelle before responding. "Yes. I'd say we are." She saw the smile that spread across Noelle's face and knew the idea pleased her. Maggie surprised herself by realizing that over the last few weeks, they had become friends.

While she was contemplating how and when that happened, her phone dinged with a text. She looked at the screen to see only an address and time. Noelle glance at the phone and smiled. "Looks like Quinn gave you the official go ahead."

"Well, we have a couple of hours. Let's have a glass of wine and talk about what's ahead."

The girls moved out onto the balcony with their glasses of wine and Noelle lit up a cigarette before they settled into the two cushioned chairs outside and began chatting and planning their next steps.

30

aggie pulled her bike into the lot that was part of the clubhouse compound, a half hour after the time Quinn told her to be there. Noelle left long before Maggie, planning on arriving early so she could be 'useful' as a way of ingratiating herself. The lot was full of motorcycles and she had to park on the far side of the building.

Maggie swung her leg over her motorcycle, stepped to one side, and pulled off her helmet just as a burly man approached her.

"I think you're lost, missy. This is a private party." He grumbled.

"I was invited." Maggie retorted.

"Women don't ride to the clubhouse. I think you'd better leave. No matter who invited you."

Quinn, who'd been inside watching for Maggie, stepped out of the building and called out in greeting. "Hello Maggie."

The man backed away, hands in the air, and returned to the building as Quinn neared.

"You made it. I was wondering if you'd show." He said in greeting, "I thought we scared you off back at the bar. Or maybe he did," Quinn finished, jerking his thumb towards the retreating biker.

112

Maggie smirked before replying, "I don't scare easily."

Quinn gave Maggie a sideways look, then mumbled under his breath, but loud enough for her to hear, "No, I don't think you do."

Quinn led Maggie up the half dozen wide steps that lead up to the porch from the gravel parking lot to the heavy double entry doors of the clubhouse. Someone had propped the doors open to allow for air flow.

The front doors lead into a large room with dusty, well worn, rough-hewn floors and an array of tables and chairs and sofa clusters. A long bar stretched down the left side of the room as Maggie entered; she noted the bartender was a skinny bearded man who was busy serving drinks. There was a wide mixture of people mingling around the room. Several girls were running back and forth to the bar, gathering and serving drinks. There was a hallway that led off to the left, with several closed doors. The right side of the room housed a wall of windows and at the back was an imposing set of double doors with the initials DE carved into them.

Maggie looked around the room and saw Noelle sitting at a table with Tiny and some others. Noelle glanced at Maggie as she entered the room, but was quick to avert her eyes. Maggie made a mental note as to Noelle's position in the room in case she needed anything. She wouldn't acknowledge her, but if Noelle was in trouble, she'd help her, and vice versa.

Maggie left her gun at home. She didn't expect she'd need it. Instead, she had her hunting knife tucked inside her jacket. The knife felt more comfortable to her, anyway. She'd still need the gun to finish what she started when she killed the man who shot Liam, but only from a distance.

She followed Quinn as he led her to a sofa on the far side of the room. As she got herself situated, he asked, "Still drinking whiskey neat?"

She chuckled and nodded. "You remembered."

"You're kinda hard to forget." He muttered as he called out to the bartender, "Kenny, a whiskey neat and a Keith's."

It didn't take long before a girl approached with the drinks on a tray. Her hips swayed in her tiny cut-off shorts. She placed Maggie's drink in front of her before turning to Quinn with his beer. She handed it to him and exposed her well-shaped cleavage before trailing her fingers along his shoulder and leaving.

Woman to woman, Maggie knew she was laying claim to Quinn, but because he all but ignored her, Maggie doubted he felt the same, otherwise, why was she here? She figured it was someone he'd slept with at some point. But according to her research, a member had to claim a woman, or she was available to anyone. Quinn fancied himself a ladies' man and she guessed at some point he'd been with most of the women in the room.

Maggie lifted her glass in the air to toast to Quinn before taking a sip. She had to take her time with her drink in order to keep her wits about her. Getting on a bike after too many drinks was a recipe for disaster. She could tell the alcohol had flowed freely for some time as several people stumbled around the room.

Maggie sensed someone was staring at her and she scanned the room until her eye landed on the woman from the bar, who had swung a punch at her the first time she met them. The woman scowled as Maggie raised her glass in a mock salute. Maggie smiled to herself, knowing she'd pissed the woman off and realized she'd have to monitor that one. The woman wasn't with Quinn, but she was with someone of importance or she wouldn't feel so entitled. She'd have to find out who she was. Maybe mend the fence so she didn't have to watch her back.

Maggie turned back to Quinn and studied him. He was busy talking to someone else, so she could take her time. Today he'd pulled back his shoulder length hair, revealing that he trimmed the underneath short. A five o'clock shadow covered his firm jaw, as it had when she'd met him before. He wore a simple white t-shirt beneath his club vest and the muscles in his arms flexed and pulled as he tipped his bottle to his lips.

Maggie appreciated how handsome he was. It made her job

easier. Having to make nice to someone less appealing wouldn't have suited her. There were two tiny tear drops tattooed below his right eye. She'd done her research and knew what they meant, but figured she should ask him about it because he wouldn't expect her to know. She wondered if he'd tell her the truth.

The fellow Quinn was talking to left, and Quinn turned towards her, sensing that she'd been studying him.

"You like what you see?" He smirked with confidence.

"Yes, it's a pleasant view." Maggie replied with a false sweetness. "I was wondering about something."

Quinn raised his eyebrows and waited for her to ask what was on her mind.

"Your tear drop tattoos. Do they mean you have a soft heart, or something else?"

Quinn threw back his head and laughed. The room became silent as everyone turned towards them at the sound of Quinn's booming laughter. When he could contain himself, he turned back to Maggie and asked, "Do you want the truth, or do you want me to make up something pretty?"

"The truth, always the truth."

"Members, get them when they've killed someone. I've killed two people, so I have two. I won't add to it when I kill again, though. Does it bother you I've killed?"

Maggie smiled at him and replied, "Not at all. I've killed over a dozen men, but I don't need to mark it with a tattoo."

Quinn burst out laughing again, thinking Maggie was joking. She was quick to join in, allowing him to believe she was teasing. At least she'd been honest with him, regardless whether he believed her.

The night progressed with no major issues. There were a couple of fights that were pushed outside. The club forbade fighting inside the clubhouse. Maggie allowed herself a second drink, which she also nursed. When she looked Noelle's way, she noticed Noelle was enjoying herself and from the looks of things, she wasn't coming home tonight. Knowing Noelle was enjoying herself eased some of the guilt Maggie had about putting Noelle in this situation. She had to remind herself she gave Noelle options, and it was Noelle's choice to be here.

At one point, Quinn slipped off to talk with the club's president, 'Butch' Barker. While he was away, Maggie never found herself alone. One or another member slipped in and out of Quinn's seat while he was gone. She wasn't sure if it was to get to know her or monitor her. When he returned, it was obvious he had something on his mind, but he wouldn't elaborate when she asked him.

It was late when Maggie excused herself, saying it was time for her to go. Quinn pressed up against her and whispered in her ear, "You don't have to leave. I have a room in the back."

"As tempting as that is, I don't just fall into bed with people, no matter how good looking and charming they are." To appease his bruised ego, she leaned in to kiss him, but was unprepared for the bear hug grasp he wrapped around her as he made the kiss deeper.

"Just a taste of what's coming." He said as he released her. Maggie's knees felt weak, and she held onto his arm for support.

He walked her to her bike and watched until she left the compound. On her way home, Maggie couldn't shake the feelings he'd awakened within her. She cursed her body for being attracted to a man she hated and may have to kill. She needed to burn off some energy, so after she got home, she went for a run. That followed by a hot shower and she fell into a deep sleep.

31

Maggie awoke to a bright ray of sunshine peeping through her window and the aroma of freshly brewed coffee. She lay in her bed and stretched before she realized the smell of coffee meant Noelle was home. She threw back the covers and padded to the bathroom to relieve herself and splash some water on her face. After throwing on some P.J.'s, she went out to the main room.

Noelle was in the kitchen busy making pancakes. She'd already set the table for them, poured the juice and cut up some fresh fruit.

"Oh good, you're up." Noelle quipped.

Maggie gave Noelle the once over. Noelle had showered and was in clean clothes.

"And you're home." Maggie replied.

Noelle blushed before answering. "Well," she paused as she flipped another pancake. "I haven't been home for long."

"I take it you had a good night?"

"Yes. I forgot how good it felt to choose to sleep with someone just because I wanted to, not because he paid me."

"So, whatever happened was your choice?" Maggie held her

breath while she waited for Noelle's response. She still felt guilty, thinking she'd just prostituted Noelle out for her own gain.

"Oh ya. Tiny wouldn't force me. He even offered to drive me home last night if I wanted to leave, but I was having too much fun." She placed the plate of pancakes on the table. "Let's eat."

"This looks great, thank you Noelle." Maggie said as she took her first sip of the steaming hot coffee.

"So, you like Tiny?" Maggie asked.

"Well, he's not who I'd pick to date, if I ever dated." She chuckled. "But he's fun to be around and seems to like me. He's good in bed, too. I think I had my first orgasm with a partner in years." She chuckled, looking at the shocked expression on Maggie's face. "Johns don't care about my pleasure, it's all about them. I fake it so they feel better about themselves, but they're selfish. I guess they can afford to be that way because they're paying for it."

"You know, if you don't want to go back to that lifestyle, you can stay here and look for work. Who knows, maybe you could go back to school."

Noelle smiled at Maggie. "That's very nice of you. I'll think about it."

After they'd finished breakfast, Maggie suggested they go for a walk. She wanted to get some light exercise and figured it would be a good way to get Noelle talking about her night. Maggie had a ton of questions she wanted to ask, but thought allowing Noelle to talk on her own terms would be best. She'd remember more if it came out through casual conversation than if she was answering a bunch of questions.

The two walked along the streets of the downtown core, chatting back and forth. Soon they found themselves back on the boardwalk.

Noelle stopped in front of the Beavertail shack, examined the sign and all the options, and turned to Maggie.

"I've never had BeaverTails before. Do you want one?"

Maggie felt as if her body moved in slow motion as she turned to look at the kiosk. She could almost taste the sweet sticky treat as her mind slipped back to the last time she stopped there. Then the rapid whoosh, whoosh as the bullets from the silencer tore her family apart. The air around Maggie became thick and darkness ebbed into her peripheral vision, closing around her. Her knees buckled, and she waited for her body to hit the pavement, but a pair of hands grabbed her and prevented her fall.

"Oh, my god! Maggie, are you ok?" Through the din, Maggie could hear the concern in Noelle's voice.

Maggie turned to look at the person whose arms held her upright and stared into the cool blue eyes of Colby Tate. Detective Tate. Her eyes widened. She had to pull herself together and put some distance between Colby and Noelle before he recognized her as the lot lizard from Chilliwack. It was a good thing she still had the curls in her hair instead of her usual spikes and was wearing large sunglasses.

"Detective Tate." Maggie said, smiling. Noelle stepped back. "I'm sorry to be such a bother. I guess I've been out in the sun for too long."

When Maggie gained control of herself, Colby let her go, but kept his hand on her lower back to steady her. He turned to Noelle with an outstretched hand.

"Colby Tate."

Noelle took his hand and shook it. "Anne." Choosing to use the short form of her middle name, Annabelle.

"Well, if you two ladies think you're ok, I'll continue on. It was nice meeting you Anne, have a great day."

Both women turned and watched him walk away, admiring the way his blue jeans fit as he went.

"That's one hot cop. How do you know him?" Noelle asked.

"You know him too. He did the interviews in Chilliwack after they found the body of that truck driver."

"Holy shit! I'm glad I used my middle name. Noelle is kinda memorable. So, tell me, what just happened? How do you know him?"

Maggie filled Noelle in on some details. Telling her that stopping for BeaverTails was the last thing she and Liam did together before he died. Also, that Colby was the RCMP detective who was investigating Liam's death. She let Noelle know he recognized her from Chilliwack and that she'd run into him when he was out with his daughter. She omitted telling Noelle that it was him she'd made a picnic for and joined a week ago.

32

Following another late night with the Dark Enders, Maggie entered the apartment and went in search of Noelle. The door to Noelle's room was open, so she walked in and found Noelle applying concealer to cover up what looked like a black eye. Noelle spun around when she heard Maggie, whose mouth gaped when she saw Noelle's black eye. The whole eye was a deep shade of purple and beginning to swell. The makeup wouldn't cover it. Before supper, the swelling would force her eye shut.

"What the hell happened?" Maggie yelled the minute she saw Noelle's face.

"I, um, ah."

"Who did this? Never mind. I already know. It was Tiny."

"Maggie, he didn't mean to. I made him mad because one of the other members was talking to me. I figured it didn't matter because he hasn't made me his old lady."

"Doesn't matter? That's bullshit! Of course, it matters." Maggie stomped off to get her concealer kit, knowing there was a shade in there that would disguise the bruising. Then she went to the kitchen and grabbed an ice pack, stopping by her medicine cabinet for witch hazel and cotton pads.

"Sit down." Maggie commanded as she came back into the room. Noelle obeyed and dropped onto the bed.

Maggie held up the concealer kit. "When you need to cover your bruises, use this. The green will help hide the purple." Then she pulled out a makeup remover wipe and handed it to Noelle. "Take it all off."

Noelle sensed Maggie's rage and complied without argument. Noelle wasn't as upset as Maggie appeared to be. In her line of work, getting knocked around was an occupational hazard. In the past, she'd covered more bruises than she cared to remember. She didn't understand why it bothered Maggie so much, but held her tongue.

She watched Maggie soak a cotton pad with witch hazel and hand it to her. "Put this over your eye. It will help with the bruising."

Noelle placed the pad over her eye, enjoying the way the cool liquid on the pad felt against her hot skin. Maggie wrapped the ice pack in a hand towel and handed it to Noelle.

"I want you to alternate between cotton soaked with witch hazel and ice packs today. Hopefully, it won't swell too much, but I doubt it." She turned to leave.

"Maggie, I'm sorry I've upset you."

Hearing this, Maggie's fists curled, but she forced them to relax.

"You didn't upset me. It's Tiny. That bastard had no right to hit you. You aren't going back there!"

"Maggie, listen to me. This isn't the first time a man has hit me, and I'm sure it won't be the last, not in my line of work."

"Then get out of your line of work!" She snapped.

"I promised you I'll think about it. But I'm continuing with your plan. You want your story and I've been getting lots of information for you. It's why I'm here, remember?"

Maggie took a deep breath before responding, "Oh, I remember." Then she stormed out of the room. Noelle flinched when she heard the door slam as Maggie left the apartment.

The rage Maggie felt was almost uncontrollable as she rode the elevator down to the parking garage. As much as she'd love to take a ride, she knew it was a bad idea in her state of mind. Instead, she slid behind the wheel of her car, pulled out onto the street and headed to the park, where she'd met with Colby and Evelyn. Tears of anger and frustration blurred her eyes, which she brushed away.

'This is all my fault.' She thought. *'I've put Noelle in a dangerous position. I either need to come clean with her or I have to stop her from going back to the clubhouse. Maybe if she knew the truth, she'd understand how dangerous it was.'*

Maggie blinked at the tears in her eyes and wiped away the ones that escaped like raindrops down her cheeks. What she needed was some time to think. She stopped at Tim Hortons and grabbed a coffee before pulling into the parking lot at the park. She wasn't sure why she chose this park, but it felt comfortable and familiar.

Maggie cracked a window and leaned back while she sipped on her coffee. She sat in her seat and considered the different scenarios. If she allowed Noelle to go back, Tiny could hurt her again, or worse. If she didn't let Noelle go back, it would make her job harder, but she couldn't wait too much longer to move on with her plan. Quinn would expect her to sleep with him soon and she'd find herself in a position where she'd either have to kill him or sleep with him. Killing him was the end goal, but she had to kill Butch first. If she didn't, she'd never get this close again. Tiny had just added himself to her short list of people she needed to kill.

"Dammit!" She slammed her fist on the steering wheel. *"I have to speed up my time frame. Everything is getting so complicated."*

Had she lost her edge after she killed Frank Carter? No, she knew she could kill again. Avenging Liam's murder was worth it. But then there was Colby. She'd been spending time with him and Evelyn. He was funny and kind and easy on the eyes. He was everything Liam was. Plus, she'd fallen for his daughter. She was a real joy to have around and filled the void Maggie felt. When Maggie was with them, she felt like they were a family, something after Liam's death she never thought she'd have. How could she keep this going on? She needed to end things before they got worse. If Colby found out who and what she really was, he'd arrest her and never look at her with the kindness and compassion she saw in his eyes now.

It was time to take action. She'd been dragging things out for too long. She knew the reason was that she liked Noelle. They'd become friends. As unlikely a pair as they were, she knew Noelle felt the same way. She hated that her need for retribution caused Noelle to get hurt. It wasn't something she'd considered when she asked for her help, but she didn't expect to like her and become friends. Everything was so messed up.

She took another sip of the still hot coffee, looked up and cursed as she saw Colby walking through the park with Evelyn. She didn't want to see him right now and put her car into reverse and peeled out of the parking lot. Hopefully, he didn't recognize her car. If he saw her, she'd just tell him she didn't see him and was on a lead for a story. She knew he'd believe her because he trusted her, which was another thing that bothered her.

As she drove, she let her mind work away at her plan. She'd take care of Tiny first. He was a small fish and would be easier to get to. At least Noelle didn't have feelings for him, so his death wouldn't affect her too much. Now she just had to convince Noelle to stay away from the club.

33

Maggie knew she'd have to find Tiny and deal with him before he hurt Noelle again. She couldn't just hurt him, because he'd tell Quinn and that would ruin everything. There was only one thing she could do, and that was kill him. She wouldn't feel guilt. He deserved it. He was a woman abuser, and a member of the gang who killed Liam. Killing him might just be the push she needed to move forward and finish this.

Quinn had invited her back to the clubhouse again tonight. She knew Noelle would be there with Tiny. With them both being present and her not saying anything to Noelle in front of him would put Noelle's mind at ease, but the information she wanted was when and where Tiny would be without the rest of the gang. She hoped Noelle would learn this and tell her, unaware of the real reason behind her wanting to know. She couldn't use any information she learned from Quinn because if anything happened to Tiny afterwards, it would put her integrity into question. Quinn might think she was a rat and then she'd lose her edge with him or find herself in a precarious position.

The other option was to lie low and start following Tiny until she

125

found him alone. She'd figure it out after tonight. For now, she needed to head back home and see how Noelle was doing. Maggie hoped her home remedy would ease what looked like a nasty shiner.

When Maggie entered the apartment, she found Noelle on the sofa with the ice pack on her eye. She turned to Maggie and pulled the ice pack away to allow her to see that the eye looked better.

"Thanks Dr. Maggie, it doesn't look as bad as I thought it would. How did you know to use witch hazel?"

"I took some self-defence lessons. In the beginning, my teacher could toss me around the room. I always ended up bruised, so it was what he recommended."

"Did you ever stop getting tossed around the room? There's not much to you," Noelle asked, looking up and down Maggie's tiny frame.

Maggie smiled, "Yes, I did. I prevented him from throwing me and pinned him to the ground. That's when he told me I was ready and could defend myself against the biggest opponent. I still spar with him once a week to keep my training up."

"You're a surprising woman, Maggie."

"Yup, and one who needs a shower before we head to the clubhouse."

"So, you're ok with everything? You won't say anything to Tiny?"

"I won't say anything," Maggie paused, "for now."

After she showered, Maggie went in search of Noelle, and found her in the bathroom trying to cover the bruise with the compact Maggie had lent her.

"Here," she said, taking the palette and sponge from Noelle, "let me."

Maggie patted and blended the cosmetics until you could barely see the bruises. If it wasn't for the slight swelling, you wouldn't know she had a black eye.

When Noelle turned to the mirror to see what Maggie had done, she squealed with delight.

"Oh Maggie! Thank you! Tiny has been texting me all day telling me how sorry he was and I told him it wasn't too bad. Now he won't know I lied."

Maggie rolled her eyes. Of course, he'd want to think it wasn't too bad. If it was, she might not come back, she tsked to herself.

"Well, if you spend the night, he'll know. When the makeup comes off, you won't be able to hide the bruising."

"Then I'll love him and leave him like I would a John. That way, my makeup won't need to come off."

Maggie sighed. "Just be careful."

Maggie wanted to give Noelle a ride, but she couldn't hide the extra helmet and they were still pretending they didn't know each other inside the club. Also, Maggie didn't want to drive her car because she didn't want any of the members to recognize her vehicle when she started following Tiny. A bike would be more noticeable, whereas a car would blend in with traffic. She needed to maintain a low profile anytime she followed a member when the opportunity arose so that she could take care of business.

So once again, Maggie arrived after Noelle and parked her bike. She'd been there enough times now that no one hassled her in the compound. This time, she pulled out a cigarette. Smoking was something she'd taken up again around the clubhouse, as it allowed her to mingle with other members when she needed to. She approached a small group huddled together. It was an opportunity to eavesdrop and get a light. It was funny how her stature made men think she was helpless. Thank God she got the short gene in her family.

This time, Maggie got lucky. Just before they noticed her standing with her smoke in hand looking for a light, she overheard them talking about a run Tiny was making tomorrow. Maggie figured if she got to the location before he showed up, she could deal with him. She needed to leave without Noelle knowing, and use her car to remain anonymous. This time she'd take her gun. She felt she might need the added protection and doubted it was an up close and personal job.

Just as Maggie stubbed out her cigarette, from the corner of her eye, she saw Quinn approach.

"Hey, I was just coming to find you. I know how you like to show up late just to make an entrance." He teased.

"Let's just say I'm never the first to arrive or the last to leave." She retorted.

"Maybe it's time you were."

Maggie knew there was a veiled threat hidden in those words. He wanted to sleep with her and expected her to do so soon. She wasn't sure how much longer she'd be able to put him off. He was a man that was used to getting what he wanted and having women throw themselves at him. She was positive that he still found comfort in the many willing arms after she'd left the clubhouse. The thought of having to sleep with him was both appealing and repulsive. He was an attractive sexual man, but he was also part of the gang that killed Liam. In the end, she knew she'd do whatever she had to in order to see this through.

34

The next morning, Maggie rose before dawn and slipped out of the apartment to avoid running into Noelle. Noelle had yet to return from the clubhouse, so she fired off a quick text to her so she wouldn't worry or message her while she was out.

'Where r u?'

'On my way home.'

'K. I'm heading out. C u later.'

'K. I'll cook dinner. Grab some wine.'

'K.'

Maggie breathed a sigh of relief that Noelle didn't ask where she was going. She figured Noelle was on her way home, and she wanted to leave before she showed up. Tiny had a job to do this morning, and he wouldn't want Noelle hanging around. But Maggie also had a job to do, so she hopped into her car and maneuvered the streets until she found a place to park with a good vantage point of where she knew Tiny would be.

Maggie leaned her seat back and made herself comfortable. She had a few hours to wait before Tiny's meetup. She'd tucked her distinctive hair up under a ball cap and had the peak low over her eyes. To anyone passing by, it would appear as though she was taking a nap. She put the gun under her seat, out of sight, but within reach so she could grab it when she saw Tiny.

She'd prefer it in her lap so she wouldn't have to reach for it, but if a cop came by to see what she was doing there, it would be the first thing he saw. Having the gun under her seat hid it from view, but still made it easy enough for her to grab when she needed it. As was her habit, she hid her knife in her coat for back up. She still wasn't sure if she was going to confront Tiny face-to-face or just take him out from here with the gun.

She'd never killed from a distance. Until now, it had always been up close and personal. She sat pondering what she should do in this situation. As long as he wore his cut (his vest with the club insignia), then she'd be able to identify him. His body type was distinctive, so she didn't think it would be a problem even from this distance. She knew it would be more complicated if someone else from the club was with him.

When she heard the roar of a Harley in the distance, she'd almost dozed off. She shifted in her seat to get a better look at the scene that was going to play out in front of her.

She watched as Tiny parked his bike and climb off. His size made it difficult for him to get off the bike and he stumbled. He removed his helmet and placed it on the seat, and left his doo-rag in place. Today he only wore his vest over a t-shirt and his black Levi's jeans. When he adjusted his pants, Maggie saw the butt of a handgun tucked into his waistband. This surprised her. It was supposed to be a simple drop, so why would he be packing a gun?

Maggie waited and watched as he pulled out a thick manilla envelope from one of his saddle bags. By the shape, she assumed it was a lot of cash. She cursed herself for not finding out what his errand was. She looked around at the deserted warehouses and wondered who he was meeting there.

Maggie reached under her seat, pulled out the gun and aimed it at Tiny, but a car pulled up, ruining her shot. Maggie lowered the gun when the driver stepped out, went to the passenger door, and opened it. Tiny stood his ground. A slim, well-dressed man stepped out of the back carrying a briefcase. He motioned Tiny over.

Maggie held the gun against her thigh as she watched the scene play out. Tiny approached the man but left several feet between them. She watched what appeared to be a verbal exchange and wished she was close enough to hear what they were saying. The man placed his briefcase on the trunk of his car and opened it. His driver kept his right hand poised on the left side of his jacket. Even from this distance, she could tell he had a gun. Tiny didn't seem to notice.

The slender man pulled out a small plastic baggie. From this distance Maggie couldn't be sure of the contents, but she saw Tiny withdraw the envelope from his vest as he closed the distance between them. They swapped items and after Tiny tucked his package in his pocket; he pulled out his gun and aimed it at the man with the briefcase.

There was a heated exchange of words between them before a shot ran out and then a second. Without thinking, Maggie raised her gun as she watched Tiny and the man with the briefcase hit the pavement. The driver ran to his passenger and checked his pulse. Tiny moved, and the driver spun around and aimed his gun at Tiny again. Before the man could shoot, the bullet left Maggie's gun and connected with the driver, hitting him in the centre of his chest. Blood bloomed as he crumbled to the ground.

Maggie was out of her car and running to the scene. She knew she'd killed the driver, but she didn't know if the passenger or Tiny were still alive. Then she saw Tiny move. As she closed the distance, she kept low. She kicked Tiny's gun out of his reach and looked at the passenger. His vacant eyes told her what she needed to know.

Behind her, she heard Tiny moan. She turned to look at him. The driver shot him in the gut and he was bleeding profusely. He squinted at her against the glaring sun.

"Aren't you Quinn's girl?" He sputtered, spitting blood as he did. She nodded. She didn't need to waste a bullet on him. He was dying. Even if paramedics arrived now, they couldn't save him.

Maggie grabbed the baggie from Tiny's pocket and tossed it into the open briefcase. She snapped it shut and grabbed it off the back of the car. She'd touched nothing except Tiny's pocket, but she was wearing gloves. As she left, she heard the gurgles of death as Tiny succumbed to his injuries.

She tossed the briefcase in the back of her car. Scanned the area for witnesses and left to the sound of approaching sirens. Somebody must have heard the shots and reported them. She needed to put distance between the crime scene and herself and sped away.

<h1 style="text-align:center">35</h1>

Maggie looked for a quiet place to pull over when she'd put enough distance between herself and the crime scene. She needed to open the briefcase and see what was in it. She pulled into the parking lot of a strip mall and chose a spot as far from the building as she could to avoid traffic and people.

Maggie slipped the gun back under her seat. Now that she'd fired it, she needed to clean it. It wasn't something she couldn't do at the condo. All of her supplies were back at her house, so she'd have to go home at some point today. She opened a bottle of water from her cupholder and took a long pull, then she reached into the back and grabbed the briefcase. It was time to see what was inside.

She pushed her seat back, put the briefcase on her lap, and flicked the locks. When it snapped open, relief washed over her. She lifted the lid and her eyes widened when she saw the case was full of the same small baggies she'd pulled from Tiny's pocket.

Her eyes darted as she looked around, checking her surroundings before she picked up a bag. She inspected it and realized what it was. It was coke. There were hundreds of baggies. She dropped the bag back into the case and picked up the manilla envelope. Just as she suspected, it was full of cash. What she didn't understand was why the Dark Enders were buying coke from an outside source. She'd listened in to enough conversations at the clubhouse to know they had their own coke business. Maggie snapped the briefcase shut.

She needed to think. The Dark Enders would think it was the High Rollers and the turf war would intensify. Maggie didn't care if there was more bloodshed between the two gangs. Maybe they'd kill each other off and do her job for her. What concerned her was the possibility of civilian casualties.

The briefcase was important, and she needed to find a safe hiding spot for it. Then she remembered the sub-basement she and Liam built at their house. It was going to be a wine cellar, but they never got around to finishing it, so they'd closed off the entrance, which was hidden behind a shelving rack of sundries. It was time to head home.

Maggie put the briefcase onto the backseat and headed straight to her house. Now that the trees were in full bloom, she'd have some privacy from the neighbours, plus it was a weekday and most of them would be at work or school. Liam's bike and SUV were in the garage, so she'd have to park in the driveway.

She turned onto her street, scanned the area to see if anyone was outside, and was relieved to find that no one was around. It didn't mean a neighbour wasn't watching from behind their curtains like Mrs. Cameron. Mrs. Cameron was the neighbourhood Gladys Kravitz, like the character from the old Bewitched TV series. It didn't matter if Mrs. Cameron saw her come home, she would just wonder where Maggie had been and tsk to herself that the poor dear was still mourning the loss of her husband.

Maggie parked her car in front of the garage and opened the door with the remote before she stepped out of the car. She grabbed the briefcase and gun and entered her house, closing the garage door behind her. The silence that greeted her was deafening. She considered the possibility of getting a pet in the future to fill the void, but she was allergic to cats and her life was too chaotic for a dog. Maybe when this was all over, she said to herself and her life returned to normal.

Still wearing her gloves, she went to the basement with the briefcase and pushed the pantry shelf to one side, giving her access to the sub-cellar door. She swung open the door, revealing a room no bigger than a closet. Shelves lined the walls to prepare for the preserving she'd hoped to do with her child. A small carpet was on the floor. She rolled it back to expose a trap door. Liam wanted to use a ladder for access, but opted for a set of stairs. Maggie flicked the switch to the right of the door to the storage cupboard and both the cupboard and the sub-cellar flooded with light. She descended the stairs to a ten-by-ten room lined with wine racks. A temperature control device was on the wall at the bottom of the stairs. Only one bottle was in the rack. A bottle of Dom Pérignon. The one they had planned to drink to celebrate the birth of their child.

Maggie saw the lone bottle and her breath caught. She forced herself to look away and slid the briefcase into the space under the stairs. She needed to figure out what to do with it, but for now, it was a safe place for it. Maggie went back up the stairs, closed the hatch and replaced the rug. She turned off the lights and pushed the shelving rack back in place. Now she had to clean and reload her gun.

Maggie gathered her supplies and prepared to clean the gun. She laid out some newspaper on the kitchen table and began the tedious process of disassembling and cleaning it. She had just finished and was preparing to put the gun back together when the doorbell rang. Her first thought was to ignore it, but her car was parked out front and when she peeked around the corner, she saw Colby looking through the sidelight of the front door. She knew he saw her, so she waved and motioned for him to hold on for a minute. He nodded at her and she went to wash the solvent off of her hands and sprayed air freshener to cover the scent. Then she tossed a towel over the scattered gun parts before greeting Colby at the door.

36

Maggie stepped to the front door and opened it after placing a big smile on her face.

"Hi detective, what can I do for you?"

"Hi um, Mrs. Mur..., um Maggie."

"Cat got your tongue? Or maybe a cougar?" She teased.

Colby's cheeks went pink, but he smiled. "Sorry you didn't look like yourself with your hair all tucked up in that baseball cap."

Maggie's hand went to her head. She'd forgotten that she was still wearing it. *'Dammit, that was careless.'* She thought. Quick to recover, she replied. "Oh well, I was doing some cleaning, and it's easier if my mop of hair is out of the way."

"May I come in?"

"Uh, sure." Maggie hesitated before stepping back from the door to allow him to pass.

She motioned to the living room. "Please have a seat, detective."

"Maggie, why don't you call me Colby?"

"Oh," she paused, "is this a social call? I thought maybe you were wearing your detective's hat."

She could tell he looked uncomfortable, but she refused to do anything to make him feel more at ease. It annoyed her he'd shown up unannounced, and the scattered pieces of the gun she just used to kill the driver were only a few feet away. She waited for him to tell her the reason for his visit. She needed him out of here before he discovered what was in her kitchen.

Colby stood still, not moving to sit in the seat she offered him, so she crossed her arms over her chest and waited for him to talk.

"Well, this is awkward." He replied.

"Only because you're making it that way. Why don't you just tell me why you're here?"

"It's Evelyn."

"Is she ok?" Maggie was quick to interject.

Colby heard the worry in her voice.

"Oh yes, she's fine." He reassured her. "It is just she has her kindergarten graduation on Friday and she wanted me to ask if you'd come." He finished, blowing out the breath he'd been holding.

Maggie stared at him. She was so touched her voice caught in her throat and she only croaked.

"It's ok if you can't, I understand. I can make excuses for you." He cut in.

"I'd love to." She responded, touching his arm. "What does one bring to a kindergarten graduation?"

"Cookies?" He replied hopefully. "She'll be thrilled. Why don't I pick you up here and we can all go together? Would 8:30 work? We have to be to the school for 9."

"Sure, that sounds good. And yes, I'll make cookies."

"Ok. Thank you, Evelyn will be thrilled. See you then."

Colby left and Maggie watched him until he pulled away. The invitation touched her and couldn't stop the smile that spread across her lips. She found she was even looking forward to it. It meant she'd have to spend Thursday night at the house baking and getting ready for Colby to pick her up. She knew Noelle would be fine on her own, so that wouldn't be a problem. The problem would be Quinn. He expected her to drop everything the minute he called or texted.

She made some quick notes on her phone about the ingredients she needed to pick up to make the cookies and went back to assemble her gun and clean up the kitchen. If she hurried, she'd be able to hit the grocery store and drop the supplies back off and still get back to the condo to have dinner with Noelle.

37

By the time Thursday rolled around, Maggie was tired of listening to Noelle complain she hadn't heard from Tiny for a few days. Maggie didn't want Noelle to know what happened to Tiny, and felt certain she wouldn't go to the clubhouse without an invitation. Maggie asked if she'd texted him.

"Of course I have," Noelle snapped. "He just hasn't responded. He must be busy with club business."

"I'm sure that's it." Maggie reassured.

Leaving Noelle to her own devices, Maggie spent most of the afternoon at her computer, writing a few articles for her paper. Just because she had gone into a self-imposed undercover assignment didn't mean she didn't have work to do. Thankfully, it also reassured Noelle that she was writing a story about the club.

When she hit send on the second article, she stood up and stretched. She had to head back to her house and bake cookies for Evelyn's graduation tomorrow. She packed up her laptop, not wanting to leave it in the apartment, and piled it with a few items she wanted to take with her by the door. In the trunk of her car, she had a gift for Evelyn. She'd gone to the Build-A-Bear in the Mic Mac mall and made her a graduation bear. Maggie would have preferred to do it with Evelyn, but didn't want to overstep her boundaries. She left it in the car because she didn't want to explain anything to Noelle. She felt bad about lying to her, but her spending time with Colby and Evelyn had nothing to do with why Noelle was here. Plus, she was aware Noelle would remind her about Quinn's jealousy, and she didn't want to hear it.

When Maggie was ready to leave, she knocked on Noelle's door. Noelle had been moody most of the day, wondering why Tiny wasn't responding to her, and Maggie had left her alone. Maggie knew the reason he wasn't responding was because he was lying in a morgue somewhere. She saw the news about the gang killing, but Noelle didn't pay attention to the news feeds, so she didn't know, and Maggie wouldn't be the one to tell her. Maggie felt guilty keeping the news from her, but Noelle had to find out from another gang member or they'd suspect her of being involved.

"Come in." Noelle called out after hearing Maggie's knock.

Maggie stepped into the room and found Noelle applying her makeup preparing to go out.

"Where are you going?" Maggie asked.

"To the clubhouse. There's a gathering tonight. Tiny invited me the last time I saw him."

"But you haven't heard from him. You shouldn't go if he hasn't been in contact."

"I have to. If he doesn't want me to be there, he'll tell me to go. If that happens, I'll text you and let you know." Noelle finished lining her right eye with eyeliner. "What I'm curious about is how Quinn let you get out of going tonight."

"I told him I have to work."

"Does he know what you do?"

Maggie chuckled. "As far as Quinton Mars knows, I work in a call centre. It's the perfect cover, as they have day and night shifts."

"Are you going to tell *me* where you're going?"

"No. But it's personal. It has nothing to do with the club or my article."

Noelle eyed Maggie and sighed. "Ok, you go on and have a nice evening. I'll see you tomorrow."

Maggie turned to leave, but went to Noelle and hugged her. "I'd prefer if you'd stay home, but if you go, be safe." Then turned and left.

Maggie pulled into her driveway and parked her car. It was a good idea for her neighbours to know she was home. She brought in her personal items and dropped them on the sofa, then went back to the car for Evelyn's gift and the cookie ingredients. She put the groceries in the kitchen and left the gift on the table in the hall so she could grab it when Colby picked her up in the morning. Then she put her personal items away in her room so Colby wouldn't know she wasn't living here at the moment. No need to stir up trouble where it wasn't welcome.

Then she pulled the gun safe out from under her bed and deposited the reloaded weapon. If Colby and Evelyn came back to her house, she wanted it locked up. She looked through her closet trying to decide what to wear the next day before opting on a sundress she knew emphasized the green of her eyes and checked to see if it needed ironing, then she hung it on the back of her bedroom door, ready to be put on in the morning.

She slipped into her PJs and went back to the kitchen to thumb through the recipe cards that belonged to her mother until she found the one for butterscotch chocolate chip cookies. They would be perfect. No nut allergies to worry about. Although these days with gluten-free, vegan etc., you were bound to upset someone, but she was making them for Evelyn and that's what mattered to her. She turned on the oven and went to work on making the cookies. As she pulled out the last batch from the oven, her cell phone rang.

Maggie picked up the phone, looked at the caller ID, and saw that it was Audrey. It had been a while since they last spoke, so she put the call on speaker and answered it while she cleaned up.

"You sound busy." Audrey said when she heard the clang of dishes being stacked.

"Believe it or not, I just made cookies and I'm cleaning up."

"Cookies? You?" Audrey teased.

"I'll have you know I'm an excellent baker. Liam used to say..." her voice trailed off.

"How are you?" Audrey asked. "When I get radio silence from you, I worry. I haven't heard from you since you mailed out the last hair clip."

"Oh, you don't have to worry. I'm doing well. I just remembered the last time I made cookies was for Liam. He was taking them into work to celebrate my pregnancy. It just got to me."

"Well, I have some good news. I think I found another child. The details are sketchy right now, but I'm hopeful."

"That's fantastic! Why don't you send me what you have so far? I'll use my resources and see what I can come up with."

"Perfect. By the way, I had dinner with your aunt and uncle the other day. They're worried about you. They say you haven't called in a while."

Maggie rolled her eyes. Now she knew what prompted the call from Audrey. Her aunt and uncle were worried, but they didn't want to seem pushy, so they got Audrey to call for them. They knew she wasn't great at keeping in touch. They should be used to it by now. Maggie sighed.

"Tell them I'm thinking of coming back for Christmas."

"Are you really? But Christmas, that's months away."

"It's the best I can do right now. I've got too much going on."

"You're going after the people responsible for Liam's death, aren't you?"

Maggie dropped into a kitchen chair. *'How did Audrey always know my darkest secrets?'* She thought.

"It's ok Maggie if you are. I understand. I just want you to know I'm here if you need a shoulder or an ear."

"Thank you." Maggie whispered as she choked back the tears that threatened to spill. "Ah, listen Audrey, I have to get going. Send me the details on that case and let's see if we can put another family's uncertainty to rest."

Maggie reached over and grabbed a still warm cookie to nibble on. Playing 'family' with Colby and his daughter was fun, but she was losing her focus. She wouldn't back out of the graduation, but she needed to create some distance between them. He was a detective, and she was a killer, one slip-up, and he'd be investigating her.

Her phone pinged with the information Audrey had gathered and Maggie set to work on her computer, gathering research to correspond with what Audrey had found out. Later, when she looked up, she realized it was past one a.m. and she needed to get to bed if she was going to be up and ready when Colby arrived in the morning. She hadn't been able to confirm the information Audrey sent yet, but her gut told her they'd found another mother who deserved to know the truth. Maggie had a generic email set up to contact the parents of potential victims of Frank Carter, but she needed to go somewhere else to send it. The IP address had to change in order for it not to be traced back to her. She gave Audrey the address and passcode and told her to take a day trip somewhere that she could get access to a public computer. Audrey could send the query and Maggie could pick up the response.

She slipped under the covers and pulled Liam's pillow to her body, and held it between her arms. It no longer smelled like him. She'd changed the sheets too many times since the shooting, but still the act comforted her as she drifted off to sleep.

38

The sound of her alarm dragged Maggie out of a deep sleep. Her surroundings confused her at first, after spending so many weeks at the condo, but then she remembered Evelyn's graduation. She rubbed the sleep from her eyes before she slid out of bed and padded to the bathroom to shower.

She stood under the hot spray of water, allowing the heat to ease the tension that had built up in her shoulders over the last few weeks. When she stepped out and dried herself, she slipped into a sundress and applied some light cosmetics. Maggie looked at the unruly curls of her hair and pulled out her hair dryer and round brush. She was going to tame her hair into soft waves for the day ahead. She just finished applying a light shade of gloss to her lips when the doorbell sounded.

Maggie took one last look at her appearance before she went to answer the door. Colby greeted her when she swung the door open and Evelyn stood on the other side, her hand in his. The child beamed at Maggie, and Maggie's heart melted at the sight before her. Evelyn wore what Maggie assumed was a party dress, shimmery pink satin and a full skirt. Evelyn spun around for Maggie's approval. She noticed the matching hair clips in the child's hair and her knees went weak. Maggie's hand clamped onto the door frame for support as she took in the sight of the sweet innocent child in front of her and felt an overwhelming need to protect her.

"Did ya make cookies? Daddy can't bake." She said, wrinkling her nose.

Maggie grabbed the platter of cookies and held it out for Evelyn's approval. "Yummy!" was all she said. Maggie handed Colby the platter and then turned back to grab her purse and the gift.

"What's that?" Evelyn asked, pointing to the gift bag.

"It's a surprise. You'll have to wait and see."

Evelyn squealed in delight and hugged Maggie's legs. Colby leaned over and whispered that she didn't have to do that, but Maggie just shrugged her shoulders as they headed to Colby's waiting car.

Maggie and Colby sat together at the graduation. Throughout, she felt many eyes staring at her. She could tell some parents wondered who she was, especially the single mothers. Maggie didn't let their curiosity bother her. She was here because Evelyn wanted her here. After the graduation ceremony, complete with paper mortar hats and diplomas, Maggie presented Evelyn with the graduation bear. She showed Evelyn the birth certificate and told her the name space was blank so she could be the one to name it. Evelyn threw her arms around Maggie and planted a sticky wet kiss on her cheek as a thank you, before rushing off to show her friends.

"You have a way with children." Colby said as she stood back up.

Maggie smiled at him. "I'd always hoped to have some, but..." She didn't finish her thought, only shrugged her shoulders. Her eye prickled with the threat of tears, so she forced the feeling away by smiling.

Colby almost said she was young and could still have children when he remembered the medical report. She'd lost her uterus and child after the shooting. He held his tongue and watched her as she moved around the room with ease, chatting with several parents. *'Yes,'* he thought, with admiration, *'she'd have made an excellent mother.'*

After the party, Colby took them out for something to eat, because it was Evelyn's day, it was her choice and she picked McDonald's. Colby groaned, but relented. Maggie teased him and said, "Sometimes you just need a Big Mac."

After lunch, Colby dropped Maggie back off at her house. She thanked them for a wonderful time, but Evelyn wouldn't let her go until she promised to go to the park again with them sometime this week. Before she answered, Maggie eyed Colby, who only shrugged his shoulders. Then Maggie agreed, giving both Evelyn and Colby a brief hug before they left.

When she was sure Colby was gone, Maggie changed out of her clothes and packed up her computer to head back to the apartment. She pulled her burner phone from the bedside table and noticed several texts from Quinn.

"Where are you? I thought you might stop by after work."

"Maggie? Are you ignoring me?"

"Don't be such a bitch."

Quinn's behaviour angered her. He was both possessive and jealous. They hadn't even slept together. She hesitated before responding. She had to think of an excuse and reply to him before she left the house. Having him mad at her would be problematic if she was going to finish her vendetta soon.

"Shit." Maggie cursed. She had to get back to the condo, change into the right gear and get to the clubhouse or she'd arouse suspicion. Maggie ran back to her bedroom and grabbed her gun out of the gun case. She felt this time she was going to need it.

39

After a quick drive back to the city, Maggie ran into the apartment to change. She checked the time on her phone and saw that she had little time to get into her riding gear and arrive at the clubhouse. As soon as she entered, she smelled the distinctive aroma of cleaners. She could tell that Noelle had cleaned the apartment since she left the day before. Maggie called out to her.

"Hey Noelle, I'm back." Silence greeted her. Maggie wondered where Noelle was, but didn't have time to deal with it now. She changed into her riding gear and slid her gun into the custom holder inside her jacket. She tied her hair back and added some liner to her eyes. The PTA mom look from this morning wouldn't pass with Quinn.

She arrived a few minutes later than she planned. The first thing she noticed was Quinn sitting on the front steps, waiting for her. When she saw the look on his face, she knew he wasn't happy. He jumped up and headed her way, and before she could get off her bike, he was by her side.

"What the hell happened to you last night?"

"What are you talking about? I told you I had to work." She quipped as she dismounted her bike.

His hand shot out, grabbed her ponytail, and yanked her head back. The force of it caused her to stumble backwards. Her scalp ached, and she yelped in pain.

"Don't get cute with me. It's been a tough week."

Her immediate reaction was to retaliate. She felt anger bubble up inside her, but it wouldn't do to show her strength and capabilities to Quinn before she needed to. Instead, she was nice and reached up to stroke his cheek.

"Quinn, you're hurting me." She said, smiling up at him.

Suddenly, he let go, and she stumbled to regain her balance. She unfastened her helmet and undid her jacket. Giving herself easy access to her gun if she needed it. She placed her helmet on the seat of her bike and watched as he ran his fingers through his hair. She knew something was bothering him and wondered if he'd tell her what it was.

"Let's go inside." Quinn ordered.

Maggie looked around the parking lot and noticed there were only a few bikes parked there. This was the first time she'd been at the clubhouse when there wasn't a party going on. Her step faltered. *'Was this a good thing or a bad thing?'* She wondered, *'he could be leading me inside to be executed. Did he find out who I am and why I'm here?'*

As she followed Quinn inside, her feet felt leaden. She fought the urge to shoot him and take off. If it was a trap, she realized she may not survive. Her head swung around as she stepped inside the building, her body tensed, waiting for the first blow. Instead, she found they were alone.

"Quinn, why don't you tell me what's going on? Maybe I can help."

"What are you playing at, Maggie?"

Maggie turned to look at him, shock registered on her face. "What?"

"I've been a patient man. You've been coming around for weeks, hanging out. You've kissed me, but that's it. Are you going to keep playing your virginal game? If so, get out and don't come back."

Maggie was stunned. Of all the scenarios she'd envisioned when he messaged her, this wasn't one of them. The last thing she wanted to do was sleep with Quinn, but she needed him to trust her if she was going to get access to Butch. It appeared as if her stalling tactics had worn thin. She looked at him and knew she'd have to sleep with him in order to continue the ruse. She struggled internally with this and knew she was out of options.

"Quinn," she purred, "it's not that I don't want to. It's just there are always so many people around. To me, sex is a private thing."

Quinn leaned his head back and laughed. "If that's all, we have the clubhouse to ourselves right now."

He closed the distance between them and pulled her into his arms, locking her body to his, his face lowered to her upturned one until his lips captured hers. She willed her body to relax as she felt him intensify the kiss. She shifted, not wanting him to feel the gun hidden in her jacket. He pressed against her and made sure she felt his growing need. There was no way she could prevent this from happening, so she played the part of the anxious girlfriend.

"Where can we go?" She said as she broke away from his kiss. He paused and looked into her eyes, then back at the empty room behind him.

"Here?"

"Someone could come in. My body is for your eyes only." She winked.

He growled and scooped her up into his arms and carried her to one of the back rooms. She noticed 'VP' painted on the door and she knew it was his room. He'd never taken her this far into the clubhouse before. She trembled. This was going to happen no matter what her previous intentions were. She'd have to disassociate herself in order to get through it. Maggie reminded herself of Noelle's words, 'sex is sex' and hoped her mind could drift away from the inevitable.

Quinn kicked open the door, strode across the room and dropped her onto the unmade bed at the far side, then he went back to close and lock the door. Maggie took off her jacket and put it to one side of the bed on the floor. She didn't want Quinn handling it. If he picked it up, he'd notice there was something off by the weight of it. She kicked off her riding boots and scooted back up to the top of the bed.

"Do you live here?" Maggie questioned him as he approached her, removing his t-shirt as he went.

"Here?" He looked around the room. "No. I only stay here when I have club business to attend to."

Before she could say anything else, he was on the bed with her, kissing her again, and she resigned herself to the inevitable, unable to fight the yearning she felt to be touched, even if it was by this man.

When they finished, Quinn laid back on the bed and pulled her to him.

"That was worth waiting for." He said, tracing his fingers down her arm. "I wasn't sure, but now I know you're a true redhead." He winked.

Maggie swatted him before sighing and accepting his embrace. Her body needed that physical release more than she realized. She wouldn't have done it if she could have avoided it, but she couldn't keep putting him off. She knew that. Now she hoped he'd finally trust her and let her meet Butch. She smiled to herself and thought, *'At least he's attractive and talented between the sheets.'* Then she silently begged for Liam's forgiveness.

His hand travelled to her abdomen and stopped, feeling the puckered skin from the bullet wound and fragments. He pulled back the sheet to get a better look.

"What's this?" He asked, pushing her back on the bed while he examined her scar and tattoo. He traced his fingers on the black inked lines reflecting shattered glass around the scar.

Her hand went to the scar, and she felt the familiar ache deep in her core. She couldn't allow herself to wallow in her grief, not here. Not now, not in front of Quinn.

"I was in an accident that took my ability to have kids. I always thought I wanted them, so I had the ink added to reflect my shattered dream."

"Um, that's kind of deep. I'm sorry. What happened?"

"I don't enjoy talking about it. But it's ok, I've come to terms with it." She said, climbing over him to get out of bed.

"Hey where are you going?"

"I have to pee." She said as she slipped into her underwear and pulled his shirt over her head. She figured by doing so, he'd think she was marking her territory.

"It would look better without the underwear." He teased as she left the room.

Later, when they were both dressed, they went back into the main area to find they were still the only ones there, so Quinn poured Maggie and himself a drink and led her to a table.

"Did you want me to stick around? Is there another gathering tonight?"

"No." He barked, startling her. Then he made his tone softer. "Sorry, I have club business tonight. Things might get messy and we don't want any outsiders around."

Maggie raised her eyebrow. "Outsiders? I think I'm more than that." She suggested motioning to the hall they just came down.

"Don't be smart. You know what I mean. I'll call or text you when we're finished. Maybe I can come to your place?"

Maggie shook her head. "I have a roommate I'd rather didn't know this side of my life."

"I see we both have a few secrets yet." He finished his drink and motioned for her to do the same. "I'll walk you back to your bike."

Maggie tugged her jacket on before he could pick it up and allowed him to drape his arm across her shoulders as he walked her outside. In the distance, she could hear the roar of motorcycles and knew the rest of the members were on their way.

She allowed him to kiss her goodbye and headed in a direction opposite from her apartment. She twisted down a few streets, turned into a parking lot to a coffee shop and watched the cars and bikes going by. She'd grab a coffee and do the same twists and turns again when she was done. Before she went home, she had to be sure she wasn't being followed.

<h1 style="text-align:center">40</h1>

Quinn watched Maggie leave the clubhouse parking lot as he waited for the rest of his crew to assemble. They had the bitch Tiny was fucking tied up in the basement, and it was time to question her. Someone had shot Tiny during the drug deal and even though it looked like it was the work of the High Rollers, the club figured there had to be a leak in order for the High Rollers to have found out about the deal. The only new person Tiny could have talked to was his new bitch. They had to find out what she knew.

When she showed up last night, the club was in shock. They assumed she'd stay away now that Tiny was dead. But she'd shown up as if nothing was wrong. The bartender slipped her a Mickey, so she'd pass out and when the clubhouse cleared out, Quinn had tied her up and taken her to the basement. Now they could take their time finding out what she knew.

The club was furious. Tiny was one of their own and someone leaked the information leading to his murder. He even considered the possibility that Maggie was involved. But after today, he was sure she wasn't. When she kept avoiding sleeping with him, he felt it was a red flag. No one holds out for as long as she had. He'd thought she was playing games, but then today she'd slept with him, and it was great.

He stared at the group of men filling the main room. The club members were restless and wanted answers. Some wanted to go after the High Rollers right off, but others wanted to kill that bitch Tiny had been hanging out with first. By the end of the day, they might have to do both. Everything depended on how she answered their questions.

Before anyone could go downstairs and deal with her, they needed a meeting to decide how they were going to proceed. Randal, their road captain, approached him. He'd suspected Maggie's motives were off since she first showed up at the Capital.

"So, how'd it go with the redhead?"

"It's all good," Quinn replied with a grin.

Randal leaned in and sniffed the air around Quinn. "Yup, I smell pussy."

Quinn pushed him back, laughing, and called the chartered members into the meeting room. Butch waited inside, sitting at the head of the meeting table. He was at the clubhouse when Quinn brought Maggie back to his room, but stayed out of sight until he was sure everything was ok with her. She may have been the one to plant information with the High Rollers. If Quinn didn't get what he wanted out of her, she'd be the next one they'd deal with.

Butch made eye contact with Quinn, looking for his signal on how things went with Maggie. Quinn nodded at him that everything was ok. Butch motioned for the members to take their seats. Quinn sat first, and the rest followed suit. The meeting was called to order.

After some back-and-forth conversations about how to deal with the girl, they decided as a whole that Butch, Quinn, and Randal would take care of questioning her. The rest of the members would go back to club business and some would head off to find out about the dealer's connections to see if there was a leak at that end.

The three men went down to the basement, leaving two members upstairs to guard the door. There was a buzzer system in place if anything happened, and the guards needed to warn those downstairs. They entered the room where they had Noelle naked and bound to a ring in the centre of the cold cement floor. As soon as the lights went on, she squinted against the glare. They'd left her gagged so no one would hear her screams. Trails from her smeared makeup ran beneath her eyes from crying.

On seeing them enter the room, her face paled and her body shook. Butch and Quinn noticed her fear and stayed back and let Randal remove her gag.

"What's going on? Why am I here? I did nothing wrong. Where's Tiny?" She pleaded.

"Tiny's dead! But I'm sure you already knew that." Butch replied with malice, spitting at her.

Her eyes widened in disbelief. Quinn saw this and a sliver of doubt crossed his mind, '*maybe they were wrong about her. Maybe she didn't know what happened to Tiny. If she did, coming back here was a stupid move.*' He thought.

Randal grabbed her hair, lifted her up and smacked her across the face, blood splattered as her nose broke.

"Tiny already had to put you in your place once, bitch. I saw him give you that black eye. Did he know you were a treacherous bitch?" He finished as he slapped the other side of her face. This time, her lip split and her mouth filled with blood. He released his grasp on her hair as she crumpled back to the ground.

"I didn't do anything." She pleaded. "Do you think I'd come here if I did?"

Randal kicked her in the stomach, watching as she curled up in the fetal position. "That depends on how stupid you are. And I think you're pretty stupid."

Tears ballooned in her eyes and rolled down her cheeks, creating rivers in the dirt, grime, and blood that covered her face. She begged for her life.

"Please don't do this. I came because Tiny asked me to. Please let me go!"

"Tiny was dead two days before you showed up. How could he ask you to?" Randal asked, kicking her again.

This time when Noelle replied, blood oozed from her mouth. "He told me the last time I was here. I didn't hear from him after that, but I knew he had club business to do, so it didn't surprise me he didn't call. I came because I knew he expected me to."

"Club business?" Randal rained a few more blows, this time grabbing his baseball bat from the corner. "Did he tell you what that club business was?"

"No." She croaked between gasps for breath. Noelle was in trouble, and she knew it. Her breathing sounded ragged. That last blow had broken a rib. Every breath she took was shallow and painful. She drew her legs back up to her chest and wrapped her arms around her knees. With her hands tied to the ring, she needed to protect her stomach and face, which she tried to do in futile desperation.

"I don't think she knows anything." Quinn cut in.

"I agree," replied Butch. "I think it's the dealers who gave up the location. They got theirs already. We need to go after the High Rollers. I want my money and product back!"

Quinn went over to untie Noelle.

"What the fuck are you doing?" Butch asked.

"We know it wasn't her, so I was going to drop her at a hospital."

"She knows too much." Butch replied, then turned to Randal, "Finish her."

Quinn knew there was nothing he could do, so he turned to leave as Randal brought his boot down on Noelle's neck. He flinched when he heard the snap as Butch joined him. "We are at war, Quinn. We can't let this slide. If we let her go, we both know she'd go to the cops."

"I get it," Quinn said, turning back to look at the body on the floor.

"Randal, dump her body somewhere. We can't leave her here to be found. Go through her bag, burn her ID and toss the rest somewhere far away from the body." Butch ordered.

"On it Butch."

Quinn paused as Randal wrapped Noelle's body in a blue plastic tarp. He felt bad for her; she knew nothing, but died anyway. Killing innocent women wasn't a typical move of the club, but Butch was under a lot of pressure because of the turf war with the High Rollers. He'd have to monitor Maggie. He didn't want her to get caught up in Butch's cross hairs.

41

Maggie paced the apartment, cursing under her breath. She twisted a lock of her hair around her finger until it cut into her flesh and she felt the pain. It was Sunday, and Noelle still hadn't returned. Noelle didn't know anyone else in the area other than members of the club, so she wasn't hanging out at a friend's house. The last time Maggie saw Noelle was Thursday afternoon when she was heading back to her house and Noelle was getting ready to go to the clubhouse. That day, she didn't give Noelle another thought as she walked out the door to head back to her house and bake cookies for Evelyn, that is until she got home and found Noelle gone.

Maggie tried calling Noelle, but her calls went straight to voicemail.

She had a bad feeling when she left the clubhouse on Friday afternoon. Quinn seemed eager for her to leave. She'd felt so dirty after being with him she didn't give his behaviour another thought. She'd gone right home and showered. Maggie had showered three times since, but still didn't feel clean. When she closed her eyes, she could still feel his hands all over her body. When she started this, she thought she could control the outcome, like she had when she hunted Frank Carter. But this time, things were different. She had to get close to someone from the club in order to gain the information she needed, and she chose Quinn. It was his position within the club that made him her obvious choice, and his looks too, if she was being honest with herself. She knew sleeping with Quinn was inevitable, or he'd have banned her from the clubhouse. One thing was certain, she wasn't getting banned before she made Butch pay, even if it meant sleeping with Quinn again.

She couldn't believe how dirty she felt when she got home. It felt like she'd cheated on Liam. Maggie's focus was on getting the feel of his hands off her body, and she didn't even think about Noelle. The guilt she felt wasn't just because she'd slept with him, it was because her body betrayed her. She'd enjoyed it! The worst thing was, she liked Quinn. He was tough, but he was also kind and he didn't seek trouble, but faced it when he had to. She knew she was more of a threat to him than he was to her. Although he could out-power her, she didn't think he'd sneak up on her and catch her unprepared if she angered him.

She plopped down on the sofa, fresh from another shower, and considered her next steps. She'd have to be on guard. After Tiny's death, she knew the club would seek revenge, and that would mean going after the High Rollers. The same turf war that cost her Liam.

All she'd done so far was to stir up more trouble. She cursed to herself. When Tiny hit Noelle, it angered her, or she wouldn't have gone after him. Her temper was a problem she'd have to learn to control. Noelle told her to leave it alone, but she didn't. Noelle got hurt by helping her, which was something she couldn't stand for. She got up and went to Noelle's room. It was time to go through her belongings and see what she could find. There was no way she'd just take off without letting her know. Something was wrong.

42

Detective Tate squatted down beside the naked body of a Jane Doe and lifted the tarp back to get a better look. Based on the amount of bruises, someone had beaten her before leaving her body behind the dumpster. From the lack of blood at the scene, he knew someone killed her elsewhere and dumped her there. He looked around at the gathering crowd at the entrance to the alley and sent an officer to move them back. Whoever did this wrapped her in a blue plastic tarp and left her leaning up against the wall; then pushed the dumpster back to hide her. From the condition of the body, he suspected she'd been dead for at least three days. The coroner would tell him more.

He scanned the area until he found the poor homeless man who'd discovered her. He saw the man rinsed out his mouth with a bottle of water and spit it to the ground. Even from here, Colby could see the man wasn't doing so well. Colby noticed the pile of vomit near the body. When asked, a nearby officer told him the homeless man threw up when he made the discovery. Colby stepped away and let forensics get back to work. He pulled out his notebook and approached the man to ask him some questions.

"Hi, I'm Detective Tate. I understand you found the body. I have a few questions, if that's ok?" Colby noticed the bottle in the man's hand was empty. "Here, you look like you could use some more water." He said, handing the man a fresh bottle.

"Thanks," the man muttered before downing half of it.

Colby watched him, noting the man's chapped lips and filthy appearance. The stench that emanated from him spoke of days without washing. Even his clothing appeared stiff with dirt. Maybe he should recommend a shelter so that the man could clean himself up, but he didn't want to offend him, so he held his tongue. There was a reason some people preferred the streets to shelters.

"Are you ok?" He asked as he watched the man nod before continuing. "Ok, can you walk me through what happened? How you found the body? If you touched it? Everything."

"Um, ah, well, I saw the blue tarp sticking out from behind the dumpster and I thought I could use it for shelter when it rained. I tried pulling it out, but it was stuck, so I pushed the dumpster back to get at it and when I tried to move it out, I realized there was some-thing inside it. I didn't think it was a body or I would have left it alone." He took another swig from the water bottle. "I pulled back the tarp and saw her." He stated, motioning with his hand to where the body lay.

Colby watched the man's reaction when he looked towards the body and took a step back, thinking he was going to be sick again. He didn't want to spend the day smelling like vomit. The man wasn't sick, and Colby considered maybe he had nothing left inside of him after being sick twice already. Colby watched the man spit on the ground before he continued telling him what happened.

Colby asked him some more questions and made some notes. He explained to Colby that this wasn't the usual area he hung out in. He'd spent the night walking around checking dumpsters behind restaurants because they sometimes left containers of leftovers outside for the homeless, but they also might throw a loaf of stale bread away, still in the packaging that he could salvage. Colby nodded as he listened. He did this willingly even though it wouldn't help with the investigation, but the man seemed comforted by talking.

Colby looked up at the surrounding buildings to see if there were surveillance cameras in the area, but didn't see any. Whoever dumped her body was careful not to be caught and chose this location because there wasn't surveillance nearby. He'd still talk to the staff at the restaurant and find out who worked over the weekend to see if anyone saw anything. Today was Tuesday, and he guessed whoever killed her dropped the body off Friday night or Saturday morning, if they disposed of her right away. Of course, the restaurant was closed on Mondays, so they could have dumped her body then. He'd come back and interview the staff at 4 pm when they opened.

He was busy making notes when he heard a motorcycle idling at the entrance to the alleyway. Colby turned and saw the rider of a motorcycle staring down the alley towards him, concentrating on the body bag behind him. He couldn't make out the face of the rider behind the tinted face shield, but the figure was slight and could have been a female or a young male. It was too hard to tell from this distance. The rider wasn't wearing any identifying markers, so he knew it wasn't a gang member. Gangs didn't go anywhere without wearing their 'cut'. He dismissed the rider as not important, chalking it up as a casual onlooker, well aware that a police presence caused gawkers, which was clear by the enormous crowd of pedestrians behind the barricade, and continued making notes.

43

Maggie paced around the apartment. The uncertainty was gnawing at her, and her guts rolled every time she thought about Noelle. It had been five days and there was still no word from her. She could have decided that the violence in this lifestyle wasn't worth the risk and made her way back to Enfield to find a ride home, but she doubted it. There was no way Noelle would leave without saying goodbye or taking her belongings. They'd become close since Noelle had moved in and Maggie knew Noelle considered her a friend. Friends didn't just leave without a word. Plus, it wasn't just her new clothes that remained, even the original bag she arrived with was still in the apartment.

Maggie donned her riding gear and headed out to ride the streets of the downtown core to find Noelle. She was a journalist with lots of resources available. It was time to put her skills to work. She'd ride the streets and see what she could learn. Maybe Noelle turned a few tricks to earn some extra money. Maggie made sure Noelle wanted for nothing, but understood it bothered Noelle to rely on her so much. She also knew if Noelle was turning tricks, her disappearance wasn't because she got arrested or she would have her from her to be bailed out. If she came up empty in her search, she'd head to the club-house. To hell with Quinn telling her to stay away for a few days. She needed to find Noelle.

She rode up and down the streets in the downtown area, even some of the smaller streets, pausing at alleyways, looking for something out of the ordinary. While stopped at a stoplight, she noticed a crowd had formed on the road ahead, and she slowed down to look, then stopped her bike when she noticed the police presence and the body bag on the stretcher. Something didn't feel right. She noticed Colby was one of the investigating officers when he turned towards her. Maggie couldn't tell if the body was male or female, so she turned away, put the bike back in gear, and returned to the condo. She didn't have a good feeling about this.

Maggie parked her bike in the underground and remained in her seat, unable to move. Her heart raced, not because Colby might have recognized her, but because deep inside she felt that the body was Noelle's. for the first time since Noelle went missing, Maggie consid-ered she might be dead. She had to find out, and that meant getting in touch with the police.

Maggie went upstairs and changed out of her riding gear and into her street clothes, then pulled her hair back into a low ponytail. She needed to see if there was any news about the body on social media. Nothing showed up after she scanned every site she could find. She wanted to head to the police station and ask questions, but until news of the body aired, there wasn't much she could do.

Then an idea struck her, her editor! She could call him and let him know what she saw. He might tell her to investigate and then it wouldn't matter that she saw the crime scene or if it came from an anonymous tip. Maggie crossed her fingers as she dialled his number.

"Ripley here."

"Ripley, it's Maggie."

"Hmm, Maggie, where have you been? You've been AWOL for a while. I was wondering what happened. Is everything ok?"

"Ya, it's just, well, everything with Liam and the shooting has been hard." She knew Ripley was tired of her excuses, but it was hard for him to fault her for it. She heard him sigh.

"What's on your mind, Maggie?"

"Well, I was out riding to clear my head and I saw the police loading a body from an alleyway into the back of a bus. I wondered if you heard anything."

"A body, eh? When was this?" Ripley replied. Maggie could hear his fingers on the keyboard doing the same search she had just done.

"About an hour ago."

"Nothing has come across the wire yet. What's your interest in this?"

"I thought I could investigate it. It's been a while and I need to get back to work."

"It's not your usual kind of story."

Maggie could hear the hesitation in his words. She needed to persuade him to let her investigate, so if the police checked, her story would be true.

"Ripley, I need something different. This will be a small piece. Who knows if they even have an ID yet? Since my follow-up piece on my gun story, I've been thinking about investigating crime. I thought this would help me see if I'm interested or if it's just morbid curiosity after what happened."

She knew she twisted the knife, but she wasn't backing down. He hadn't dismissed her yet, which meant he was going to relent and let her do it. She breathed an inward sigh of relief when she heard his response.

"Ok. Look into it. After you speak with the police, if you think there's a story there, send me what you have and we'll find a spot for it."

Maggie thanked him. With a heavy heart, she hung up the phone. Now she had a legitimate reason to show up at the police station.

She slipped her notepad and pen into her bag and headed to the station. Halifax wasn't a stranger to bodies, but it wasn't as common an occurrence as in some of the bigger cities across Canada. She'd slip into the station and try to get some answers. She hoped she'd run into Colby there. Maybe he wouldn't talk to her on the record, but she could use their friendship and get some information off the record. If the victim was a woman, she knew Noelle well enough that she could identify her. If it was Noelle, the problem was she wouldn't be able to tell the police. She couldn't let anyone know she and Noelle were friends. It could cast suspicion on herself. She'd have to be careful, but she'd get the answers she needed. The basic description of the body would tell her if it even could be Noelle, but the tattoo of the hummingbird on her right shoulder would confirm it. When this was all over, she vowed that if the body in the morgue belonged to Noelle, she'd do right by her.

She knew Noelle didn't have any family, but there was no way she deserved to go to an unmarked grave. If it was Noelle, once she'd dealt with Butch and whoever killed her, she'd send a tip to the police so they could identify her.

44

Maggie walked up to the front desk of the police detachment and flashed her credentials. The officer behind the desk looked up and frowned.

"I heard they found a body behind a restaurant downtown. I'd like to speak to someone about that."

"Who told you that?" The officer asked.

"We got an anonymous tip. You know I can't reveal my source."

"Just a minute. Have a seat over there." He replied, motioning to the row of chairs. "I'll see if someone's available to talk with you."

Maggie sat down on one of the hard plastic chairs and began flicking through social media while she waited.

Maggie thought the officer had forgotten about her and was about to approach the main desk again to ask him how much longer when she saw Colby enter the building. His attention was on his phone and he didn't see her. She stood up and stepped in front of him before he could pass her by.

His step faltered as he realized someone had blocked his way. He was about to step around the person until he looked up and saw Maggie. A smile crept across his face.

"Maggie!" He leaned forward to hug her. "It's good to see you. What brings you by?"

"Work actually. I'm on assignment."

"Oh? What could be newsworthy enough to bring you here?"

"Well, I'm waiting to speak to someone now." She responded looking down at her phone, "I've been waiting a while though, maybe you can help me."

"Tell me why you're here and I'll see what I can do."

Maggie smirked to herself. Running into Colby was perfect. She knew he could help her and would have the answers she needed. She saw him at the crime scene earlier and knew if anyone could help her, it was him.

"Can we go somewhere more private?" She asked, motioning around the very public waiting area.

"Sure, why don't we go get a coffee? You can hop in with me."

"Will I have to sit in the back in handcuffs?" She teased, putting her wrists together and holding them up in front of her.

"I think I can let you sit in the front if you promise to be good." He replied with a chuckle.

"No promises."

Colby picked a coffee shop close to the station and parked out front. They went in and Colby bought them each a coffee while Maggie picked a table. She picked one at the back, far from the entrance, and slid onto the bench so her back would be against the wall. Unless it got busy, it would give them some privacy and if they kept their voices low, the background chatter would drown out their conversation.

After a few pleasantries, Maggie dove right in.

"We had an anonymous tip that you found a body this morning. What can you tell me about that?"

Colby raised his eyebrows, looked around the room, and he leaned in closer before responding.

"How could you know that already?"

"This is the social media age, Colby. It wouldn't surprise me if there aren't pictures of the location all over Facebook, Instagram, Twitter and YouTube, maybe even videos. If I wait a bit, I can google the information, but I'm writing an article and need facts."

"OK. I'll tell you what I can. This morning at oh five hundred, a call came in that there was a body behind a dumpster. It was the body of a woman. I'd guess late twenties, early thirties."

"Was it foul play? Do you have an ID?"

"Yes, we're sure it was foul play and for now, she's a Jane Doe."

"Are you going to release a description to see if anyone can identify her? Can you tell me how she died and when?"

"Someone beat her, judging from the condition of her body, but I can't confirm if she died from the beating. Until they complete the autopsy, and then we'll know how and when. If I had to guess, I'd say a couple of days. We will release a description after we check missing persons. I don't want her family to find out about this from a news article."

Colby's voice was firm. She knew he wouldn't give her anything if she continued talking to him as a journalist. So, she switched gears and made it personal.

"That's horrible Colby. Do you think it is someone hunting women? Should I be concerned?"

Maggie watched the look in his eyes soften as he reached out and took her hand.

"I don't have an answer to that, Maggie. I think it's always important for you to be aware of your environment. When I know more, I'll let you know."

"Colby, can I ask something off-the-record?"

"Shoot."

"Did she have any identifying marks on her?"

Colby paused. "Off-the-record?"

Maggie nodded.

"She had a tattoo of a hummingbird on her right shoulder."

Maggie slumped back, and her jaw slackened. A ball formed in the pit of her stomach as she fought back the urge to cry. She suspected the body was Noelle, and now she knew. The Jane Doe was Noelle. Maggie struggled to regain her composure. She couldn't let Colby see how much the news affected her. She had to get through the coffee and get back to her car without showing emotion.

"That should help in identifying her." Maggie said, before taking a sip of her coffee. She couldn't talk about this anymore without crying, so she changed the subject.

"So, how is little miss graduate doing? Is she in daycare for the summer while you're at work?"

"She loves school, so she's missing seeing all of her friends already. She's never been in daycare. My hours are crazy, so either my mom or Stephanie's mom comes over to be with her. They are both retired and love spending time with her, and Evelyn loves her grandmas."

"You're lucky they live nearby. All of my family is in Ontario, what there is of it. I moved here to go to school, then I met Liam and stayed."

"Do you think you'll move back to Ontario to be with your family?"

"No, I like Nova Scotia. My home and work are here now. I haven't been back for a few years. Maybe it's time I went back and visited with my aunt and uncle. It's been too long. They're all I have. My parents are both dead."

Colby nodded at her, then paused before mumbling he was sorry. Maggie saw the look in his eyes when she revealed her parents were dead. That's when she knew he'd checked into her background. Not that she blamed him. If she was a cop, she'd check the background of anyone who came in contact with her child as well.

45

Maggie returned home before the emotions that bubbled up inside of her released with a flood. She tossed her purse on the table and then kicked the closest chair with such violence it toppled and slid across the floor. She opened her mouth and screamed at the top of her lungs before collapsing onto the sofa.

Tears broke free from her eyes, smearing her mascara, leaving black streaks down her checks. She grabbed one of the throw pillows and pressed it to her face, screaming into it to muffle the anguished sounds that escaped her lips. When she gained control of herself, she made her way into Noelle's room, sat on the edge of the bed, and looked around for a clue she may have missed.

'How could I have been so stupid?' She thought as she looked at Noelle's meagre belongings. 'I thought I could handle this situation and that everything would be all right. My cockiness got Noelle killed. She didn't deserve to die. She was a kind, good person.' Maggie punched her fist into the quilt and wondered who would miss her? She didn't have any family. The whole time they'd been together, the only call she'd made was to the person who'd sublet her apartment while she was away. Maggie would miss Noelle and she would mourn her.

Maggie opened the bedside table and dug through it until she found Noelle's personal phone. The one she carried was a burner like the one Maggie had. She turned it on, but it was password protected so she couldn't access it. She sat looking at the blank screen. Maggie didn't think anyone would look for Noelle or notice her gone. It had been 5 days since she last saw Noelle and there wasn't one message on the phone. This tore at Maggie's heart. She vowed to do right by her. Once they identified her and this was over, she'd send an anonymous donation to cover her cremation and then she'd scatter her ashes to the sea. Noelle loved looking out at the ocean. She'd even told Maggie that the reason she came to Nova Scotia instead of stopping in a busier location was to see the Atlantic Ocean.

Maggie went to the closet and pulled out Noelle's clothing. Most of it was new. She only carried a small bag when Maggie met up with her. She found it therapeutic to fold the clothing and place them in neat piles on the bed. Once she emptied the cupboard and drawers, she went into the washroom and tossed all of Noelle's toiletries in the trashcan. She wouldn't be needing them anymore and Maggie couldn't donate them in the condition they were in. She placed all the clothing into an empty cardboard box and put it on the floor of the closet in the back. When this was over, she'd take it and donate it to a shelter. Noelle would've liked that.

Packing up Noelle's belongings had calmed the rage, even if it was only temporary. The deep sorrow that tore at her heart left her feeling raw and exposed. There was only one person she could call about this, and she needed to talk to someone.

Maggie stepped out of the bedroom and closed the door. She'd strip the bed and change the sheets, but not now. Now she had a phone call to make. She picked up a package of Noelle's cigarettes and her father's zippo lighter, poured herself a double shot of whiskey and stepped out onto the balcony. After lighting a cigarette, she took out her phone and selected the number from favourites. She sipped on the whiskey while she listened to the ringing and waited for the call to be answered.

"Hello?"

"Hi Audrey, it's Maggie."

"Maggie? Is everything ok?"

"No." Maggie couldn't prevent the tears that followed as she took another sip of her whiskey.

"Maggie, I'm sure it will be all right."

"You don't understand Audrey. It's my fault she's dead."

"Who's dead? Maggie, start from the beginning."

Maggie plopped down on the balcony chair and told Audrey about her plan to avenge Liam's murder and Noelle's part in it. She also told Audrey she was sure the gang killed Noelle and that her death was all her fault.

Audrey listened to Maggie, allowing her to vent her anger, frustration, and sorrow. If she allowed Maggie to talk long enough, Audrey knew Maggie would calm herself down and find peace. Maggie may have asked Noelle to help her and not explained everything to her, but Noelle made the choice to help. From what Maggie said, Noelle went back even after Maggie asked her not to. After Tiny gave her the black eye, she knew the risk.

Maggie may have gotten her involved, but it was Noelle's choices that got her killed. When Maggie finished with her rant, Audrey would reassure her it wasn't her fault. Guilt was a horrible thing to carry around, and Maggie already had her fair share.

Right now, Audrey's primary concern was Maggie's safety. The Dark Enders sounded scary, and Maggie had wormed her way inside and was in danger. She knew Maggie could take care of herself under normal circumstances, but not against an angry gang with a grudge. Maggie had to be careful, which she would reiterate when Maggie finished talking and calmed down.

When Maggie stopped talking and all Audrey could hear were the soft sobs from her crying, Audrey responded.

"Maggie, from what you just told me, Noelle knew full well what she was up against and didn't care. You told her to stay away, and she went back anyway. Did you ever hide how dangerous they were from her?"

Maggie hesitated before responding. "No, I told her. I wanted her help, but I wanted her to know what she was getting into."

"Then you did what you could. What you have to consider now is, did she tell them anything about you?"

"She wouldn't."

"Maggie, they beat her. How long do you think she held out until she gave you up? I think you're in danger and should leave their capture to the police."

Maggie laughed a dry, harsh laugh. "You and I know firsthand how inept the police can be at catching killers. They have too many restrictions. They know who's responsible for Liam's death, but because they don't have the physical proof, they can't help. No, this is my fight. I have to see it through."

"Be careful Maggie, this Quinn sounds like a tough character."

Maggie laughed bitterly. "He bragged about killing two people. For a tough gang member, that's almost sad. We both know my numbers are higher than that."

"Yes, Maggie, but so far, you've only killed deserving people. You can't save the world and if you're not careful, you'll cross a line from where there's no coming back."

"I'll be careful Audrey. Thank you for listening. It's helped a lot. I'll call you again soon."

Maggie hung up the call and stared at the cigarette that had burned to ash in the ashtray. She didn't bother to light another. She finished the whiskey and went back inside. It was time to push her plan forward and finish this, so Noelle's death meant something.

46

Maggie stepped back inside the apartment and placed her glass in the dishwasher. She picked up her burner phone and saw that she'd missed texts from Quinn. He was the last person she wanted to talk to right now.

<blockquote>Maggie, I need to c u.

Where r u?

Message me back.</blockquote>

Maggie rolled her eyes. He'd barely sent one message before he sent another. She debated letting him wait a little longer when he texted again.

<blockquote>Where the hell r u?

Cool ur jets. I was outside having a smoke.

Come to the clubhouse.

When?</blockquote>

Now.

Maggie paused. She needed some time to figure out her next move. She'd need to stall.

I'm working.

When can u get here?

I'm off at 5.

Come straight here.

K

Maggie tossed the phone on her bed and hopped into the shower to clean the smeared makeup off her face and refresh herself. She thought about her next move as the water rinsed away the tear stains and her sorrow of losing someone she considered a friend. By the time she was done, she'd gathered a newfound resolve. She'd survived so much tragedy in her brief life, and she wasn't sure how much more she could take before the darkness took over for good.

By the time she'd dressed, she had decided she needed to spend more time at the clubhouse. It was the only way she'd have to gain access to Butch. It meant she'd have to be Quinn's girl until this was over. A small shudder rang through her at the thought of having to be intimate with him regularly. Not that he was unappealing, it was just that it felt like a betrayal to Liam. But she'd vowed to do whatever it took to see this through. She now had two deaths to avenge.

Later that day, when she pulled into the clubhouse parking lot, she found it full of bikes. She had a bad feeling; it was too early in the day for a regular gathering. *'Was there an official club meeting going on? Why would Quinn want her here for a meeting?'*

She swung off the bike, and her hand slid inside her jacket to touch the knife. Maggie left her gun at home, knowing it would be difficult to explain if Quinn found it, but the knife would pass without question. She unhooked the clasp that held it in place in case she needed to withdraw it in a hurry. She pasted a smile on her face and headed towards the building.

There were two prospects positioned to guard the main doors. Maggie stepped up, expecting a confrontation, but they stepped aside and held the door for her. She realized they expected her. She braced herself for what lay in store and went inside.

Maggie's step faltered when she entered the main room and found it was full of women, many Maggie had seen before, but others she figured were the 'old ladies' of members she hadn't met. A silence crept across the room as all heads turned her way. She saw the woman she had the initial confrontation with at the Capital whisper in someone's ear and point her way. The woman nodded before getting up and approaching Maggie.

Maggie braced herself and held her ground as she watched the tiny woman approach. Maggie estimated they were about the same height, but the woman wore high-heeled boots that gave her the advantage. She wore skin-tight black denims and a black t-shirt with the club insignia on the right side. She had a slight hook to her nose and her hair was a mass of burnished yellow from over bleaching. Maggie knew this must be Butch's old lady. Maggie struggled to recall her name, but before she could, the woman closed the distance with her hand outstretched.

"Name's Sadie. I understand you're Quinn's girl."

Maggie took her hand and replied, "I guess I am."

"Here, come sit with me. I'm Butch's old lady. They're having a big club meeting and all the old ladies have been told to be here."

Maggie followed Sadie to her table and sat in the only seat remaining. After a quick round of introductions, the women began chatting amongst themselves. Maggie remained quiet while she listened to them talk about their men. When the conversation turned raunchy, Sadie leaned over to whisper to Maggie.

"This lifestyle takes some getting use to. Quinn has taken a liking to you, so if you're not in it for the long haul, get out now. You don't want to get on the club's bad side."

Maggie allowed herself to look shocked. *'Had she raised suspicion?'* she thought, before she spoke her next words. She was tough, and they needed to know it.

"I don't play games. Quinn knows what I'm all about."

Sadie's eyes narrowed, but then she smiled. "You're different from what I expected. The girls have been talking about the first time Quinn met you. You're a tough cookie and that's a good thing. You'll need it."

Maggie nodded, then said, "Are we supposed to stay dry until they're done or can we drink?"

Sadie chuckled. "We drink! Girls, line them up and bring them out." She called out to the usual serving girls, twirling her finger in the air.

It wasn't long before the drinks were flowing and the mood changed to a more social atmosphere. Maggie forced herself to relax, knowing she'd passed the old lady test. Now she would drink, socialize and wait for Quinn and gather some much-needed information while she did.

<h1 style="text-align:center">47</h1>

The women were several drinks in by the time the club members exited the meeting room and joined them. The men came out joking with each other and were ready to party. But first they had a little business to take care of and called a prospect over. He looked around, worried, not sure what they wanted, as he approached Butch and Quinn. They knew he worked hard at becoming a full patched member and thought they were going to kick him out.

Butch stood at the back of the room, with Quinn by his side. Maggie craned her neck to get a better look at the man who'd ordered the hit that took her husband from her. She felt her fist curl and had to force it back open before anyone noticed, so she grabbed her knee and squeezed.

Butch droned on with a long, convoluted speech that left the prospect looking even more confused. Soon Quinn cut in.

"Get to the point, Butch."

Which was followed by a bunch of whooping and hollering.

"Ok, ok. Give it to me, Quinn."

Quinn handed Butch some patches. Who then handed them over to the prospect.

"Congratulations, you've earned full patch status."

The prospect looked as though he was going to fall over. Then he grabbed the patches and held them up over his head as he turned towards a room full of cheers.

Quinn stepped forward and grabbed the prospect's vest. He slipped a large knife under the stitching of his 'prospect' patch and removed it. He tossed the patch onto the table and turned back to the man.

"You're on your own for sewing those patches on. Maybe you can convince one of the girls to help you." He teased.

Another round of laughter erupted as the new member looked around at the girls, hoping for an offer. One girl took pity on him and took his vest and patches to a corner to sew them in place.

Now that they concluded their business, Butch and Quinn approached Sadie and Maggie. Butch grabbed Sadie and gave her a deep kiss before eyeing Maggie up and down.

"Where have you been hiding this one, Quinn?"

"I haven't been hiding her. You've just been elsewhere when she's been at the clubhouse." He replied before he turned to Sadie, "Thanks for taking care of her while we finished up."

Sadie beamed at the praise before she responded, "She fits right in."

The others at the table moved to let Butch and Quinn sit down. Soon, Randal joined them. He winked at Maggie as he took his seat.

"I guess I didn't stand a chance with ole Quinn here knocking about." He teased, "All I was doing was stopping some trouble, but girl, you can handle your own."

They continued drinking and socializing, and before the night was over, Quinn took Maggie by the hand and led her to his room in the back. She felt apprehensive, not sure if his good mood was an act or not. His texts had sounded angry. But he put her mind to rest as soon as the door closed. He wrapped his arms around her and pulled her close and kissed her.

"I've been waiting for days to do that."

"I'm always a phone call away." She replied, smiling up at him.

He pushed her back to look at her. She sensed the mood change and regretted mentioning the phone.

"A phone call? So maybe I need to call instead of text. You take a while to respond to those."

"Quinn, baby. I need to work. How about I let you know in advance when I'm working? That way, you won't be concerned." She replied, stroking his cheek.

He pulled her to him, and she expected him to push her back towards the bed, but he didn't. Instead, he kissed the top of her head and said, "deal."

When he kissed her again, she willed herself to relax, waiting for him to continue. But he didn't pursue it, instead he took her hand and led her back to the main room.

"We're not going to..." Maggie's voice trailed off.

Quinn turned and smiled. "Not yet. We have some partying to do. We gained a new member. I just wanted a minute alone with you before we got going. You're spending the night." He said with an air of finality.

Maggie knew she didn't have a choice. But now she could relax and have a few more drinks. Not too many. She didn't want to loosen her lips, but she'd be an active listener to anyone else who started talking. Maggie touched the hilt of her knife. She'd love to bury it in Butch's chest, but now wasn't the time. If she did, she'd never make it out alive.

Maggie spent the rest of the evening making the rounds, chatting with different people, letting them feel her presence. They accepted her as Quinn's 'old lady' and spoke freely in front of her. She continued to nurse her drinks, watching the crowd fall into drunkenness. When it was time to retire, Quinn stumbled and fell into bed. Maggie thought about leaving him dressed but undressed him and then herself and crawled in beside him. If she was lucky, he wouldn't remember they didn't have sex and she could get away with the excuse of work in the morning.

48

The next morning, when Maggie found herself alone in Quinn's room, she gathered her things and made her way home. Maggie had only feigned being asleep as she watched Quinn get up to leave. She knew he had club business to take care of and hoped he wouldn't notice that she was awake. She wanted him to get moving so she could leave without having to be intimate with him. Today Maggie had some finishing touches to do on an article she was writing, and she wanted to call Colby to see if they had a cause of death on the 'Jane Doe'.

As she rode the streets home, she kept a watchful eye out for a tail. She expected Quinn to have someone follow her. So far, he hadn't asked where she lived, but he would soon. Last night, he officially marked her as his. The advantage of this was they'd expect her to spend more time at the clubhouse, and with her journalistic skills, she could listen to one conversation while participating in another. Soon, she'd know how to find Butch and when he'd be alone. When she did, she'd kill him. She hoped by then she'd find out who Liam's actual shooter was and take care of him, too.

Maggie travelled a few back roads, when she was sure she wasn't being followed; she pulled into the underground and parked her bike in the space beside her car. She might be paranoid, but in case someone was inside the lobby watching the elevator to see what floor she got out on, she took the stairs. Her adrenaline was high as she jogged up the flights until she reached her floor. She opened the door and peered out to see if anyone was in the hall before she left the stairwell, entered her apartment, and locked the door behind her.

This was the first time she felt she was being followed, and she wondered if she was being foolish. She didn't know if Noelle said anything and it worried her. Audrey was right. She knew Noelle would talk if the club asked the right questions when they beat her. She wasn't a trained military person who could hold out under such duress. The one thing that allowed her to relax was that Quinn wasn't acting suspicious, and the club hadn't confronted her, but if they found out where Noelle was staying and had her keys, then Maggie would be in trouble. She slid the chain in place, knowing if someone wanted in, it wouldn't stop them. Tomorrow she would change the locks.

She felt the nervous energy vibrate through her. What she needed was a proper run and a workout. She changed into her workout gear, piled her hair up under a ball cap, and set out for a run. She'd pop into the GoodLife on Barrington and get a full workout in before running back home.

Maggie was dripping with sweat when she returned home. She peeled her sodden clothes off and stepped into the shower, allowing her mind to clear while she rinsed away the sweat and grime. When she was done, she slipped on a sundress and sat in front of her computer. She checked both of her phones and found a message from her aunt Julie checking in on her. She'd call her back later.

Maggie pulled up google to search if there was any mention of the body. The body she knew was Noelle. Other than the short piece she wrote, there was nothing else. She called Colby to see if he could tell her anything more.

"Tate here."

"Hi Colby. It's Maggie."

She could sense him hesitate before he responded. "I can't talk now. Can you meet me at the park in two hours?"

"I'll be there."

Maggie disconnected the line and went to work on the article she was writing. She needed to get it in to her editor by the end of the day, so she planned to finish it and submit it before she left to meet with Colby.

Maggie checked the time as she hit the send button and dashed out of her apartment. As long as the traffic wasn't bad, she'd make it with time to spare. She didn't want to keep him waiting as she hoped his wanting to meet in person meant he had more information on how Noelle died.

When she pulled into the park's parking lot, Colby was already waiting for her. She stepped out of her car and he called for her to hop in with him.

"You wanted to know more about the Jane Doe, right?"

"Yes, anything…"

Colby cut her off. "This has to be off the record, at least for now. I'll let you know what you can and can't print."

Maggie nodded.

"I need a verbal response."

"Yes, for now it's off the record."

Colby handed her a manilla envelope.

"Before you open that, I want to warn you the pictures are gruesome. If you don't have the stomach for it, let me know now."

Maggie assured she'd be okay and pulled the pictures out of the envelope, her guts clenched and a sourness filled her mouth as she stared down at the crime scene photographs. There was no doubt it was Noelle. Someone had beaten her face almost beyond recognition. There were restraint marks on her wrists, and bruises covered her body. The close-up picture of the hummingbird tore at her and her eyes welled with tears. This was all her fault. Noelle suffered and died because of her. She vowed she'd find out who did this and make them pay.

Noting her tears, Colby said, "They're pretty tough to look at. What that poor woman endured. Someone wanted her to suffer and pay for something. We're looking into it being a domestic situation. That much rage is personal."

"Do you have an ID yet?"

"No, but the coroner estimates she died late Friday or early Saturday morning."

"Did she die from the beating?"

"Here's the strange part. She took a bad beating. Which is why my guess is that it was personal. She had internal bleeding, but what killed her was, according to the coroner, was Atlanto-occipital dislocation."

"Atlanto what?"

"It means internal decapitation. Someone used enough force to separate her skull from her spinal column."

Maggie gasped. Her hand flew to her mouth as she swallowed back the bile that rose in her throat. She felt horrified at the violence Noelle underwent in the last hours before she died. Maggie struggled to find the words to continue. Colby's hand slid out and grabbed the one on her lap and held it.

She turned towards him when she gained control of her emotions and said, "that poor woman. Who could do something so horrific?"

"If it wasn't a domestic partner, it might have been someone who hated women. No one has reported her missing. Her prints aren't in the system and we haven't matched her up with any other cases."

That's when Maggie knew she had to leave an anonymous tip so they could identify Noelle. She knew there was a vineyard in the valley that had an old English phone booth where you could make one call to anywhere in North America for free. Using that phone would guarantee they couldn't trace the call back to her and Noelle would no longer be a Jane Doe.

A slight sob escaped her lips, and Colby lifted her hand to his mouth and kissed it. She stared at him and her lips parted to say something, but he cut her off as he leaned in and kissed her. His free hand wound into her hair and pulled her closer, intensifying the moment. Maggie felt the awakening of desire that she wanted to succumb to, but she pulled away.

Colby pulled back and looked at her, before saying, "I've wanted to do that for weeks."

Maggie kept a hold of his hand and replied, "Me too. It's just things are complicated right now."

"Life's complicated and we both know how unpredictable it is."

"Colby, I like you. I'm just not sure I'm ready."

She reached out and held onto the door handle as she felt the world around her spin. She couldn't deal with this right now, not with everything going on with Quinn and the club. Maggie didn't want to hurt Colby like that. It suddenly dawned on her how much she liked him. Before he could respond, she added.

"Let's start by being friends, get to know each other and see where things go from there."

He lifted her hand up to his lips again and replied, "I'm good with that. I just can't promise not to kiss you again." A hint of mischievousness flashed in his eyes.

Maggie smiled at him. Getting involved with a detective would complicate things, but she couldn't help being drawn to him. First, she had to finish her business with the club before she saw where things went with Colby.

"We have to go slow, for Evelyn's sake." Maggie insisted.

"But Evelyn already loves you. She's always asking when we can see you again."

Maggie's heart warmed at the thought. Evelyn was adorable, and she couldn't explain it, but she felt drawn to her. But if she wasn't careful, she would mess up their lives. Until her vendetta was done, she'd have to create some distance between herself and Colby. If someone from the club saw her talking to another man, let alone a cop, there would be trouble.

"Then it's even more important to take things slow. We don't want to hurt her if she gets more attached and things don't work out."

Colby sighed, "You're right. We'll take things slow. Now back to our Jane Doe."

"Yes?"

"My captain has agreed to release Jane Doe's description and see if it helps prompt someone to come forward."

"Perfect! If I get moving on it, my editor might squeeze it in the next edition. It will be nice to give her a name."

"Ok, only a description. Don't mention the tattoo. That piece of information will help confirm if the tips are accurate. Only someone who knows her would know about the tattoo."

Maggie slipped the pictures back into the envelope and handed it to Colby. She touched his cheek and said, "You're a good man."

"Oh, oh, that sounds like the kiss of death!"

Maggie chuckled. "Liam was a good man too, so you're ok. I have to write this piece and get it to my editor. I will reach out to you later."

Maggie got back into her own car and watched him drive away. She made some notes for the article and fired off an email that described 'Jane Doe'. Then she took a drive down to the valley.

49

Colby left Maggie and headed back to headquarters. He wanted to spread the crime scene photos out on his desk and take a better look. There was something bothering him. He knew he'd gone against protocol by showing the pictures to Maggie, but he hoped to get some of the information out so they could identify her, but not too much. But what bothered him was how Maggie reacted to the pictures.

He knew the pictures disturbed her, which he'd expect, but there was something more. The way she reacted to them; it was as if she knew the victim. But if she did, why wouldn't she identify her? In the end, he brushed off his suspicions about her and wrote it up to her compassion for Jane Doe.

Next, he pulled out the coroner's report and reviewed it. He thought about the injuries, especially her internal dislocation. How much force and pressure did someone need to inflict to create such an injury? What could she have done to create such rage in her killer? Colby made a list of questions he needed to ask the coroner when he spoke to him next.

Just then, his captain stepped out of his office and approached.

"Tate, any news on the Jane Doe?"

"I was just going over the photos and coroner's report."

"Ok, put that aside for now. There's been another gang related shooting down by the docks. This time it was a High Roller. I want you to look into this. Take Chisholm with you. We need to find out what's going on before we end up in an all-out war between the two gangs. It was only last week we found Tiny Britts' body with those two drug dealers. My guess is it's a retaliation."

"Right captain." Colby replied, as Chisholm joined them. Colby gathered up the information on the Jane Doe and put it back in the file.

"What are your thoughts Tate?" Chisholm asked, "Do you think the captain is right and they're heading into a gang war?"

"Ya, I think he's right. There was that mistaken identity shooting last year. Then we discovered the body of 'Patch' Cummings, who we think was the original target, floating in the harbour. Last week, we had Tiny Britts and now this new victim from the High Rollers. I wish we had some evidence that would stick and we could lock them all up."

"If we're lucky, they'll start killing themselves off, and then our lack of evidence won't be a problem."

Colby laughed, "That would work, but the unfortunate thing is they'll take out too many innocent people, like Liam Murphy."

"Ya, that was unfortunate. I saw a picture of his widow. She's a hot little number. I heard you did a follow-up interview with her. Is she as hot in person?"

"Hotter." Colby replied with a smile.

Chisholm let out a low whistle. "We'd better get moving. Hopefully, the witnesses are more reliable than they've been in the past. Whenever there's an incident involving either of these two gangs, the witness testimony is questionable."

Together, Colby and Chisholm left the building and got into Colby's car on their way to the docks to investigate this latest victim.

50

Maggie pulled into Luckett's Vineyard and parked in the gravel lot. She looked around at the beautiful vista before stepping out of her car and going inside to wander the store and allow the staff to escort her to a table. She couldn't just walk up to the phone booth in the field without having something to eat after coming all this way. At least the food was tasty, and the wine was interesting.

The hostess sat her at a table with a view of the vineyard and the phone booth. She watched various people as they made their way over to it and take photos. She'd wait until after she finished eating, and the crowds to lessen, before using the phone booth. Maggie scanned the menu and then ordered herself the charcuterie board and a glass of The Old Bill.

She took her time, enjoying the change of pace, while she ate her charcuterie, and even ordered a second glass of wine. Maggie enjoyed the wine so much she figured she'd purchase a bottle in the store on her way out to bring home.

While she ate, she took some pictures with her phone and made some more notes for her article. When she had finished, she paid her bill and made her way to the now deserted phone booth. She dialled the tip line and did her best to disguise her voice as she called and gave them Noelle's name, and told them Noelle was visiting from BC. Now the cops could put everything together. She only hoped they wouldn't assume because of Noelle's background a John had killed her. The other thing that concerned her was that they ran into Colby on the boardwalk. If he remembered and put two and two together, he'd realize she knew who the Jane Doe was and said nothing. It would make her look guilty.

Maggie felt confident that although the police wouldn't know Noelle was working with Maggie or her involvement with the Dark Enders, she'd no longer be a Jane Doe. It was the least Maggie could do for Noelle for the time being. Later, when she could, she'd do more.

After hanging up the phone, she went back to the store, picked up the bottle of wine and some interesting cheeses to bring home, and headed back to her house. She needed a break from the apartment and all the drama and to give herself time to rethink her strategy. The home she shared with Liam would give her the strength she needed to continue.

She entered her house through the garage, walked past Liam's bike and SUV, and paused. It was time to think about selling them. It had been over a year since he died, and keeping his belongings wasn't helping her heal and move on. What frustrated her the most was that she was still no closer to killing the man responsible for his death than she was when she first woke up in the Hospital. So much had changed over the last year. She needed time to think.

She opened the bottle of wine she'd brought home and poured herself a glass. It didn't matter how much she drank because she wasn't going back to the apartment tonight. She picked up the wedding picture of her and Liam from the mantel and sat on the couch. Looking at the picture, she began telling Liam everything that had happened over the last year. From her infiltrating the club, sleeping with Quinn, getting Noelle killed, and her growing attraction to Colby. By the time she finished talking to the photograph, she was sobbing. Now that she'd let everything out, she felt raw and exposed. She wondered what Liam would think if he'd known her true nature. She'd tried so hard to put her demons at bay only to have this happen. If he'd lived, they'd have their baby by now. The guest bedroom would be a nursery and their lives would be full of love. But in the blink of an eye, everything changed.

Maggie wondered if she was just a killer by nature and didn't deserve happiness. Then she thought about Colby and Evelyn. How could she be a part of their world with her true nature so dark and twisted? She didn't hesitate when she killed. She enjoyed it, felt an innate satisfaction when someone who she felt deserved to die, perished by her hand. There was no place in her life for a child, especially the daughter of an RCMP detective.

Maybe she should sell everything and start over. Put some distance between herself and the memories that shadowed her. Maybe even go back into trucking. Then she wouldn't have to stay in one place again. But first, she needed to take care of business. When this was over, she could reevaluate her life and figure out her next move.

Feeling raw and emotional, she finished the last of the bottle and stumbled off to bed. Tomorrow night, she decided she'd head to the clubhouse and make herself a regular until she took Butch out. Someone would get chatty and she'd find out who fired the bullet that killed Liam and who killed Noelle. She knew Quinn could answer those questions, but he wouldn't talk shop around her. No matter what, she vowed she would discover the truth.

51

Maggie entered the compound where the clubhouse was located and parked her bike. She'd taken extra care with her appearance to appease Quinn. He'd text her earlier in the day to let her know there was a celebration happening that night and to dress in something nice. She wouldn't wear a dress, because she'd be riding, so her leather pants and leather halter would have to do. A fancy dress is what she'd wear to an event outside of the club, like she did for Evelyn's graduation, but this was a unique situation. She preferred to wear her blue jeans, but the leathers were safer on the bike.

Maggie noticed Quinn standing outside talking with Butch, and when they saw her, they headed her way as she got off the bike. She removed her helmet and the sheath that protected her hair and brushed it out. She pulled off her jacket, exposing her bare back, and pasted a smile on her face as she turned back towards them.

Quinn let out a low wolf whistle and Butch slapped him on the back.

"That's a fine ride you have there." Butch said with double

meaning while he eyed her Indian Chieftain. "You handle it well. Have you been riding long?"

"I got my license when I started driving. My uncle loves his bike, and I used to ride dirt bikes when I was younger. I have my class 1 as well. You could say I'm a well-rounded driver." Maggie replied with a wink.

"Class 1? Little thing like you?" Butch's tone sounded condescending, which irritated Maggie. She let the annoyance of his words wash over her before she responded.

"I'm full of surprises. I drove a truck for 8 years, even owned my rig. Then I gave it up, moved to Halifax and slowed down my life."

"I think you'd better keep an eye on this one, Quinn. Looks like she'll give you a run for your money."

Quinn draped his arm around Maggie's shoulder and replied, "She's not boring." Then he leaned in and kissed her.

"I guess it's a good thing I'm not wearing lipstick. I don't think a smear of it would go with your bad boy image." Maggie said with a chuckle.

"You need to keep your lips lipstick free so I can kiss them anytime I want." He replied before kissing her again and leading her to the clubhouse. She looked back and saw Butch still staring at her bike. Maggie made a mental note not to go straight home when she left. She'd need to find somewhere to park and do a thorough examination of her motorcycle. She felt he was up to something and her guess was a tracking device. If she found one, it meant Butch didn't trust her or her involvement with Quinn. There was nothing he'd find if he searched for the last name she used on her fake driver's license, so she was certain that bothered him. Butch liked to be in control and Maggie knew for him, not knowing everything about her, made her a wild card.

Throughout the evening, Maggie made the rounds in the club house. She wanted to get to know more of the members and eavesdrop on some conversations. By the end of the evening, Maggie learned Butch was going on a run for the club a few days from now, but he wasn't going alone. Maggie thought if she followed him and learned his habits, where he lived when he was away from the clubhouse, she might get him alone and take care of him.

Her ears perked up when she heard Randal telling Butch the cops had identified the girl's body. She knew they were talking about Noelle, and because it was a quiet conversation, she realized it wasn't general club knowledge that they'd killed her. Maggie also assumed by their conversation that Randal and Butch were the ones who'd killed Noelle. She probably didn't die by Butch's hand, but he ordered it. She looked at Randal's knuckles and saw the dead give-away that he'd been punching something or someone recently. Her guts rolled; she knew he took pleasure in what he did. He didn't care who he killed or why. At least when she killed, she chose people who were deserving. Randal's name was now added to her list.

Maggie felt her fist clench, a subconscious reaction to her anger. She couldn't do anything right now with a room full of club members, but she'd make sure Randal paid for what he did to Noelle. She relaxed her fist and made her way back to where Quinn was. A part of her hoped she could take care of Randal first.

She had to put distance between herself and Randal before she did something foolish. Playing the part of the dutiful 'old lady', she climbed onto Quinn's lap, wrapped her arms around his neck and whispered in his ear, "Take me to bed or lose me forever."

His eyes widened. Then he slid his arms underneath her, scooped her up, stood and called out, "night," as he carried her off to his room in the back.

<h1 style="text-align:center">52</h1>

Quinn rolled over in bed and reached for Maggie. She felt his arms wrap around her and allowed him to pull her close. She wasn't sure how much longer she could keep up the act of being his 'old lady,' but for now, she had to make do.

He kissed her neck and whispered, "Let's go for a ride."

"A ride? Together? Do I get to ride my bike, or are you expecting me to be the bitch on the back?"

Quinn leaned back and laughed. "You can ride your own bike. I figured it would be nice to get out of the clubhouse and go for a ride. Maybe even stop for something to eat. You know, like an actual couple." He teased.

"Don't you have club business to take care of today?"

"Nope, today I'm all yours."

Maggie smiled and pretended the idea pleased her. She needed to check her bike for a tracking device and she couldn't with Quinn around. It would only delay things, but she had to keep this pretence going. She also needed to persuade Quinn to pick somewhere to stop where she'd be unlikely to run into Colby. Running into him would ruin everything.

"Is there somewhere I can shower?" Maggie asked, after donning one of Quinn's t-shirts, which came halfway down her thighs. He smiled at the sight of her in it.

"Sure, down the hall. Wait a sec," Quinn said, throwing back the covers and getting out of bed. "I'll join you."

This time, Maggie had prepared to spend the night and brought a change of clothing. She slipped into her jeans and t-shirt and rolled up her leathers. Maggie had her chaps in her saddlebag, but she couldn't get the leather pants over her jeans and the halter wasn't right for a long ride.

She reached for her jacket, but Quinn beat her to it, trying to be a gentleman. When he grabbed it, he stared at it and shook it in the air, saying, "What the hell's in there?"

Before she could respond, Quinn searched the inside of her coat. When he found what the extra weight was from, he pulled out her hunting knife and turned towards her. "What's this for?" He demanded.

Maggie had prepared herself for this scenario, and replied, "I learned as a trucker, a girl alone can be a target. I've always carried a knife to protect myself. You can never be too careful."

Quinn nodded and put the knife back into the designed holder and fastened it closed. "I guess Butch was right. I'll have to keep an eye on you."

Maggie smiled and took the coat from him. "I think you're safe," and winked, "for now." Then she turned and breathed a sigh of relief that he excepted her answer.

Together they left the building and Maggie found someone had moved her bike from where she'd parked it the night before. She noticed the sun gleaming off the freshly washed paint. She turned to Quinn to ask him about it when a 'prospect' came up and started cleaning another bike near hers.

With her question answered, she put her pants and halter into the saddlebag and pulled out her chaps and put them on over her jeans. Then she pulled back her hair, snapped the long leather sheath around its length, and clipped it in place. She plopped her half helmet on and tightened the chin strap before sliding her sunglasses into place and starting her bike. Maggie turned to look at Quinn and found he was already on his Harley waiting for her.

"You lead baby." Maggie purred.

"Try to keep up." He called out as he left the lot.

Maggie was quick to follow him, expecting that he was going to make her work at keeping up the pace, but it surprised her to discover that he was a good leader. She realized she missed riding with someone else. Maybe when this was behind her, she could find a friendly riding group to join. People without gang affiliations who just liked to ride.

Her heart ached with missing Liam as she followed Quinn. Liam always led when they went on their rides together. A part of her felt like a traitor to his memory first by sleeping with Quinn and now riding. Everything with Quinn was betraying Liam's memory, because of his murder and her need for retribution.

They rode along the South Shore. A road Maggie was well familiar with. It wasn't long ago she'd taken the same route with Noelle. Maggie followed Quinn when he pulled into the Finer Diner just outside of Peggy's Cove and suggested they have lunch. Maggie relaxed, knowing it was unlikely she'd run into Colby here. Quinn picked a table by the window, ordered the Cheese burger while Maggie picked the falafel. Quinn's 'cut,', which he always wore, made him recognizable as a member of the Dark Ender's, and she noticed the way people turned and looked at them. She knew he took the lead when they went inside, choosing to sit by the window so he could monitor anyone approaching the front door. She didn't enjoy having her back to the room, but Quinn wanted his back to the wall so he could face the room, and she relented.

Once people adjusted to their presence, and realized they wouldn't be disruptive, they had a pleasant uninterrupted lunch and were soon back on the road. They continued on until Bridgewater, where Quinn turned to cut through the province and head back into Middleton and then follow Highway 101 towards Halifax.

By the time they returned to the clubhouse, it was after 10 pm. Maggie was hungry for supper and eager to get going. She still had to check her bike over. But Quinn expected her to follow him back inside the clubhouse. She complained she was hungry, but he just replied that they could send the 'prospect' out for something or order a pizza.

Maggie knew he wouldn't take no for an answer, so she resigned herself to another night with him and went inside. This time, there weren't as many people as the previous night, so Quinn led her to the couch and sat down. He leaned back and waited for Maggie to lean into him.

"You handle your bike well." He said after telling a girl to get them something to drink.

"You're not too bad yourself." Maggie replied with a chuckle.

"You're spending the night." Quinn stated, leaving no room for negotiation.

Having already resigned herself to it, she nodded in response. Maggie wanted to go home and not have to sleep with him again so soon, but she didn't have a choice. She had to play the part of his dutiful 'old lady' until this was over, so for the time being, she'd play nice.

The next morning, Quinn told her she needed to go home because he had club business. Maggie was relieved, she hadn't planned to spend two nights. She allowed herself to relax as she prepared to leave. The first thing she'd do was go somewhere to search her bike, then head home and clean herself up. Afterwards, she'd check in with Colby. He'd wonder if she didn't, especially now that they'd identified Noelle from her anonymous tip.

Maggie rode her bike to the park where she'd met Colby before and got on the ground to search for a tracking device. She heard a car pull up beside her, as she was on her back, on the pavement, looking at the underside of her bike. She glanced up, but dismissed the car before focusing back on her task. Then she heard the car door slam and Colby's voice.

"Having bike trouble Maggie?"

Maggie raised her hand to block out the sun and squinted up at him. "No, I just like to check things over from time to time."

Colby walked to the rear door of his car and fumbled in the back seat, while Maggie refocused on the undercarriage of her bike. She only had a minute before she'd have to get up and greet him. Then she spied it. Snuggled up beside the Gremlin Bell, that Liam had fastened to her bike when they were still dating. She plucked it off and shoved it in her pocket just in time for Evelyn to run up to her and squeal, "Maggie, come play!"

Maggie was quick to get up and brush herself off. Evelyn grabbed her hand, and Maggie allowed Evelyn to lead her to the playground. Maggie looked back at Colby, who only shrugged his shoulders as he followed them. It was then she realized she should have found somewhere else to examine her bike. Running into Colby and Evelyn wasn't what she'd had in mind. She felt dirty from her last two nights with Quinn. She needed a shower and a change of clothing.

Resigning herself to the situation, she pushed Evelyn on the swing while Colby watched. Soon Evelyn wanted off to play on the slide, something she could manage on her own, and Maggie walked over to where Colby sat.

"You're good with her." He said as she sat down, "She's taken a real shine to you."

"She's adorable and easy to like," Maggie said, tucking a strand of hair behind her ear.

"I called you yesterday, but you didn't answer." Colby said.

"Oh, sorry, I was out riding all day to clear my head and I didn't check my phone."

Colby frowned at her. "Ok." He thought it was strange a reporter wouldn't check her phone, but he said nothing.

"No really. I don't even have my phone with me today."

"I thought maybe you were avoiding me after I kissed you."

"I just have some things to sort out. A lot has happened over the last year. Riding is a way of clearing my head."

"So, is you head clear now?"

Maggie laughed, "About as clear as it's going to get for today. I was going to call you later, anyway. I heard you identified your Jane Doe."

"Yes, we got a tip and checked it out. Turns out she was a prostitute from BC. What she was doing here, we don't know, but we think it was a John who killed her."

Maggie flinched. That's not what she wanted to hear. She may have to make another call to the tip line, linking Noelle to the Dark Enders.

"So, what's going to happen to her?"

"She'll stay at the morgue while we try to find her family. So far, we haven't come up with anything. But here's something strange, I've seen her before. You have too."

"What? Where?" Maggie felt an uneasiness creep over her. *'Did Colby connect Noelle as the woman that was with me on the boardwalk?'*

"She worked the truck stop in Chilliwack. I interviewed her when I was there to investigate that murder. You must have passed her a bunch of times when you parked there."

Maggie paused before responding, "Oh my god! That was her? I would never have recognized her. Her face was so messed up. She didn't deserve to die like that."

"No, she didn't."

53

Before she left the park, Maggie took the tracking device out of her pocket, ground it under her boot heel and tossed it in the trash. She knew she was lucky that whoever put the device on her bike hadn't followed her to the park. If anyone in the Dark Enders saw her with Colby, it would be over. By the time they figured out the device wasn't working, she'd be home, but she'd have to be careful when she went to the park in the future. Someone might check it out if they saw it was the last place the device was working.

Colby told Maggie he was taking Evelyn home for lunch, but not before asking her to have dinner with him. Maggie knew she was walking a fine line. Quinn couldn't find out about Colby and vice versa. Because she needed a break from Quinn, she'd told him she was working tonight, so Maggie suggested Colby come to her house, and she'd cook for him, even including Evelyn in the invitation. That way, it wouldn't be an actual date and Evelyn could act as a buffer between them.

When Evelyn heard the news, she jumped up and down with excitement. Colby smiled at Maggie. He knew what she was doing, but appreciated the gesture, and mouthed 'thank you' before he left.

Having Evelyn there would make things easier. She couldn't deal with him and Quinn at the same time. She had to keep them separate.

'*Soon.*' She thought, '*soon I'll have this mess with the club behind me and I can see where things with Colby lead. It's not a good idea, but I'll put away my knife and gun and try to live a normal life again. Like the one I'd planned with Liam.*'

Back at the condo, Maggie switched out her bike for her car and headed to her house. She slipped the burner phone she knew Quinn would use to contact her into her bag. She wouldn't answer it while she was with Colby, but she needed it close by. On her way home, she stopped for some groceries so she could make dinner. She only had frozen and dry staples at the house because she'd spent most of her time at the condo since spring. When she was in the parking lot, she fired off a quick text to Quinn, reminding him about her shift that night. Her not being available shouldn't bother him since he was busy with club business. She ended the text with 'I'll C U tomorrow,' followed by a heart emoji. She hoped that would satisfy him.

For dinner Maggie planned to make a lasagna because she knew Evelyn liked pasta. She had some homemade sauce in the freezer she could thaw and she'd pair it with a Caesar salad and fresh bread. She'd also make crème brûlée for dessert. It was super easy and never failed to impress.

She walked into her house with her groceries and noticed the layer of dust on the furniture. She'd have to get moving if she was going to have time to clean, cook supper and get showered too. But first she had to make the crème brûlée, so it would have time to cool.

Twenty minutes before Colby and Evelyn were due to arrive, Maggie finished getting dressed. She walked out and surveyed her work. The house was sparkling; the table set and she could smell the lasagna in the oven. She picked a bottle of red wine from her wine rack, opened it and emptied it into the carafe to breathe. She wasn't sure if Colby drank or not, but she'd have a glass after he left if he didn't.

As she waited for the doorbell to ring, she felt her mouth go dry, and butterflies of possibility fluttered in her stomach. She took a few deep breaths to calm herself, then pulled out an apron to protect her dress and cracked a clove of garlic, to rub on the inside of the wooden salad bowl before she tore the washed lettuce into it. Maggie added some freshly crumbled bacon and shaved parmesan and squeezed some lemon juice on top. She would add her homemade dressing and croutons just before she served it.

The doorbell rang when she was wiping her hands dry on a tea towel. She untied her apron and smoothed out the skirt of her dress before answering the door. She swung the door open to greet Colby, who was standing on the porch, holding Evelyn's hand. In Evelyn's other hand, she held a bouquet of fresh flowers, which she offered to Maggie. Colby had paired a dress shirt with a nice pair of jeans and Evelyn was wearing a pretty dress and sandals.

"Dees are for you." She said with her hand outstretched. Maggie took the flowers, then Evelyn spun around in her party dress and said, "I picked it out myself."

"And you look beautiful." Maggie replied, stepping aside for them to enter.

"Something smells good." Colby said, leaning in and kissing Maggie's cheek, eyeing her up and down. "You look great."

Maggie beamed and reached for the bottle of wine he held out for her. "You don't clean up half bad yourself."

Dinner was a hit. Evelyn wasn't fond of the candy crackle on top of the crème brûlée, but loved the custard underneath. When Maggie cleaned up the dishes, she brought out a game she picked up just for the occasion: Chutes and Ladders. They played and chatted until Colby noticed Evelyn yawning and announced it was time to leave.

Colby picked his sleepy girl up in his arms and thanked Maggie for a lovely evening. Maggie touched Evelyn's head to say goodbye, and Evelyn leaned over with her arm outstretched, "hug" she said. Maggie leaned in and hugged Evelyn as Colby's free arm wrapped around her and connected them in a group hug. The feeling warmed her heart. How nice would it be if this was her life?

Before he left, Colby leaned in and whispered, "Next time, it's just us."

54

Maggie arrived at the clubhouse a little earlier than she planned and settled down at a table with Quinn, Butch, Sadie and a few of the others. The club members were congratulating themselves on a good run. Maggie tried to learn what they were talking about without asking questions but soon discovered everyone but her already knew what was going on and no one was going to fill her in. She could tell they didn't trust her yet. She'd have to work hard to change that.

Maggie observed Sadie's behaviour. If she kept a close watch on Sadie, she'd learn how to behave the way the club expected her to. Only then would they trust her and talk more freely in front of her.

She lowered her gaze. She hated the fact that being with Quinn made her feel she was cheating on Colby. Not that there was anything going on with Colby, but there could be. *'When had she let her guard down and allowed Colby to get under her skin?'* she wondered. Before she left her condo, she secured her personal phone in the safe with her gun. The last thing she needed was for Quinn to know she had two phones. She couldn't have it with her if she was at the club. There was too much personal information on that phone.

"So, where were you yesterday?" Quinn asked. All heads turned her way. She'd texted him she was working last night and wondered why would he ask her that? Then she remembered the tracking device. It would have stopped working after she smashed it in the park.

"I texted you. I had a shift last night. You were busy. I thought you were ok with it, at least you didn't say otherwise. Working helps me pay my bills." She chuckled.

"I meant during the day. I went out after you left to catch up with you, but I lost track of you."

Maggie knew Quinn was lying. If he'd followed her, he'd have found her in the park with Colby and Evelyn. '*Dammit*,' she thought, '*that was close*'. From now on, she had to distance herself from Colby at least until she settled the debt with the club. It was for his own good. If she wasn't careful, and the club found out, it could be Evelyn who paid the price.

But now she was certain they were tracking her movements. She was quick to think and came up with a plausible story.

"Well, when I left here, I went for a quick ride and stopped at a park to stretch my legs. It was a nice day, and I wanted some fresh air and exercise. When I left the park, the undercarriage of my bike got hooked up on the curb after some jackass cut me off. I stopped to check it out, and I found I knocked off my Gremlin bell and I saw this electronic thing was on the ground beside it. I didn't know what it was, so I left it there, then I picked up my bell, which I put back on when I got home. The rest of the afternoon I spent cleaning my bike and checking it over."

"I'm glad you're ok," He replied gruffly.

Maggie realized she wouldn't get away with removing another tracker without it looking suspicious. She needed to find somewhere else to park her bike other than the parking garage at her condo. One advantage to where her house was located was, she had a post office box delivery address on her driver's license. In Nova Scotia, it was your mailing address that was on your driver's license, not your civic, so if they searched her pockets, they'd only learn what area she was in from her driver's license, not her actual street address.

She thought she could pay a superintendent at one of the nearby buildings to park in their lot. Then she could walk home. She'd have to make those arrangements as soon as she left the clubhouse, because she knew there'd be another tracker in place by the time she did.

Maggie kept a watchful eye on Butch as he interacted with the club. She could tell something big was brewing, but was quick to realize they didn't discuss club business in front of women. The other target of her revenge, Randal, was a different story. He liked to brag, and he didn't go for the tear drop tattoo. Instead, he preferred to keep a running set of notches on his baseball bat. She watched as he carved a fresh one in beside one that wasn't too old. She could tell by the shade of the bat blood had worn through the surface and had embedded into the grain. Her stomach rolled when she realized some of those blood stains could be from Noelle.

A member called out to Randal as he hung his bat up. "Is that one for the High Roller?"

Randal just turned and grinned. Maggie looked at the dozens of notches and knew he was going to be a formidable foe, but in her gut, she knew the last notch he'd made before today was for Noelle. For that reason, she was going to enjoy killing him the most. They all had their hands dirty, but Randal was their enforcer. He took pleasure in his kills. Maggie couldn't blame him for that. She also enjoyed killing her victims, but her victims had been pedophiles. Tiny abused women. Randal just liked the idea of killing, which made him even more dangerous. Maggie risked looking up at him again and noticed for the first time the deadness behind his eyes. There was no emotion. He was a psychopath.

That was when she realized she had to kill him next. He was the one who threatened her existence the most. Maggie also knew she had to use the gun to deal with him. She'd never get close enough to him to use her knife and survive. She needed a better disguise than the one she wore when she killed Tiny. Maggie was lucky that no one saw her that day. As soon as she could get away, she needed to buy a wig to hide her hair. A hat was too risky. It wouldn't take much to knock it off. Her red hair that Liam loved so much was too distinctive.

Maggie continued to listen to the stories that went around the room, monitoring Sadie to learn from her, until she finished this self-imposed assignment.

Sadie leaned over. "Stick with me Maggie. I'll show you the ropes."

That was when Maggie realized Sadie had been watching her, too. She knew Maggie had listened to everything and was picking up on Sadie's signals. Maggie made a note to watch her more carefully in the future.

55

Maggie found a parking spot at an apartment building three blocks from her unit. It was a short walk, and the building's directory didn't list the tenant's names. This was a relief because if the gang came here looking for her, they'd have trouble getting in and finding her. Or finding out that's not where she lived.

Maggie switched out of her riding gear and took her car to the mall to buy what she needed for a disguise. She decided on a dark brown wig cut into a bob with bangs. She even found some coloured contacts in a costume store and picked up a brown pair. They'd cover her green eyes. Then she went in search of black jeans, a black t-shirt and a black jacket. Maggie was careful to ensure there were no reflective surfaces on any of her purchases. She didn't want to call attention to herself. She needed to hide in the shadows, and the dark hair and clothes would help.

Maggie locked her purchases in the trunk of her car so they'd be available when she needed them. Then she remembered she had to return her aunt Julie's call. If she didn't, because her aunt worries so much, she might call the police and report Maggie missing. The last

216

time she'd spoken with Audrey, she reminded Maggie it had been too long since she'd called home. She turned her ignition on as she told her Bluetooth to call her aunt at the shop.

"Hello?" Julie barked into the phone. Maggie rolled her eyes. Julie never looked at the caller ID.

"Hey aunt Julie."

"Maggie girl, it's been a while. How are you doing? Are you back to work?"

"I'm good and yes, I've written a few articles. It's just I miss him so much aunt Julie. I never knew how empty I'd feel without him. It's hard to pretend things are normal."

"Aww Maggie, time will heal. You'll never forget him, but eventually it will hurt less."

Maggie paused, "aunt Julie, I was thinking,"

"Yes."

"Would it be ok if I came home for Christmas?"

"OK?" Julie hooted. "Your uncle and I would love that! It's still months away, though. Are you sure you won't be off on assignment somewhere?"

"I'll work things out with my editor. I think I need a little distance from everything here."

"Ok Mags, whatever you need. By the way, Dr. Coleman left another of those envelopes for your uncle to mail. It's nice that you're both helping all of those families."

A hitch caught in Maggie's throat and before she could reply, Julie said, "I gotta go Mags, they need me in the back. Thanks for calling. Love you, girl."

"Ok aunt Julie, I love you too and I'll call again soon."

Maggie disconnected the call and pulled her car into a Starbucks parking lot. She wondered what her aunt would do if she knew what those envelopes represented. She and Audrey had devised a cover story they were sending encouragement to families of victims, using Maggie's journalistic skills and Audrey's connections with law enforcement. As a psychiatrist, Audrey was once one of the first people the police contacted to help with child victims. Julie and Bobby thought it was a therapeutic decision and were glad to help. They were unaware of the dark reality behind those packages.

Maggie entered the Starbucks and bought herself a caramel macchiato and went back to her car to enjoy it in peace. She figured it was a good time to catch up on all of her calls back home, and called Audrey next. Audrey answered on the second ring.

"Maggie, it's good to hear from you. Maybe you should send me a daily text so I know you're still alive."

"You're hilarious Audrey. I heard you identified another victim. I'm surprised you didn't call me and tell me yourself."

"So, you finally called your aunt. That's good, I'm glad. Maggie, you have so much going on right now. I didn't want to distract you with this."

"To me, it's a pleasant distraction, Audrey. I want those families to have closure."

"Ok, I'll keep that in mind. How are you making out with the biker gang?"

"I had to sleep with Quinn." There was a hitch in her voice as she spoke.

"Oh Maggie, I'm sorry."

Maggie heard the saddened tone in Audrey's voice.

"I knew it was inevitable, but what bothered me was my body's response."

"You liked it." Audrey paused before continuing. "Maggie, that's normal. It's a biological response to stimuli. Women have experienced orgasms during rape. Don't beat yourself up about it. It's best that your body enjoyed it. Some men can tell the difference."

"That sort of makes me feel better. It just feels so disrespectful to Liam's memory."

"You could always stop what you're doing and let the police handle everything. Then you wouldn't have to sleep with him again and I wouldn't have to worry about you."

Maggie chuckled, "Audrey, you of all people know me better

than that. The police have already had over a year to catch Liam's killer and they're no further ahead. They have to wait for physical evidence. I don't. I know which member killed Noelle, and he's next on my list. At some point, I'll find out who pulled the trigger that killed Liam and our child, but in the meantime, I can take out the man who ordered the hit, which was 'Butch' Barker."

"I know you can take care of yourself, but please be careful. These are evil men you're tangling with."

"Audrey, they all were."

56

A few days later, Maggie overheard a conversation revealing a location where Randal would be. He wouldn't be alone, but that didn't bother Maggie. She was going to find a hiding spot in the area and shoot him. She wished she could use her knife. The idea of feeling Randal's blood spilling over her hands and watching the realization she was the one to kill him would have brought her great pleasure. But it was too dangerous.

Maggie led Quinn to believe that she worked that day, so he wouldn't expect her at the clubhouse until later. She'd had to put Colby off a few times, claiming she was busy working on a story. Luckily, he was busy with work and caring for Evelyn that he accepted her excuses at face value. But she wouldn't be able to carry on with the ruse for much longer. Colby had a way of showing up when she least expected it.

To prepare, Maggie slipped into her disguise several hours before the time she expected Randal to be at the location, the one where she planned to kill him. She admired herself in the mirror, noting the disguise made her unrecognizable, took a chance and coated her lips with a dark red lipstick. Not a colour she'd wear, but it worked with the dark wig. The end look was perfect, although she had to use a dark brown eyebrow pencil to cover her own naturally red ones. In this disguise, even Liam would have walked past her.

She pulled her gun from the safe, loaded it, and slipped some extra rounds into her pocket. She looked at her hunting knife and grabbed it as an afterthought. If she only wounded him, she could use the knife to finish the job without creating a greater disturbance.

She circled the area where he'd be until she found a place to park her car and went in search of a good hiding spot. With the war between the Dark Enders and the High Rollers, everyone was on alert, and even a woman sitting in a parked car would be a red flag to them. So, she left her car in a parking lot with other cars and made her way back to the location. It was another deserted building. Things had changed since the virus. Lots of foreign companies were coming in and buying up properties to set up businesses in. New business was good for the economy, but bad for the gangs.

Maggie found a broken window and knocked out the rest of the glass to give herself easy access. She climbed up and dropped to the floor inside. The broken glass crackled under her feet as she kept her back to the wall and took in her surroundings, making sure that she was alone before she found the best position to watch from and take her shot. But first she had to find a second exit, one that took her out the rear of the building. Maggie needed a quick escape in case the police were called when the gun fire started or someone else came to investigate. She might need to abort if there were more gang members present than she expected, and then the back exit would come in handy.

She discovered a back door, unlocked it, and surveyed the area outside, noticing the overgrowth that would help hide her. If she was fast enough, she could make it to the cover of the next building unde-tected. This door was the perfect escape. Maggie stuck a piece of wood in the doorway to prop it open. If she was in a hurry to leave, she wouldn't have to fiddle with the door knob. She made her way up the stairs to the second floor. She'd have a better view of the meeting area to watch for their arrival. Maggie found a broken window with a few boards nailed over it. It was the perfect vantage point. She could still see the surrounding area, but the boards would help to obscure their view of her. She checked her gun and slid the safety off. Now all she had to do was wait.

Her legs began cramping from squatting when, in the distance, she heard the roar of approaching motorcycles long before she saw them. She rolled her shoulders back and peered out of the cracks in the boards. Maggie cursed as she saw the fourth bike pull into the abandoned lot. She wasn't expecting that many people. Maggie waited and watched the interaction between the men. She knew which one was Randal, but from here the identity of the others wasn't clear. In order to be sure she killed him with one shot, he needed to remove his helmet. A head shot would guarantee he died. It was difficult to hit him in the heart while he moved around and wounding him wasn't what she wanted.

Maggie sighed with relief as she saw all four take off their helmets. Maggie recognized two of the other three from the times she'd been at the clubhouse. She didn't know who the fourth man was. Not caring about the other men, she aimed her gun and fired. Maggie watched as Randal's body bowed from the impact before he collapsed in a heap on the gravel lot. She didn't have time to revel in his death. The others were quick to pull out their guns and return fire.

Maggie continued shooting until the gun was empty. The man she didn't know took off on his bike, but the other two kept firing. Her body jerked back as she felt a searing pain in her left shoulder. There wasn't time to investigate her wound. The club members were advancing on the building. Maggie reloaded her gun and took her time to aim the next two shots. Each one rang true, and the men collapsed to the ground.

In the distance, she heard the wail of sirens. She had to get out of there. Maggie looked down at her left arm and saw the blood dripping off the fingers. She shoved her hand into the pocket of her jacket and kicked construction debris and sawdust over the droplets that landed on the floor.

With her heart pounding, she ran down the stairs and out the back door of the building. As she got to the edge of the structure, she peered around the corner to make sure the coast was clear. She still needed to get back to her car before anyone saw her.

Her arm burned where the bullet hit. But she couldn't take the time to stop and access her injury. She had to put as much distance between herself and the carnage she left behind. Allowing her pocket to act as a sling for her injured arm, she slowed her pace as she approached the occupied buildings.

People stepped outside to gawk as the emergency crews arrived. Maggie again slowed her pace so as not to attract attention. She looked at her blood-soaked sleeve and was thankful she chose a black jacket to go with her black jeans. She only hoped she could get back to her car, then home, and slip into the garage unnoticed. Then she could see how bad it was.

Maggie pulled her car up as close to the garage as she could. Her left arm was stiff, and she had to reach across her body with her right arm to open the car door. She saw the bloody mess on the inside of the driver's door and realized she'd have to get right on that to clean it up, but first she needed to see what she was dealing with. Maggie grabbed some clean rags from the garage and wrapped them around her hand and arm to prevent any more blood transfer as she entered her house.

She stood in her tiled bathroom and peeled the jacket from her body, easing her arm out of the sleeve. Next, she had to take off her t-shirt. The fabric stuck to the wound, and she had to pull it free, flinching as she did. They were both ruined, so she tossed them into the bathtub to deal with later. She looked at the wound on her upper arm by the shoulder. Thankfully, the bullet only grazed her flesh, but it was deep. She should seek medical attention, but the hospital would have to report a bullet wound to the police, even if it was only a graze.

'Dammit!' Maggie thought, *'The bullet! It has my DNA on it.'* Maggie knew she'd have to go back when the police finished investigating the scene. She hoped they'd miss the bullet that hit her when they investigated. If luck was on her side, the bullet would still be there. There'd be plenty of other bullets to find from all the gunfire. She had an idea where it went and hoped the police would miss it.

Maggie washed the blood away from her arm and noticed the bleeding had slowed. It was a nasty-looking gash. She applied some Polysporin and a gauze pad, then swallowed some of the pain meds she had left over after her surgery. Maggie had to clean the blood from the car before it set into the carpet.

She tied her arm up in a makeshift sling and went out to clean the mess in her car. Every movement caused her arm to throb as she worked diligently to remove all the blood. When she was done, she was certain only a forensic team could find any traces of her blood. As long as it wasn't visible to the naked eye, she was fine. Then she went back inside to toss the clothing she wore into a black garbage bag that she could toss out later in a dumpster downtown.

When she'd cleaned up, she sat on her sofa and poured herself a shot of whiskey. Her body shook, and her head spun. She had some things to figure out. She peeled back the bandage and decided she would FaceTime with Audrey. Audrey was a doctor, all-be-it a head doctor, but she had a medical license and could advise her. She couldn't send her a picture, as it would leave a record of her wound. A face-to-face conversation on the computer was the best choice.

57

Maggie logged onto her laptop and waited until she saw Audrey's smiling face as FaceTime connected. "Hey Maggie, it's good to see you. Wait, what's wrong?"

Maggie sighed. It was uncanny how Audrey could do that, so she lowered the screen so Audrey could see the wound.

"Maggie! What the hell happened? Have you seen a doctor? That looks bad."

Maggie told Audrey about Randal, what he did to Noelle and the gunfight. When Audrey heard it was a bullet graze, she replied, "You can't see a doctor. I have a suture kit here. Give me a few minutes to see if I can get a flight out of Montreal. I'll try to be there tonight. I'll rent a car at the airport. On my way to the airport, I'll stop and pick up some topical freeze. That will help and I can stitch it up when I get there, but it will hurt like hell."

Maggie was about to refuse, when she thought better of it. She would have to explain the injury to Quinn and if she left it as it was, it would be obvious that a bullet grazed her. Stitching it up was the best way to conceal that it was from a bullet and it would heal better, but she would still have to come up with a plausible cause for her injury.

"Let me know when you land. I'll keep putting Polysporin on it in the meantime."

Around 10 pm, Maggie's phone rang. It was Audrey telling her she landed and was on her way to Avis, which was located inside the airport, to pick up her rental car. Maggie ordered a pizza to be delivered and knew it would arrive right after Audrey did. She was starving and figured with all the running around Audrey had done, she wouldn't have had time for supper. Thankfully, Audrey was lucky enough to find a seat on the first flight out of Montreal, but she had to drive to the airport first, which meant Audrey had been on the go since they'd hung up.

About 10 minutes before the pizza arrived, Audrey entered the house carrying a small duffel bag. They argued because Audrey wanted to stitch up Maggie's wound before they ate, but Maggie was several shots of whiskey in and needed food first. She justified it with 'at this point what's a few more minutes?'

Maggie poured them each a shot of whiskey, then pulled out some plates for the pizza. Meanwhile, Audrey pulled a small medical kit out from her duffle and put it on the table. She'd added some gauze and medical tape to her bag as well, unsure what Maggie had on hand.

Although Audrey had lots of questions, Maggie said she wasn't interested in talking. Instead, she kept going over everything that had happened earlier that day while they ate in silence. Audrey struggled to hold her tongue, but honoured Maggie's wishes for silence. When they'd finished, Audrey removed the pizza box and plates to the kitchen and washed her hands.

"Ok Maggie. Let me take care of this before it heals much more and we have to open it up."

Maggie winced as Audrey pulled back the gauze. A scab had formed, and adhered to it. Removing the bandage caused the wound to bleed again.

"We'd better move to the kitchen. You don't want blood on your sofa. But it bleeding again is a good thing. It will help the edges attach when I stitch it."

Maggie clutched the bandage to the wound so she wouldn't get blood on the floor and made her way into the kitchen while Audrey gathered up her first aid supplies. Maggie plopped down on a chair at the table and bumped her arm. She let out a yowl of pain.

Audrey frowned and laid out the supplies, then poured Maggie another shot of whiskey. She cleaned the wound and sprayed it with antiseptic. Maggie grimaced. Audrey threaded the needle and sprayed the area with a topical freeze, before she inserted the needle, she turned to Maggie and said, "This is going to hurt."

As the needle punctured the skin and pulled the edges closed, Maggie grabbed onto the table's edge with her right hand and held tight. Her eyes watered and she clenched her jaw. Her knuckles were white from the pressure of her grip on the table. A few more jabs and pulls, and Audrey had closed the wound. Then she sprayed it again with antiseptic and redressed it.

"Well, it was bigger than I first thought. If we waited much longer, I don't know if I could have just stitched it up. I had to use 9 stitches. It's going to be an ugly scar, but not your first. Here," she handed Maggie a couple of pills, "I snagged you some Oxy. Only for tonight, though."

Maggie swallowed one and palmed the other. "I'm going to bed. Thanks Audrey, I don't know what I'd have done without you." Her head was already foggy from the whiskey as she stumbled off to bed, beginning to feel the effects of the Oxy. "Make yourself comfortable. You know where the guest room is. We'll talk in the morning."

Audrey watched Maggie head off to bed, then she cleaned up the kitchen. She put the leftover pizza in the fridge, the plates and glasses into the dishwasher and tidied up the first aid supplies.

Audrey picked up her duffle bag and put it in the guest room. What she didn't tell Maggie was she planned on staying until Maggie finished what she set out to do. If Maggie got hurt again, she'd be there to take care of her. She knew Maggie was letting her rage take control, and she needed to help Maggie get her focus back.

Audrey began to unpack and put her belongings away into the dresser. In the car's trunk was a full suitcase, but she could get it in the morning. She pulled out the case she kept the hair clips in and put it in the bedside table drawer. She'd left them attached to the ribbon, as it became a chronological representation of Frank Carter's victims. While Maggie avenged Liam, she could still work at matching up the victims' families so they could return the clips and bring the families' closure.

58

The next morning, Maggie crawled out of bed and inspected her arm in the bathroom mirror. Dark bruises formed around the wound; the muscles felt tight from the swelling and she couldn't lift it straight out or up to the side. Maggie cursed and wondered how she was going to ride. She knew it wouldn't be long before Quinn messaged her and expected her at the clubhouse. She needed to come up with a story to put him off and give her some time to heal.

Maggie splashed some water on her face and brushed her teeth, then she swallowed the second Oxy Audrey gave her the night before. She slipped into some yoga pants and one of Liam's tees and went out to the kitchen to make coffee.

As soon as she left her room, she smelled the aroma of fresh coffee and realized Audrey had beaten her to it. Maggie peered around the corner of the kitchen doorway to find Audrey at the stove, flipping pancakes. Her stomach growled, and she realized how hungry she was. It wasn't until she looked at the clock on the stove that she realized it was after 10. No wonder she was hungry.

Audrey turned to her as Maggie pulled out the coffeepot and poured herself a cup. "Oh good, you're up. How are you feeling?"

"My arm's stiff, swollen, and bruised, but I guess I got off lucky. It could have been a few more inches to the right."

"You were very lucky. I've put together a meagre breakfast, considering what you have in the house! I think we need to go grocery shopping."

"We?" Maggie asked, taking a sip of her coffee.

"Yes, we. I'm staying until this is over. You may need me again."

"NO!" Maggie snapped. "You can't stay. It's too dangerous. I've already lost one friend."

"I won't infiltrate the club, Maggie. Being at the house is what I am talking about. You've told me you're staying downtown at the condo, and only come back here when you need to."

"But..."

"No buts. It's settled. I brought my suitcase in from my rental car this morning and I'm unpacked. This way, if you get into trouble, I can get to you and patch you up again if need be."

Maggie knew it was senseless to argue with Audrey. So instead, she watched her finish making the pancakes and serve them. Then she had a thought that might persuade Audrey to go home.

"What about our search for the families of Carter's victims?"

Audrey chuckled. "Maggie, you should know me better than that. I brought everything with me. While you're out seeking your revenge, I can continue seeking justice." Audrey finished with an air of finality.

While they ate, Maggie filled Audrey in on where things stood with the club. She chose not to bring up Colby, hoping to put him off for a while longer and hoped while Audrey was there, he didn't just show up at her door.

"I have to contact Quinn soon. He'll get suspicious if every time a club member dies, I go AWOL. The problem is, I don't know what to say. I can't ride for a few days, and he'll see the stitches when I show up."

"Why don't you tell him your grandmother showed up for a surprise visit?"

"My what?"

"Your grandmother." Audrey finished, pointing to herself. "Send him a picture of us in a text. Tell him you sliced your arm on something and I came out when I heard to help you. That should put him off for a couple of days."

"Oh, my god! That just might work. Let's take a picture. Hold on, we need a blank wall behind us so there's nothing for him to recognize. I'll say I was riding in a t-shirt and something flew off a truck in front of me and sliced my arm. It's just plausible enough to be believable."

Maggie took a couple of shots with her burner phone until she found one, she thought would work, then she sent it to Quinn, followed by:

'Hey baby, sorry I've been MIA. I got hit by a piece of road debris and needed stitches. My grandma came for a few days to make sure I was ok.'

'R U OK?'

'Yes'

'Did it mar your beautiful face?'

'Nope, hit me in the arm. Serves me right for not wearing my jacket.'

'K. Lot of shit going on here. When will I c u?'

'Give me a couple of days. Then grandma will be gone and when I'm sure I can ride, I'll be there.'

'K. Keep in contact.'

Maggie smiled as she put the phone away.

"He's tied up with Randal's death. Quinn was short and to the point. He didn't get pissed off or demand to see me. I don't know how long until he does, but I'll take it. Let's get some food for the house and then we can look for the owners of the hair clips."

Audrey agreed and waited while Maggie got ready. She'd drive, so that Maggie didn't pop her stitches. But this would give them the opportunity to work together on some of the more difficult searches.

59

With the groceries all put away, Audrey checked Maggie's wound and changed the dressing. First, she cleaned and disinfected it again, then she made a poultice of witch hazel to help with the bruising and swelling. While Maggie sat holding the poultice to her arm, Audrey pulled her files up on her tablet so they could continue matching hair clips to victims to bring closure to the families.

"How many more do we need to find?" Maggie asked as Audrey sat down on the sofa beside her.

Audrey picked up the bag containing the ribbon of hair clips and handed it to Maggie. Maggie opened it and was both happy and sad. They'd found the families of so many of the missing and exploited children, which made her happy, but there were still five families left who didn't have closure and that bothered her. From the position on the ribbon, they were the oldest cases, which was why it was more difficult to find them. Some were from over twenty years ago.

"Can you look at the top file for me?" Audrey asked, motioning to the pile of files she put on the coffee table. "I need a pair of fresh eyes. I keep thinking I'm missing something."

Maggie picked up the file and realized it included copies of police reports. She looked up at Audrey and asked, "How did you get these?"

"I have a friend on the force who was happy to do me a favour. How do you think I've found so many families already?"

"I thought you were using google." Maggie replied, "Here, let me show you something."

Maggie took the laptop and entered the colour, and description of the last clip and hit send. A variety of images and articles popped up. Maggie scanned the headings of the articles, searching for one that looked relevant.

"I think my way is better." Audrey said, "That looks like a lot of work scanning, hoping to find a clue. At least my files are of actual cold cases of missing or murdered children."

Maggie continued to read through several articles, while Audrey worked on a file, knowing that Maggie would look at the file she needed her to see after she tried searching the internet. Audrey made some notes in her notepad and picked up the file that concerned her.

"Oh, my god!" Maggie exclaimed, turning her laptop towards Audrey.

"What?" Audrey asked.

"Listen to this. 'Laura Christie finally brought her daughter home. Lily Christie went missing 21 years ago and yesterday they put her skeletal remains to rest. Hikers found her remains in a wooded area off the interstate, three states away. The recent rain storms had washed away most of the soil, revealing the grisly find, exposing her partially buried body. DNA was used to identify her.' The article continues to go over what she was wearing when she disappeared, including a green hair clip with ladybugs on it." Maggie picked up the ribbon and held out the faded green clip covered with ladybugs.

"Lily Christie?" Audrey asked as she dug through the case files until she came to the one she was looking for and passed it to Maggie.

Maggie flipped through the file until she came to the photograph of Lily Christie, complete with the clip holding back her hair on one side. She had been a pretty child with a beautiful smile. Maggie looked up at Audrey.

"We found another one." She couldn't help it as tears pooled in her eyes.

"Let's find out where the mom is living and bring her the closure she deserves."

60

Colby leaned back in his chair at his desk and looked at the crime scene photos, from the shooting at the warehouse district. He knew the death of Randal Reece was a big hit to the Dark Enders and wondered how long before the retaliation began. It was only a matter of time before the detachment would feel the heat from the inevitable gang war. The other two victims were minor players, but by his count, the Dark Enders were down four members in the last month. It wouldn't be long before the High Rollers started seeing a drop in their membership once word got out. The Dark Enders may even ask other charters to come in to fight the battle. It was something they'd have to monitor.

Colby drummed his fingers on his desk as he considered the timeline. The whole thing started after Liam Murphy got shot instead of Parker Cummings. Cummings' body turned up a few days later, but that didn't change what happened. He wished he could prove what he knew, but they'd been unable to find any evidence to link the Dark Enders to Murphy's shooting. He'd love to be the one to call Maggie and tell her they caught Liam's killer.

"Hey Tate."

Colby lifted his head as his partner, Mark Carlson, approached.

"DNA's in from the blood at the warehouse shooting. The blood analysis from the second floor came back. It's female, but there are no matches in the National DNA Data Bank. It's possible it was a homeless person who was in the wrong place at the wrong time."

"Female, eh? Now that's interesting. Why do you think it's a homeless person?" Colby asked, turning his chair to face Mark.

"Biker clubs don't have female members, and I can't imagine why else a woman would be in the building or be involved."

"A grudge?"

"Ok sure, but a woman with a grudge who took out three bikers and got away unseen?"

"Ya, you're probably right. People overlook the homeless. Still, we should contact the local hospitals and see if anyone came in with a bullet wound." Colby replied, looking down at the photos that showed the bullet's trajectory.

"Hey hold up Carlson. According to the bullet trajectory, they were shooting up at the second floor and the bullets came from the second floor."

Carlson shrugged his shoulders. "That just proves the shooter was on the second floor. The female may have been sleeping and had gone unnoticed until she got shot. If the shooter wore a disguise, he wouldn't have cared about her presence."

"Yes, that's possible. The bullets that took out Tiny and Randal are not a match. That means we're looking at two different shooters. It's probably the work of the High Rollers." Colby said as he closed the file.

"My gut tells me the gang war has started and we're going to have a lot more victims in the coming months. I just hope no more civilians get caught up in it. Let's head to the warehouse and have another look around."

61

Maggie's arm was still swollen and stiff the next morning. She flexed her fingers to keep the blood flowing and knew she'd have to ice it. She picked up the envelope she just addressed and used a wet sponge to seal it. No need to leave her DNA on it.

Getting dressed proved to be a difficult, although not impossible task, and when she was ready, she went out to the living room to talk to Audrey.

"Why don't we take a drive down to Digby for fresh scallops?" Maggie suggested. "Then we can pop this in the mail." She finished holding up the small package containing the card and hair clip addressed to Laura Christie.

"Sounds good."

As they prepared to leave, Maggie's personal cell phone rang. She picked it up without looking at the caller ID, knowing it wasn't Quinn, and answered it.

"Hello?"

"Hey Maggie. It's been a few days."

Maggie's heart raced when she heard his voice. "Colby! How are you?"

"I'm good. I was just wondering if you're free for dinner?"

"You know I'd love to, Colby, but..."

"No buts."

"I have a friend visiting from Ontario for a few days and we have some touristy things to do. After she leaves, you can take me out."

"I'm going to hold you to that."

Maggie chuckled, "Oh, Colby?"

"Yes?"

"Give Evelyn a hug from me."

"She'll be happy to hear that. She's been asking to see you. Maybe you and your friend want to meet at the park on Saturday? The weather looks good, and I promised to take Evelyn."

"I'm not sure I'm up to playdates right now. I got hit by something that fell off a truck while out on my bike. There are 9 stitches in my arm and it's quite sore and swollen right now." Maggie replied, keeping to the same story she told Quinn.

"Maggie! I'm sorry to hear that. Are you ok?"

"Yes, I'm fine. I'll be off my bike for a while yet, but it happened a few days ago, and it's getting better each day."

"That's good to hear. Well, think about Saturday and let me know if you're up to it. I've got to get back to work, chat soon."

Maggie disconnected the call and turned to find Audrey staring at her. There was a look of disapproval on her face.

"Say it." Maggie suggested.

"Ok I will. With your, shall we say, 'colourful history,' do you think going out and meeting up with a detective is a wise thing to do?"

Maggie sighed. "No, I know it's not, but there's something there. He kissed me and I felt something I hadn't felt in a long time. And don't tell me it was just a chemical reaction to stimuli! Plus, there's Evelyn. She enjoys having me around, and I really like her. This might be the only way I can have a child in my life."

"That's another reason to put a stop to things now. It would devastate Evelyn if you end up in jail for murder after you became a part of her life. You know firsthand how damaging childhood trauma can be," Audrey huffed.

Maggie sighed. Audrey was right, but it seemed fate kept throwing them together. In the future, she would try to distance herself from Colby Tate no matter how appealing he was.

The drive along the coast was pleasant because of the sunny, warm weather, so they drove with the windows down. Maggie and Audrey took the leisurely route down the South Shore towards Digby, where they enjoyed some fresh scallops at a restaurant downtown. Before they ventured home, they stopped at The Fish Market on Birch Street for some fresh scallops and other goodies. Audrey planned to make a seafood linguine for their supper. Maggie found the day's outing was a perfect distraction from all the drama with the Dark Enders and Quinn. She knew she'd have to get back to reality soon. Quinn had been texting her and had suggested picking her up so that he could see her. Soon she'd be able to lift her arm well enough to ride again and she couldn't keep putting him off. She needed to finish this so she could move forward.

62

They pulled into the driveway, tired from their trip to Digby, and noticed a bunch of flowers on the front porch. Audrey, who was in the driver's seat, turned to Maggie and teased, "A secret admirer?"

Maggie's mouth went dry as she thought back to the last time she found flowers on her porch. *'Could they be from the same person?'* She stepped out of the car, her legs were heavy as she walked to the front of the house. Meanwhile, Audrey went to the trunk to retrieve their purchases, unaware of the change in Maggie's demeanour.

Maggie picked up the flowers and knew they were from the same person. Not wanting to worry Audrey, she plucked not one, but this time two black roses from the centre of the bouquet and shoved them into the hedge under her front window out of Audrey's sight.

"Who are they from?" Audrey called out.

"It doesn't say."

"My guess would be this Colby fellow. He seems real keen on starting a relationship with you."

"You're probably right. I'll take them in and put them in water." Maggie replied as she opened the door. It was the last thing she wanted to do. She looked over her shoulder at the surrounding neighbourhood and wondered if anyone saw who delivered them. Later, when Audrey was asleep, she'd check the video footage to see if she could identify the delivery person. If she couldn't recognize the delivery vehicle, she'd call all the florists in the area to see who made up the bouquet. Maybe then she could figure out who sent them.

The next morning, Maggie found she had more flexibility in her arm, so she left Audrey at the house and returned to her condo. Maggie worried that whoever left the flowers would come back, but it had been months since the first delivery, so she hoped it would be months before another bunch appeared, if at all. The cameras only showed a nondescript van and the man who delivered the flowers kept his hat low over his face and she couldn't make out his features.

They returned Audrey's rental to the airport. There was no reason for her to keep paying for it when Maggie had a spare vehicle around. Audrey would use Liam's SUV. That way she could be independent, and able to come to Maggie's aid if she needed her to. In the meantime, Audrey would continue the search for more families. They'd mail nothing else from Nova Scotia. Instead, if they found another match, they'd send it to Julie so that Bobbie could mail it out on his travels.

Once Maggie had settled back at the condo, after buying some groceries, she pulled out her gun, cleaned and reloaded it. She needed to be prepared for whatever lay ahead. Quinn had gotten impatient with her while she healed, so she'd promised to go to the clubhouse this evening. From the conversations she'd had with him over the last few days, she knew the club had to regroup following Randal's murder.

Randal had been their road captain and a powerful enforcer. His loss was an enormous blow to the club. Added to the fact it was less than a month ago, somebody killed Tiny. The club was feeling the pressure. They were sure it was the work of the High Rollers, and had ordered a hit out on Warren Blithe, the new President.

When Maggie heard this, she wondered if she should sit back and let the two clubs take care of things themselves. At the rate they were going, several members from each side would die. Unfortunately, there were no guarantees such a war would take out the right players. Maggie needed Butch dead. She knew he'd ordered the hits that cost Liam and Noelle their lives. When Butch was dead, then she could move on. Quinn could step up and take Butch's place. She didn't care about that, but if Quinn got in her way, she'd kill him too, even if he didn't have a part in all of this.

When she finished cleaning the gun, she loaded it and slipped it into her jacket, and donned her riding gear. She checked the angry healing wound on her arm and wrapped it again. The stitches hadn't come out yet, and she knew Quinn would want to see it to verify she was telling the truth. She'd pack a fresh roll of gauze into her saddlebag. Maggie felt she was going to need it.

It took some doing, but she braided her hair into a single plait that ran down her back and left the apartment. Not wanting to go straight to where she parked her bike, she took her time and walked around downtown before ending up at the outdoor parking lot. The casual walk would be misleading if she was being watched, and she could keep her apartment's location a secret. She'd had a message from the superintendent where she parked that he'd seen several men on bikes checking hers out. That meant the Dark Enders were snooping around. Now she was glad she found an outside lot. If she'd been in an underground, who knows what they would have done to gain access.

When she settled into the seat of her bike, she felt the familiar sensation of home that always spread through her when she rode. She felt at ease on her bike and rode when the weather permitted over the last six years. It was her primary mode of transportation. Now it was part of the persona she'd become to catch Liam's killer. It worried her how easily she'd slipped into the lifestyle and killing again. This time she didn't have the personal touch to her kills, but she still felt the sense of satisfaction knowing the victims deserved what they got.

She had plenty of time before Quinn expected her at the clubhouse, so she went for a ride first to clear her head. Maggie rode for about an hour and, without realizing it, found herself at the park where Colby brought Evelyn to play. She turned into the parking lot and parked her bike. Colby's car wasn't here, so she took a walk and stretched her legs. Her mind rolled, contemplating how she would get Butch alone so all of this could be over.

The burner phone in her pocket pinged, and she knew it was Quinn. She left her real phone back at the apartment for safety. She sat down on a bench, pulled it out, and read his text. He had some club business to attend to, and let her know she could still arrive at the same time if she wanted or she could come a little later. She picked to arrive later and texted him her reply. If they suspected her of anything, arriving when he wasn't there could be a problem.

Just as she was putting her phone away, she heard someone call her name. She looked up as Colby approached and cursed.

"Where's Evelyn?" Maggie asked as he sat down on the bench next to her.

"She's with my mom. I took a chance that I'd find you here and checked. When I saw your bike in the parking lot, it was easy. I just looked for the most beautiful woman in the park and there you were. You've been avoiding me."

"Colby, I haven't been avoiding you. I told you I had a friend visiting me, and I was lying low while my arm healed."

"Let me see it."

Maggie eyed him with suspicion. "You don't believe me?"

"I didn't say that. I just wanted to see how bad it was."

Maggie shrugged and removed her jacket, then pulled her sleeve up to reveal the gauze bandage, which she lowered to expose the stitches along what would be a jagged scar.

"Oh, my god! That's worse than I thought. Did you report it?"

"Seriously, Colby, what good would that do? I always carry a first aid kit. I pulled over and wrapped it up and sought medical attention as soon as I could. The stitches will be out in a few more days. You should have seen it the first morning afterwards. My arm was black and blue and swollen. I could barely lift it. I was lucky my friend came to visit. She helped me out a lot around the house."

Colby slid his hand over and wrapped it around Maggie's right hand, holding it. She felt the warmth of his touch radiate from where their hands connected. She turned towards him, her mouth open to speak, when he lowered his head and kissed her. It was gentle and sweet, and Maggie knew if she allowed it, it would intensify. She felt it. Her body wanted the kiss to continue, but she broke away. Colby held up his hand before she could say anything.

"Maggie, I like you. And I know you like me. I'm not pushing things here. I realize it hasn't been that long since you lost Liam, not like with me and Stephanie, but I want you to know I'd like to see where this could go, so I'll be patient. It's not my strong suit," he chuckled, "but I can learn."

"You're right, I do like you. There is just so much going on right now I'm finding it hard to concentrate. Why don't you let me sort things out and I promise I'll call you for that 'real' date you wanted."

"Deal." He squeezed her hand then let go and stood, "Oh and Maggie, you know if you need anything, anything at all, I'm just a phone call away."

Maggie smiled up at him. "If I need anything, I'll call."

She watched as Colby turned and walked away. His stride was purposeful, and she almost sensed a small skip of joy in it. When he was out of sight, Maggie pulled out her phone to check the time and realized she needed to get moving if she was going to arrive at the clubhouse without raising suspicion. When she got back on her bike, she looked around to ensure Colby was long gone before she left the park, but to be safe, she did her evasive riding in case she was being followed. She didn't like how paranoid she felt, but keeping her two lives separate was becoming more and more problematic.

63

When Maggie arrived, there were only a handful of bikes parked at the clubhouse. She couldn't see Quinn's bike and wondered if she should wait for him, but parked and went inside. Maggie stepped into the room and looked around. She saw Sadie was sitting at the back with a couple of other 'old ladies.' Sadie nodded at Maggie and motioned for her to join them.

"Hey." Maggie greeted as she approached.

"Hey yourself." Sadie countered. "I heard you got hurt. All better now?"

Maggie went through the same procedure she'd done with Colby that morning and showed them the row of stitches along her upper arm.

"Ew, that looks nasty." One woman stated. "I'm glad I don't have any ugly scars."

"Felt pretty nasty when it happened." Quipped Maggie as she told the story about the shrapnel falling from a truck and bouncing up and hitting her in the arm. It was a good cover story and so far, everyone believed her.

"Is Quinn back?" Maggie asked, glancing towards the meeting room door as she made herself comfortable.

"He's with Butch. They should be back soon. Did you hear about Randal?"

Of course, she heard about Randal. She'd killed him, but they didn't know that, so Maggie hesitated while she tried to remember if Quinn mentioned it to her. Then she remembered the call where she lay in bed talking to him on the phone, and he told her about Randal.

"Yes, Quinn told me. It's horrible that the High Rollers have killed so many members in such a short time. Should I be worried about Quinn?"

"Oh honey," Sadie said, "in this lifestyle, you always have to worry. Club rivalries, road accidents, deals gone bad. You never know what's going to happen. That's why when we party, we party hard. Come on, you can give me a hand setting everything up for when they get back."

Sadie grabbed Maggie's hand and led her to another area of the clubhouse to get things ready for later. Every movement she made setting up pulled at her stitches, her arm ached and Maggie thought if she wasn't careful, she'd rip the stitches out. It wasn't long before her arm throbbed so much, she had to beg off doing anything else. Maggie wondered if Sadie picked her to help as a way of punishment, but she couldn't be sure.

It wasn't long before various members started rolling in and their boisterous laughter filled the room, but there was still no sign of Butch and Quinn. Maggie caught Sadie's reflection and saw the worry in her eyes. She liked Sadie, and for a fleeting moment, regretted the pain she would cause the woman when she killed her partner. But 'Butch' deserved what was coming to him.

Maggie went over to the bar and got Sadie and herself a drink, and brought them to the table. Sadie took the glass from Maggie's hand, and raised her hand in a toast, when a commotion broke out behind them as Quinn and Butch strolled in. Sadie squealed with delight as she tossed back her drink before jumping up and running to greet Butch. To keep up appearances, Maggie followed suit.

Quinn greeted Maggie not with a hug and kiss, but by grabbing onto and digging his fingers into her forearms. She winced as his fingers dug into her healing flesh. "Ouch." She said, pulling back, tears springing to her eyes.

Quinn let go of her and pushed up the sleeve of her shirt to examine the wound. He scowled when he saw the jagged row of stitches. "Sorry," he mumbled, before pulling her into a kiss.

Maggie knew it was both a test and punishment. Maggie stayed away longer than Quinn wanted her to, and he expressed his annoyance by hurting her. All Quinn needed to do was ask to see the stitches, not inflict pain. The pain was her punishment.

"That's a lot worse than I thought. You're lucky it didn't hit your face. You could have lost an eye wearing your half helmet."

"I won't be riding without full gear again. I can tell you that."

Maggie traced her fingers along his jaw and purred. "I've missed you."

Quinn growled, "I'd take you right back to my room and show you how much I've missed you, but first we celebrate."

"Celebrate?"

"Yup, we avenged Randal's death and made sure the High Rollers know we won't take anymore shit."

Maggie's step faltered. "The High Rollers? Are you sure it was them?"

"It had to be them. We've been in a turf war with them for years. We've called out to another charter to come and help us out."

"What did you do to them?"

"Maggie, you know I can't tell you that. Trust me, we took care of it."

Quinn draped his arm across her shoulders and led her to the bar to refresh her drink. The rest of the night was a celebration, and the clubhouse filled with music and laughter. Quinn led Maggie around so she could show everyone her war wound. One member commented to her, 'that's why men should do the riding.' Which she ignored.

When the night was over, Maggie slid into the bed beside Quinn and realized he'd still never taken her to his home. She didn't think he lived here all the time, but maybe it was his responsibility as VP to make sure everything ran smoothly. Quinn had never elaborated on what the club did to earn money. The only information she had was what she'd learned when she was researching them. Not that she cared. It wouldn't be long before she took care of Butch and distanced herself from this life.

<h1 style="text-align:center">64</h1>

In the morning, Maggie rolled over and stretched before she slipped out of bed, leaving Quinn sound asleep. She needed a shower and some coffee. Maggie headed to the main room to put on a pot so it would be ready when she got out of the shower. She couldn't just get up and sneak away without causing suspicion, so she'd have to hang around until Quinn woke up. But staying in the room while he slept didn't appeal to her. She wasn't a fan of boredom, and watching someone sleep was boring.

She stepped out into the hall and the aroma of coffee drifted towards her. Smiling to herself that she wouldn't have to make the coffee, she made her way down the hall. She was about to enter the main room and grab a cup when she heard Butch's voice as he talked to someone on the phone. She pushed back against the wall to stay out of sight so she could eavesdrop on his conversation.

"We took out their VP last night. You know they're going to retaliate. They haven't recouped since they lost Patch." Butch paused while he listened to the other end.

"Be aware. Quinn's staying here to monitor things. I have to go to the port today. There's a shipment coming in, and I have to be there when they offload it." Another pause while he listened. "No, I'll be fine on my own. There's a lot of security at the port. I just need to get the product out before anyone asks questions."

Maggie's heart pounded. This was her chance. She knew the layout of the port better than most people after all the loads of cars she'd picked up there. The only difficulty would be Quinn. He'd expect her to stay with him if he was staying at the clubhouse. She had to think of a reason to leave and decided she could always claim she got called into work. She pulled her phone out of her pocket and pretended to take a call. It would be a dual purpose; one, it would alert Butch she was coming into the room and he wouldn't suspect she'd been listening and second, he'd hear her accept a shift at the call centre and verify it with Quinn.

She ensured her voice was loud enough that Butch heard her as she held the phone to her ear and pretended to be speaking with someone. On seeing Butch, she nodded at him as she passed him on her way to the coffee machine. He was quick to put his phone away. She hung up and made herself a cup of coffee before mumbling, 'good morning' to Butch.

Before she could head back to Quinn's room, she heard him call to her, "Come sit." It sounded like a command as he motioned to the empty chair beside him. Maggie had no choice but to oblige as she walked over and sat down.

"I haven't seen you here for a while. I figured Quinn was tired of you. Although I can't imagine why."

Maggie scowled. "You saw my scar and stitches. It was difficult to ride with my arm swollen and bruised. Then my grandma came to take care of me."

"You don't have a car?"

"I live downtown. I can walk everywhere I need to go. The bike gets me out of the city."

Butch nodded and continued to watch her as she sipped her coffee. She suspected he didn't believe her. Luckily, she took a selfie with Audrey that showed her fresh bandages and bruises the day after Audrey stitched her up and sent it to Quinn. She picked up her phone and scrolled through the texts until she found the picture and held it up for Butch to see.

"That's my grandma and I. I sent it to Quinn right after it happened. You can see how fresh my wound is."

Butch grabbed the phone from her and enlarged the picture so he could see the swelling and bruising on her arm. He then scrolled up to see the date of the text.

"That's the day after Randal got shot."

Maggie only nodded. Butch handed her phone back to her when Quinn joined them. Maggie looked up at him. Sleep still blurred his features. He'd passed out the night before and she'd left the bed before he woke up because she hoped to avoid having sex with him again. She figured he was coming to tell her to get back to bed, but he grabbed a coffee and plopped down beside her and said, "Good morning."

"We need a minute, Maggie." Butch said.

"No problem, I need a shower before I go to work, anyway." She replied as she leaned forward and kissed Quinn's cheek before he could comment.

After her shower, Maggie said her goodbyes and promised to return later when her shift was over. She made her way to the downtown lot where she parked her bike and went over it, checking for another tracking device. She found one on the back side of her saddlebag and removed it. She wouldn't destroy this one, instead she'd leave it here, so they'd think she'd walked to work. As long as the tracking device didn't move, they'd think her bike was still parked there. To avoid detection, she also removed her license plate and slipped it into her saddle bag.

She checked the time and headed to the port so she'd be early.

Maggie got back on her bike, knowing she needed to find an inconspicuous place to wait and watch for Butch. It was going to be difficult to kill him and get away in such a busy port, but she wouldn't let this opportunity pass her by. Who knew how long she'd have to wait for another opportunity to find Butch alone and away from the club?

Maggie pulled into the Tim Hortons, located just down the street from the port, and parked her bike. She grabbed a coffee and a seat by the window to watch for Butch. From what she'd gathered, he was picking up drugs. She knew workers hid the drugs inside other legitimate products and she hoped that what he was picking up would fit inside his trunk and saddle bags so she'd recognize him. If he came in another type of vehicle, he could go by unnoticed.

65

aggie was sipping her coffee, staring out at the ships in the harbour, when she heard the rumble of a motorcycle and turned to watch as it approached. The familiar sensation of calm spread through her when she recognized Butch on his bike. He was alone! This was going to happen. Today, he would pay the price for taking Liam from her and killing Noelle. She watched Butch turn up Howard Avenue and park his bike to the side. The area he chose was wide open. She'd have little to no coverage, but she'd take her chances.

Maggie slipped out of the building and made her way on foot across the rail yard. She felt the weight of the gun in her holster reminding her of its presence. She'd only use it as a last resort. The sound of a gunshot would attract too much attention, with the port full of workers. She felt for her knife and withdrew it from inside her jacket. It wasn't the same one she'd used in the past, but it was sharp and true and would do the job. She just had to get close enough to Butch in order to use it. Maggie hurried her pace, needing to find a place to hide where she could observe him until she made her move.

She saw him up ahead, and she positioned herself behind a rail car. From there, she watched Butch as he met up with someone from the port. Butch got into the front seat of a car with the man, and they conducted their business out of sight. When Butch stepped out, he was carrying a large package. Maggie watched while he divided it into smaller packages and put them in his trunk and saddle bags. She was about to step out of her hiding space when the man with the car stopped and spoke to Butch again. Maggie pressed herself against one of the rail cars and stayed in her hiding spot. She slipped her knife into the sheath on her leg and withdrew her gun. It looked like she was going to need it after all.

Before she could make her move, she watched as Butch took a quick look around and then ran towards where Maggie was hiding. She felt her heart pounding in her chest.

'*Did he see me? Does he know I'm here?*' She thought. Then he stopped beside a nearby rail car and she heard the familiar sound of urine on the pavement. A smile crept to her lips as she slid her gun back into the holster and pulled out her knife.

Maggie stepped out and quietly approached Butch from behind, keeping her knife hidden. When he turned and saw her, he didn't seem surprised. Her step faltered with this development, but Maggie continued on with her plan. A dark smile stretched across Butch's face when he saw her.

"Shall I keep this out?" He called out while shaking drips of urine from his penis. "I knew you had the hots for me." He said with a sneer. "What did you do? Follow me here?"

Maggie felt her guts roll at the audacity that he thought her showing up here was because she wanted him. But it would serve her purpose and allow her to get close enough to use the knife, which she held against her leg.

"Well, I couldn't come on to you at the clubhouse now, could I?" she asked, smiling at him.

Butch eyed her, "Quinn will forgive you, because it's me, but Sadie won't. It's too bad too, because I think she likes you."

Butch leaned over to kiss her when she was close enough for him to reach her. Repulsed, she stepped back and swung her arm with the knife in her grasp up and buried the blade to the hilt in his neck. The shock that registered on his face made her smile. He grabbed the wrist of the hand holding the knife, so she twisted the blade, ensuring she severed his carotid artery. His hand dropped from her wrist as he tried to stench the flow of blood as she withdrew the blade.

"You fucking bitch!" He hissed.

"That was for Liam, you bastard!"

With his hand clutched to his neck, Butch looked around for someone to help him. His other hand reached out and grabbed her arm with a steely grip, wrapping around her sutures, digging his fingers in. She howled with pain and struggled to break free. *It's taking too long for him to bleed out.* She thought, *I must be losing my edge.* Maggie turned back towards him and kicked him with everything she had. She watched his eyes roll back as both hands went to his crotch, exposing the wound in his neck, that now bled freely as he crumpled to the ground.

This was her chance. Maggie turned and raced back to the Tim Horton's parking lot, where she parked her bike. Butch's blood had splattered over her leather jacket and gloves, but she could take care of that when she got home. She needed to get out of here and put as much distance between herself and the scene as she could before someone found Butch. As Maggie pulled out of the parking lot, her red hair flowed in the wind behind her, unaware of the bike that had pulled into the port as she left, witnessing her departure.

<h1 style="text-align:center">66</h1>

Quinn's jaw sagged as he saw the flash of red hair of the familiar figure pull away. *'What the hell is she doing here?'* He thought. *'She said she had to work.'* He pulled up and parked beside Butch's bike. Quinn waited a few minutes before he searched for Butch. He didn't agree with Butch when he said he could handle this alone. Taking out the High Rollers' VP had upped the ante. With everything going on, he felt they should pair up wherever they went.

He checked Butch's bike, found the packages, and knew the deal took place. He scanned the area but couldn't see Butch anywhere, so he went to look for him. Quinn saw the trail of blood before he found Butch's body. He rushed to his side, but knew by the vacant look in Butch's eyes it was too late. He examined the wound in Butch's neck. This wasn't a deal gone bad, this kill was personal. The image of Maggie fleeing the scene flashed through Quinn's mind. *'Maggie must be involved in this,'* He thought, *'but why?'* He debated his next move. Should he call for reinforcements? Or take matters into his own hands. The need for revenge bubbled within him. He knew he could handle Maggie on his own. She wouldn't expect him to know what she did. The only way she could have killed Butch was to have caught him off guard.

He looked down at Butch's body and left it there where the port workers could discover him, and went to retrieve the merchandise from Butch's bike. The cops couldn't find that. His duty was to protect the club at all costs. He debated again whether he should call for backup, but Maggie was tiny. He'd have no problem overpowering her. Taking care of her on his own would give him great pleasure.

Quinn pulled out his phone and checked for the tracking device. His phone showed the tracker in a downtown lot, but he just saw her. Maggie must have found the device. *'Who the hell is she?'* Quinn wondered. *'Could she be an undercover cop? No, cops don't stab their targets in the throat or sleep with them. No, there was another reason she'd stepped into the Capital that night, and if her beauty didn't blind me, I'd have figured it out before now.'*

He'd head downtown to where she parked her bike and take care of her. There were a lot of alleys nearby where he could hide out. This was personal.

Maggie pulled her bike into her underground parking at her building and parked. She'd take the back entrance and double back to the lot where she left the tracking device. She needed to destroy it before some unsuspecting person picked it up. But first, she needed to remove her jacket and gloves. They were covered in Butch's blood.

She went up to her unit and changed her clothes. She didn't want to lose the custom leather jacket, but getting the blood out of it would be difficult, so she cut out the tag and hidden pockets from the lining and stuffed it in a green garbage bag and tied it up. Maggie wrapped up the gloves in with her kitchen garbage and tossed it down the garbage chute. Then she brushed her hair into a ponytail, checked herself in the mirror, and left the building. She'd drop the garbage bag with her jacket in it in a dumpster on her route.

Maggie decided that when she got back to the apartment, she'd call Audrey to come pick her up. She needed to lie low for a while. Her bike was ok in the underground. What worried her was she glimpsed someone pull into the port riding a motorcycle when she left the scene. *'Who was it? Did they see her? Was it someone from the club?'* Her mind raced as she stepped into the elevator. For the first time, she realized her life would be in danger if anyone suspected her of Butch's murder.

Maggie slipped out of the back door of the building, not wanting to be seen exiting the front, tossed the garbage bag and hurried to the parking lot. She went to the spot she'd been parking in and saw the device was where she left it. A quick look around to verify she was alone, and she lifted her foot and crushed it beneath her heel. Twisting until she'd ground the pieces as small as she could. Then she picked them up and scattered them around the lot. Satisfied that she had destroyed the device, she headed back to her apartment building.

Meanwhile, Quinn had parked his bike on one of the side streets and went to the lot where the tracker showed Maggie's bike was. He followed the app on his phone to the device and found it on the ground.

'She's found and removed it.' He thought, *'I'll leave it there. She'll have to come back and either retrieve it or destroy it.'* He smiled to himself, knowing that he had the upper hand. She didn't know he knew. He'd slip into one of the alley's nearby and wait for her, then he'd take care of her once and for all.

It wasn't long before his patience won out and he saw her walk by his hiding spot on her way to the lot. *'She's parked elsewhere and is going back for the tracking device.'* He thought. He moved closer to where the alley opened to the street and watched for her to return. *'It all makes sense now. She must have found and destroyed the first device.'* He clenched his fist, feeling the rage within, and rolled his shoulders in anticipation. *'Whatever the reason, she's doing this; I'll make her pay for her actions. When I'm done with her, even her own mother wouldn't recognize her.'* He flexed his fingers before rolling them back into fists, embracing the anger that radiated down his arms to his clenched fists.

Having destroyed the device and not wanting to draw attention to herself, Maggie slowed her pace as she walked back to the apartment. She'd left her gun, but still had her knife hidden in the sheath of her leather pants. She'd need to scour and bleach the knife to remove all traces of Butch's blood, but there was no hurry. Maggie could deal with that when she was back at her house. She noticed it was getting dark. Where had the day gone? She hadn't realized it was so late. Maybe she would wait and call Audrey to come get her in the morning. She'd be fine by herself in her apartment for the night. No one from the Dark Ender's knew where she lived.

Maggie reached into her pocket to pull out her phone and checked the time when her head snapped backwards as someone grabbed a handful of her hair with extreme force. She couldn't prevent herself from being pulled into the alleyway she was passing, and her body slammed hard against the brick wall. The air expelled from her lungs from the force and a hand slammed against the side of her head, forcing her face into the brick facade of the building. She tasted the blood that filled her mouth.

"You fucking bitch." Quinn hissed in her ear. "You're going to pay for killing Butch."

"Quinn? What are you doing? Butch is dead? What are you talking about? I did nothing."

"Bitch, I saw you there!" He seethed, spit flew from his lips, spraying her cheek. "I'm going to kill you for what you did."

Maggie heard the rage in his voice and her face went ashen. She had to think if she was going to survive. Maggie tried to twist from his grasp, but he held her in place. She kicked back at his shin with the heel of her boot and heard him howl in pain. She hoped it would cause him to loosen his grip on her, but he held even tighter.

He pressed against her and snapped her head back as he pulled her hair so he could look at her. Loathing filled his eyes as he spun her around and punched her in the stomach. She doubled over as a wave of nausea overcame her. Maggie tried to stand upright when his fist connected to her jaw, forcing her backwards and off her feet. Her shoulder connected to the concrete. Pain radiated through her, her eyes stung with tears. She curled inwards to protect her abdomen as he began kicking her body, cursing her as he did. Just a few feet away, people walked by, oblivious to the violence a short distance from them. She sensed he was dragging this out to make her suffer as long as he could. She felt helpless against his assault.

A kick to the back of her head caused Maggie's vision to blur, and she knew if she lost consciousness, it was over. Quinn paused his assault. She heard the heavy breaths he took from exertion and Maggie knew this was her only chance. Maggie slid the knife out of its sheath and unfurled her body in time to see Quinn coming towards her with a brick. She slashed out at him and her knife connected with the back of his ankle. Quinn collapsed to the ground screaming in pain, and she realized she'd severed his Achilles tendon. The brick dropped from his hand, landing on her chest. She heard the snap as ribs broke. Air expelled from her lungs and she struggled to get a breath. She knew if she didn't get up, Quinn could still kill her, even with a severed Achilles tendon.

Maggie tried to rise, but her body betrayed her and she collapsed to the ground, so she tried crawling away, but he grabbed her foot and yanked her backwards. Her face hit the pavement and blood spurted from her nose. She rolled onto her back before he crawled on top of her, his face contorted, unrecognizable from the hatred that filled him. Her breaths came in short, raspy gasps as he sat on her chest. The pain was unbearable. She felt his hands wrap around her neck; her arms pinned beneath his legs. She was at his mercy. She whispered, "I'm coming Liam."

Hearing her words, Quinn paused and leaned forward until his face was inches from hers. "Just die already." He hissed.

His movement freed her right arm. She gasped from the weight of him on her chest, and the hands that still tightened around her throat. This was her only chance. She still held her knife, so she looked him in the eyes and, in one quick movement, buried her blade into the underside of his jaw.

His eyes bulged before they rolled back, and he slumped forward on top of her. She struggled against the weight of him, but she couldn't push him off. Her breathing became shallow, and she welcomed the darkness that enveloped her.

67

When Maggie regained consciousness, she found herself still pinned under the weight of Quinn's body. His dead, vacant eyes stared down at her. She struggled to push him off, but couldn't. Her whole body ached. Her breathing was shallow as she gasped for air under his added weight. Then she felt Quinn's body shift, and for a moment, she thought he was still alive. Not having the weight of him centred on her chest allowed her to take an unimpeded breath of air, but doing so caused her to gasp from the intense pain caused by her broken ribs. She could now wiggle out from beneath him and tried to get up, but failed. She needed help, and she wondered where her phone was.

Suddenly, a hand reached out to her, and she froze. There was a witness to what she'd done. But then she looked up into the saddened eyes within the weather-beaten face of the old man who offered his hand. She took it. He helped ease her into a sitting position.

"Thank you." She croaked through her damaged vocal cords as she leaned against the wall. Maggie's throat was swollen and ached from where Quinn's hands had strangled her.

She looked up at the man who'd helped her. From his tattered, filthy appearance, she realized he must be homeless. *'How much did he see?'* Maggie wondered as the man squatted down beside her and looked back and forth from her to Quinn's body.

"Are you ok?" He asked.

"Not really." She replied, "Did you move him off me?" Motioning towards Quinn's body.

The man nodded. "I sleep back there." He said, pointing to a lean too at the back of the alley that she hadn't noticed before. "I was coming back for the night when I saw him on top of you."

"You saved my life." Maggie said to him. "How can I repay you?"

Maggie slid her hand into her pocket and pulled out the small wad of bills she had and offered them to him. He held up his hand and shook his head, but Maggie insisted. Shoving the bills into his hand. "It's all I have on me. If I had more, I'd give it to you."

His eyes widened when they landed on the pink $50 folded over a couple of $20 and he nodded, then put it in his pocket before backing away.

"I had to help." He said, "I didn't want you to end up like that lady behind the restaurant."

"Thank you, I'm glad you did. I have to get out of here and get some help. I can't stay with the body. Will you be, ok?"

The man nodded and retreated to his lean too. Barricading himself to avoid viewing the body.

Maggie didn't like the idea of leaving the man there to deal with the police when they found Quinn's body, but she had to get out of here. She searched until she found her phone on the ground and called Audrey. She needed her help before the police showed up. Maggie knew she couldn't get out of the alley on her own. Her injuries were too great. This time she couldn't avoid a visit to the ER. When Audrey got here, she'd have her to take her to Hants Community Hospital. If the Dark Enders were looking for her and knew anything about what happened today, they'd search the local ERs.

Receiving Maggie's call, Audrey didn't ask questions, just hopped in the SUV and made her way downtown. Maggie sat leaning against the wall of the building for support and fought to maintain consciousness while she waited. It wasn't long before Audrey pulled up in Liam's SUV and parked in front of the entrance to the alley with the four ways flashing. Maggie motioned to Audrey as she stepped out of the vehicle and called to her, her voice little more than a croak.

Audrey's eyes widened when she saw Maggie and Quinn's body just a few feet away. Audrey tried to help Maggie get to her feet by putting her hands under her arms to lift her. Maggie struggled to stand, but collapsed back to the pavement.

"Maggie, I can't lift you. You have to help me get you to the car." Audrey pleaded.

Audrey turned to look out at the waiting vehicle and debated what to do next. She spun around when she heard the clatter of a fallen board from further up in the alley. She switched the flashlight on her phone on and aimed it in the noise's direction. A movement caught her attention as a man came out from behind a tarp with his hands up, demonstrating he meant no harm. He nodded at Audrey, then bent down in front of Maggie and pulled her upright motioning for Audrey to help him. With him on one side and Audrey on the other, they got Maggie into the backseat of the vehicle. Maggie, her chest rising from the exertion, turned to the man.

"Do you have somewhere else to go tonight?" She asked him.

"Yes, I have another spot."

"Go there. I don't want you here when the police show up and find his body. There is no reason for you to have to deal with this. Please don't tell anyone you saw me here."

The man nodded, then pulled something from his coat pocket and offered it to Maggie. She looked down and realized it was her knife. He must have taken it out of Quinn's jaw. She reached out and took it from him, noting he'd taken the time to wipe it clean.

"I'd tell you to keep it, but it would only get you in trouble. When I'm better, I'll be looking for you so I can thank you." She reached out for his hand and gave it a squeeze. "Now get moving. I'm going to call the police when we are on the highway and report the body."

Maggie leaned her head back and watched as the man gathered his grocery cart of belongings and started off down the street. She looked up and saw Audrey, who was now sitting in the driver's seat, staring at her through the rear-view mirror.

"You look like shit," Audrey quipped as they left the city.

"I feel worse."

"We're going to a hospital, so you'd better figure out a story."

"I'll direct you to one outside of the city." Maggie flipped open the burner phone and called 911 to report Quinn's body. Then she wiped it clean and dropped it out of the window, watching as it broke apart on the road.

"Can I assume it's over?" Audrey asked as they pulled up to the hospital in front of the ER. When she didn't get a response, she looked into the back seat and saw Maggie crumpled into a heap.

Knowing she couldn't get Maggie out of the car alone; she ran into the building for help. Two orderlies came out with a wheel chair and struggled to get Maggie out of the car and into it. Audrey watched as they wheeled Maggie inside before she parked the car. Tonight, Maggie's recklessness had almost gotten her killed. Audrey decided when Maggie recovered, she was going to suggest a visit back to Ontario with her aunt and uncle. It was time for Maggie to put some distance between herself and what happened.

68

Colby paced back and forth in front of his desk, clutching the photographs from the two crime scenes. He wondered when they'd put an end to these gang wars. Colby paused, leaned over his desk, dropped the pictures, and spread them out to get a better look. He sorted through them until he came to the one of Bradley 'Butch' Barker's body, picked it up and examined it.

Police were called to the scene when workers found his body next to a rail car and reported it. Butch's open fly and neck wound reminded him vaguely of the truck driver's murdered by who the press dubbed 'The Trans-Canada Killer,' but he was dead. Doubt flickered as he looked at the photograph, then he pushed it away. The wounds were different. The coroner would give an official cause of death, but based on the amount of blood at the scene, he bled out from the stab wound to his neck.

Although they recovered Butch's bike at the scene, he figured they wouldn't find anything. Both saddle bags and the trunk were empty.

Colby dropped the picture back on his desk and picked up the one of Quinton Mars' body.

"Two of the most prominent members of the Dark Enders murdered in one day." He whistled softly. "This war is getting bloody." A nagging shadow of doubt slipped in.

'Was this retaliation? Both kills felt personal.' He thought, *'maybe there was a vigilante taking care of the gang members. But who could get that close to both Butch and Quinton?'*

He picked up a magnifying glass and examined Quinton's knuckles. Blood crusted both hands. The split open skin revealed he'd been in a fight before he died.

He spread out the remaining pictures of the wounds Quinton suffered before he died. Both the severed Achilles tendon and the wound in his jaw were from a knife.

'Could it be the same person who killed both Butch and Quinton?' He wondered, but dismissed the thought. *'It's unlikely it's the same person, but we'll know more when forensics gets back to us.'*

The only reason they found Quinton's body so soon was from an anonymous tip. Now the entire department was on high alert. They knew the Dark Enders would call in reinforcements to strengthen the club now that they'd lost both their president and vice president.

Colby suspected that because both of the victims were members of The Dark Enders, this was the work of the High Rollers. There were rumours that the Dark Enders killed the previous president of the High Rollers, and although there wasn't enough evidence to prove it, he was sure they were the ones who wounded Maggie and killed her husband. Colby ran his hands through his hair as he watched his partner approach and toss an evidence folder on the desk.

"We got lucky. A street camera caught an image of the someone fleeing the scene where we found Barker's body, although it's not much to go on. The picture is blurry, but it could be a woman because of the slight frame and long hair, but these days, who knows? Also, it could be a wig. Of course, no one is talking. Whoever it is, they'd better hope the Dark Enders don't find out, or there'll be a bloodbath. We don't need more innocent civilians getting caught up in this."

Colby nodded to his partner and sighed before he reached across his desk, picked up the photograph and stared at the grainy image. He saw the long copper hair trailing out from under the helmet and his heart sank. Even though the photo wasn't clear enough for a positive identification, Colby knew in his heart who rode that bike, despite the license plate being removed.

He dropped into his seat and stared at it. His chest tightened and his palms became clammy as his phone rang. He looked at the call display and hesitated before answering it. He wondered two things as he did. One, could he protect her and two, did she do what the evidence was pointing too. He stood, gripped the edge of his desk, and took a deep breath before he spoke.

"Hello Maggie."

About the Author

J. E. Friend is an emerging author of crime thrillers. She lives in beautiful Annapolis Valley, Nova Scotia, with her husband Steve and their dog, Hartley. There she can enjoy the peace and solitude offered in order to immerse herself in her writing, whether she's writing in her writing room or out on the deck. She has a Bachelor's Degree from Waterloo, where her field of study was psychology. This enables her to delve into the mindset of her killers when writing.

She is a member of Author's Ink, a writing group in Nova Scotia, consisting of published and non-published authors, and for the past few years, she has also been The Municipal Liaison for NaNoWriMo (National Novel Writing Month) for her geographical area. NaNoWriMo promotes writers with an annual challenge to write 50,000 words in November, which she has won each year since 2017. She is an active member of the Writer's Federation of Nova Scotia, where she has reviewed and short-listed emerging authors in several competitions.

Design of Deception was her debut novel. Her second book, Redemption, the first in the Trans-Canada Killer Series, released in 2022. Retribution is the second in the series. She is currently working on the third book in the series.